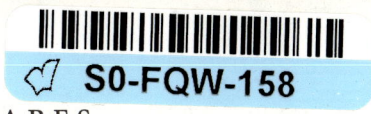

PLOUGHSHARES

Fall 2003 · Vol. 29, Nos. 2 & 3

GUEST EDITOR
Alice Hoffman

EDITOR
Don Lee

MANAGING EDITOR
Gregg Rosenblum

POETRY EDITOR
David Daniel

ASSOCIATE FICTION EDITOR
Maryanne O'Hara

FOUNDING EDITOR
DeWitt Henry

FOUNDING PUBLISHER
Peter O'Malley

PLOUGHSHARES, a journal of new writing, is guest-edited serially by prominent writers who explore different and personal visions, aesthetics, and literary circles. PLOUGHSHARES is published in April, August, and December at Emerson College, 120 Boylston Street, Boston, MA 02116-4624. Telephone: (617) 824-8753. Web address: www.pshares.org.

ASSISTANT FICTION EDITOR: Jay Baron Nicorvo. EDITORIAL ASSISTANT: Olivia Kate Cerrone. PROOFREADER: Megan Weireter. BOOKSHELF ADVISOR: Fred Leebron.

FICTION READERS: Maureen Cidzik, Kathleen Rooney, Megan Weireter, Joanna Luloff, Asako Serizawa, Nicole Kelley, Simeon Berry, Wendy Wunder, Leslie Cauldwell, Eson Kim, Michelle Mulder, Matthew Modica, Christopher Helmuth, Erin Lavelle, James Charlesworth, Cortney Hamilton, Hannah Bottomy, Jeffrey Voccola, Erin Hagedorn, Scarlett Stoppa, Patricia Reed, Coppelia Liebenthal, and Laura Tarvin. POETRY READERS: Megan Weireter, Simeon Berry, Zachary Sifuentes, Kathleen Rooney, Erin Lavelle, Robert Arnold, Joanne Diaz, Jennifer Thurber, and Chris Tonelli.

SUBSCRIPTIONS (ISSN 0048-4474): $24 for one year (3 issues), $46 for two years (6 issues); $27 a year for institutions. Add $12 a year for international ($10 for Canada).

UPCOMING: Winter 2003–04, a special *Emerging Writers* issue, will appear in December 2003. Spring 2004, a poetry and fiction issue edited by Campbell McGrath, will appear in April 2004.

SUBMISSIONS: Reading period is from August 1 to March 31 (postmark dates). All submissions sent from April to July are returned unread. Please see page 207 for editorial and submission policies.

Back-issue, classroom-adoption, and bulk orders may be placed directly through PLOUGHSHARES. Microfilms of back issues may be obtained from University Microfilms. PLOUGHSHARES is also available as CD-ROM and full-text products from EBSCO, H.W. Wilson, Information Access, and UMI. Indexed in M.L.A. Bibliography, American Humanities Index, Index of American Periodical Verse, Book Review Index. Full publisher's index is online at www.pshares.org. The views and opinions expressed in this journal are solely those of the authors. All rights for individual works revert to the authors upon publication.

PLOUGHSHARES receives support from the National Endowment for the Arts and the Massachusetts Cultural Council.

Retail distribution by Bernhard DeBoer (Nutley, NJ) and Ingram Periodicals (La Vergne, TN). Printed in the U.S.A. on recycled paper by Capital City Press.

© 2003 by Emerson College   ISBN 0-933277-38-5

CONTENTS

Fall 2003

Cover art:
Detail of Book Damaged by Water by Abelardo Morell
Duotone, 2001
Courtesy of Bonni Benrubi Gallery

Ploughshares Patrons

This nonprofit publication would not be possible without the
support of our readers and the generosity of the following
individuals and organizations.

COUNCIL

William H. Berman
Denise and Mel Cohen
Robert E. Courtemanche
Jeff and Jan Greenhawt
Jacqueline Liebergott
Turow Foundation
Eugenia Gladstone Vogel
Marillyn Zacharis

PATRONS

Johanna Cinader
JoAnne Trafton

FRIENDS

Anonymous (4)
Jim Bainbridge
Joseph David France
Tom Jenks and Carol Edgarian
Nancy Packes

ORGANIZATIONS

AOL Time Warner Book Group
Emerson College
Houghton Mifflin
Lannan Foundation
Massachusetts Cultural Council
National Endowment for the Arts

COUNCIL: $3,000 for two lifetime subscriptions and
acknowledgement in the journal for three years.
PATRON: $1,000 for a lifetime subscription and
acknowledgement in the journal for two years.
FRIEND: $500 for a lifetime subscription and
acknowledgement in the journal for one year.

Introduction

As a beginning writer, I had the good fortune to study with Albert J. Guerard, the greatest teacher of creative writing in the twentieth century. Guerard—novelist, teacher, and critic with equal intensity—taught at Harvard for twenty-three years, then at Stanford for another twenty-three, and was a mentor to many of the century's most esteemed writers, including John Updike, John Hawkes, Maxine Kumin, Alice Adams, Alison Lurie, Frank O'Hara, Mark Mirsky, Tobias Wolff, Ron Hansen, and the hundreds of other talented fiction writers and poets who came to his classes in Cambridge and Palo Alto.

Professor Guerard believed that his primary duty as a professor of creative writing was to help each student find his or her unique and enduring voice. This personal voice was made up of energy, imagination, and language—it was the very core of who a writer was. Although Guerard was a great lover of ambiguity, a modernist who particularly enjoyed Hardy's comment that "realism is not art," he never pushed any theoretical mode on any of his students. He did not favor "fabulists" over "realists," "experimental" writers over "traditionalists."

Surely there are writing programs where students are encouraged to take on the nuances of their teachers rather than explore the intricacies of their own inner voice. Such instruction makes it difficult to move from imitating an admired writer's language and method to a more personal style. Guerard would have never approved of a literary copycat world. He loved rebels—Dostoyevsky, Dickens, Faulkner—and he broke all the rules of teaching creative writing. His motto was "Tell, not show." Write not just what you know, but what you imagine. The concept of a personal voice was at the heart of Guerard's philosophy. Much the way Gide spoke of an author's gait, Woolf an author's rhythms, Guerard believed in this concept of the voice, the writer's most authentic self.

In 1966 Guerard started the Voice Project at Stanford, headed by John Hawkes, to explore the relationship of personality to the diction and rhythms of writing. In Guerard's view, the author's voice came from the very same psychological impulse as his or her impulse to write. The elements that formed both the writer's themes and obsessions and the expression of his or her material included childhood fantasy life, stories heard in childhood, personal experience, and, perhaps most importantly, dreams. Professor Guerard encouraged dreaming as the ultimate freedom, insisting that "discipline, clarity, and control" could all be taught eventually, but dreams, always unique and individual, were what literature was made of. "Without free dreaming," Guerard told us, "truly excellent fiction is hardly possible." As no two individuals had the same experience, in life or reading, nor the same dreams, none could possibly have the same fictional voice. The writer's voice was like a fingerprint or a heartbeat: no two were the same.

As a graduate student I began to understand the true and practical meaning of "voice" for myself as a novelist-to-be when reading the text we used, which contained the work of only two women writers. One was Flannery O'Connor, the other, Grace Paley. I was twenty-one at the time, convinced that great literature was written by men, for men, that it was about war mostly, peace, less often. I had no understanding that domestic life is indeed political. Certainly, I had no real comprehension of the deep and lasting value of voice, until I read Grace Paley's astounding and brilliant fiction. Reading Grace Paley's work, hearing her singular and unique fictional voice, changed my life. It helped give me the freedom to search for my own voice, my own story to tell. That, of course, is what great fiction does: it opens a door you never even knew was there, it reminds you that the world isn't always what you had assumed it to be, and that it is our job, as writers of fiction, to report from a front no one has ever visited before.

In this fiction issue of *Ploughshares*, there is great variety, many voices, real vision. What I looked for, and what I found in these stories, was a unique voice, a true surprise in language or tone or point of view. Powerful, haunting, heartbreaking, hilarious, cool, complicated, emotional, cerebral, transforming, each of the stories creates a universe, each is unique in its telling. In reading for *Ploughshares*, I was also searching for a reminder of why we tell stories in the first place, and why we read them. How does fiction matter in a world of terror and loss? If books themselves may not last, if paper may go up in flames, why do we still write? Why do we turn to reading fiction in the search for answers of what it means to be human?

As a child, I'd always looked to books for solace. It was fiction which helped to explain why the world worked the way it did, much the way dreams explain our waking lives. My first response after 9/11 was to take down from the shelves two books I had loved as a girl. I read Ursula Le Guin's masterpiece, *The Left Hand of Darkness,* an emotional anthropologist's vision of a world that, no matter how far away it might be, mirrors our own conflicts and hopes. I turned next to *Fahrenheit 451,* the masterful and visionary work by the author who made me want to be a writer in the first place, Ray Bradbury.

Reading had convinced me, long ago, that it is in fiction we find the purest voices. I agree with Professor Guerard's declaration that "a writer's truest self is not the person you meet, it's the person you read"; that it is through fiction, and by breaking the rules of reality, that we find the greatest truths. Clearly, I went back to *Fahrenheit 451* because I needed to remember that even in a world that is fractured beyond belief, a universe in which voices are silenced by terror and loss, there was a place in which people were willing to die for books, to live for books. They were willing, in fact, to become the books they loved, memorizing each one, word by word, voice by voice, so that literature could live on, even in a world without paper and print, reminding us once more: we are the stories we tell.

A special thank-you to Abelardo Morell, whose photograph is this issue's cover. Morell's brilliant A Book of Books elevates books to sacred objects, ruined or perfect, old or new, the treasures in a reader's life, the repository of our dreams.

The Party

There were a bunch of us who had drawn together into a corner of the dining room. It was a big party, and none of us had met before. But a tiny core of women of a certain age had drawn more women until there were enough of us that we needed to be democratic about talking—each of us needed to be careful not to take up too much airtime.

We were talking about kissing, and we spoke rapidly and excitedly and laughed loudly. This was T-shirt and jeans laughter, not cocktail dress laughter—it came from the belly, not the chest. It was size fourteen and not size two. When one of us made moves toward some wilting hors d'oeuvre, the rest would stall, so that nothing good was missed by anyone.

We seemed to like best telling about our first times. There was a glamorous blonde wearing huge diamond studs who said she first kissed at age eleven, while playing spin the bottle on a hot Texas night. The rule was that after the spin, the chosen couple would go into the kitchen, stand by the washing machine stationed in the corner, and kiss. No tongues. The blonde modified the rule to include no lips. Cheeks. That was all. But a certain Paul Drummond was too fast for her that night, and smacked a kiss right on her mouth. She said she'd intended to get angry, but instead backed with pleasant shock into the washer hard enough to make a noise that roused the supposedly supervising parent from sleep. The kissing stopped; the party broke up, and the blonde went home, where she stayed awake much of the night reenacting the scene in her mind, and telling herself that the sin was venial, venial, venial.

A woman named Vicky said she spent years in practice with her best friend Mary Jo. "We would put a pillow between our faces, kneel down on my bed, rub each other's backs, and kiss that pillow to *death*." We all laughed some more, because we'd all kissed pillows, it seemed.

One woman wearing a seductively cut black dress that now seemed beside the point ventured bravely that she and her best friend Sherry had dispensed with the pillow and gone at it lip to lip. You could tell from the ripple effect of lowered eyes that she wasn't the only one. I thought of fourth grade and my friend Mary, whom I asked to be the wife so I could be the husband. I liked to be the husband—you got to say when about everything. While she dusted, I went to work. When I came home, we kissed hello for what became long enough that we decided we'd better start playing outside.

There was a serious, shy-looking woman named Jane who hadn't said much of anything, and who, when she laughed, had actually put her hand up over her mouth. *Oh, honey,* I wanted to say to her, when I saw her do that. *Sweetheart, come here and let's give you some tools.* She wore a dress with buttons that went high up on her neck, and each one was closed. I was pretty surprised to hear her say, "Oh well, kissing was one thing, but do you remember the first time you touched a dick?"

Now we were all into high gear. We were beside ourselves in our eagerness to share our experiences. We drew closer.

A roving rent-a-waiter dressed in tight black pants, a blindingly white shirt, and a black bow tie offered us little bundles of something from his tray. All of us, to a woman, took one. The waiter seemed very pleased. I waited for him to move on, then greedily opened: "I was forced. This guy called 'Telephone Pole Taylor,' for the very reason you might suspect, pulled my hand down and held it there until I had touched it for five seconds. We counted together. I almost threw up. I was a serious virgin, and I damn near passed out at the thought that kind of thing would someday... But after I got over the size, I became kind of intrigued by the texture."

Vicky's eyes widened. "Yes! Like damp velvet, right?"

Jane, standing next to me, sighed quietly. "I don't know," she said. "Men's bodies are just not *pretty.* That makes it difficult. I think women's bodies are, though, and I'm not, you know..." We knew. She took a sip from her drink, leaned her head against the wall, frowned in a contemplative sort of way. "It turned out that penises weren't so bad, really, although it did take me a long time to get used to that rising and falling routine. I mean, it was grotesque the first time I saw an erection. It was like a monster movie."

The gorgeous blonde spoke up. "I *liked* it! I thought it was so *magical.*" But then, as though protecting Jane, she added hastily, "But not beautiful, of course." We drank to that.

"It's the balls that get me," Vicky said. "They're like kiwifruit gone bad." We burst out laughing again. I think we felt that we were becoming dangerous, careening in our conversation, and we liked it. We were ready to reveal anything about ourselves. Almost imperceptibly, the circle tightened again.

"I think it's all a matter of cultural conditioning," I said, and was met with a friendly collective groan. "No, I mean it. If we'd been taught to go after a penis by a mother who winked at us when she talked about it, and if all the boys at those drive-in movies had covered their privates with both hands and moaned little protests into our ears, we'd have been *wild* to touch them. Instead, we pulled their hands down from our tits and up from their crotches."

Jane put her empty glass on the floor. "I think men and women are just hopelessly different. It's a wonder we get along at all. Sometimes the smallest things can bring out the biggest things. I had a horrible fight with my husband last night, and you know what started it?" We were all listening hard, and we didn't notice the approach of Jane's husband from across the room. But Jane did. She stopped talking and stared at him: in her eyes, it was as though a shade had been pulled.

He stood at the edge of our circle, a little wary. "What's going on over *here?*"

There was a beat; no one answered. And then Jane said, "Oh, you know. Just girl talk." I think we were all miffed by her response, but no one challenged it.

Her husband looked at his watch. "It's time to go."

Jane didn't budge. "I'd like to stay for a while."

"Oh?" He put his hands in his pockets. "All right. That's fine." He didn't move. Another beat. Silence all around. Then two of us simultaneously moved toward the food table. Someone else walked off toward the bathroom. Vicky waved to a man across the room and started for him. Our group fell apart in a sad, slow-motion sort of way, as when petals leave a blossom past its prime. And then I heard Jane say, "I guess it is late."

I listened to her say goodbye to the people around her. I was dragging a piece of pita bread through the leftover hummus tracks at the bottom of a pottery bowl. I was hoping the potter used no lead. I was wondering what my children were doing.

I thought about what I had to do the next day as I finished my drink. Then I looked around for my husband. He was in the living room discussing the Middle East conflict with a short, mildly overweight, balding man. I imagined the man in the front seat of a car at a drive-in, thirty years ago. I gave him hair, but otherwise I didn't change him much.

I sat in a chair close-by and heard my husband say emphatically that Israel fought only defensive wars. I fiddled with the hem of my skirt and wondered what it was Jane and her husband had fought about. Several possibilities occurred to me. I heard the short man ask my husband what he did for a living. Sports would be next. I turned my head away from them and permitted myself a yawn.

I thought, Here is how I feel about men: I am angry at them for the way they sling their advantage about—interrupting, taking over, forcing endings, pretending to not understand what equality between the sexes necessitates, thus ensuring that they are always and forever the ones who say when. But I feel sorry for them, too.

I remembered a redeye flight I was on recently. At about four a.m., I fell into one of those poor quality sleeps. I woke up about twenty minutes later and took a stroll down the aisle. The plane was packed with businessmen, and they all lay sleeping, their briefcases at their feet like obedient dogs. They had blankets with the airline's imprint over them, but the too-small covers had slid to one side or the other, revealing gaps between buttons on the dress shirts, revealing fists slightly clenched. They looked so sweet then, so honest and vulnerable. I felt a great love toward all of them, and smiled warmly into each sleeping face.

The Bad Shepherd

The shepherd is perched on a stile, one eye on his paper, one eye on the lane below the *ffridd,* the meadow, beyond the flock. His dogs lie at his feet, their heads between their paws, panting softly in the unseasonably warm May weather and batting their ears occasionally at the horseflies attracted to the moisture of their eyes.

He glances at the front page of the paper, *The Caernarvon and Denby,* something about the men fighting the fire at Chernobyl, then flips impatiently to a grainy photo on the back page taken at a local sheepdog trial. The picture is part of a weekly competition called Spot the Dog, modeled after the staple newspaper contest, Spot the Ball, in which a photograph of a recent football match is reprinted with the ball airbrushed out. The challenge is to draw an X where the ball should be, based on the positions of the players, their feet, their heads, their eyes. Weather conditions (blustery, fine, drizzly) and even the condition of the pitch (soft, heavy, dry) are given below. In the local version of the game, it's the sheepdog that has been erased. Somewhere on the photographed hillside there's an invisible dog. The shepherd studies it for a long moment, reads the caption which describes the direction of the wind (northeast) and breed of sheep (Welsh blacks, although he could have told that from their slightly spiderish gait), then finally takes a chewed blue Bic from the top pocket of his coat and makes a neat X, then four more. You get five crosses for 50p. He could buy more, but he never does—as much for sporting considerations as reasons of economy. Later he'll clip the coupon out, mail it in with a check made out for "Fifty pence only."

He glances up for a second, watches a lamb jockeying for position against its mother, before turning back to his paper. He's been doing the competition since it began seven years ago now. The prize is two hundred and fifty pounds, and he's won five times, which is pretty decent, he reckons, even after you deduct all those 50p's a week and a round for the fellows down the pub.

Twelve hundred and fifty quid. That's a tidy sum, even spread over the years, what with a single sheep selling for less than thirty-five. At the pub they thought he was fluky the first two or three times, but now they keep wanting to know if he's got a system. Forty years of experience is all, he says. That and common sense. Everything happens for a reason, after all, he thinks, even if the reason is unknown. If you know enough about any effect, in this case the movement of a flock, you can always eventually spot the cause, even an invisible dog.

Now, he sees a white van come around the shoulder of the hill and weave along the lower lane. The Man from the Ag., he reckons, getting to his feet and starting down to meet him, the dogs trotting through the grass, one ahead of him, one trailing, the same way they work the flock. The last time the Ag. Man was here was to administer a warning. The shepherd had been reported selling a wether to a local butcher. Just the one to tide him over a bad fortnight, it was. But he'd forgotten the new Ministry of Agriculture rule. "It's illegal," the fellow explained, "to transport a single sheep to market these days. It's considered cruel to the animal to let it travel alone."

The shepherd considered asking if that was true even if you were taking it to be slaughtered, but all he said was that he'd take two the next time.

The Ag. Man shook his head slowly.

"The minimum is three," he explained. "That way if you want to sell one, there are two to travel back to the farm together." He held up one finger of his right hand and two fingers of his left. "You see?"

The shepherd stared at him, until the other said, "I can see my way to letting you off the fine this time, all right? So long as it doesn't happen again."

"Oh, no," the shepherd said. "I couldn't let you do that." He counted the notes out carefully in Welsh—*pum, deg, pymtheg, ugain*—and put them in the man's soft palm.

"Twenty," he explained, as the other wrote out a receipt.

At any rate, he has found he rather likes the new rule. He felt a little lonely himself driving back in an empty van.

This morning the Man from the Ag. is a boy. He looks like a recent graduate from agricultural college. His wellies are still a glossy green, his cheeks rosy. In the pub the shepherds call these young fellows Herries, meaning city kids who learned their love of the land from James Herriot books. "Stands to reason, don't it? If they learned it on a farm of their own, they'd still be there, wouldn't they, not sticking their noses in our business." But beneath the mockery, the shepherd knows, is fear. For serious enough infractions, the Man from the Ag. has the power to ban any of them from owning stock for life. During the last scabies epidemic, farmers had even taken one inspector hostage for a few hours until the Minister himself telephoned them and agreed to replace him.

"Bob Bell," the young man says, and they grip, more than shake, each other's hands over the bars of the gate.

"Nice place," he says, and the shepherd thanks him. "Had it long?"

"Since my grandfather." The shepherd leans across the gate, which is made from an old iron bedstead. "This was his marriage bed," he says.

"Really," Bell says, studying it like an antique. He slaps the metal lightly, making the frame shiver and exhale a thin powder of rust. The dogs twitch at the noise.

"His deathbed, too," the shepherd says dryly.

"This them, then?" Bell says, motioning to the flock, and since the answer is obvious, the shepherd just shrugs. "Any other livestock?" Bell asks.

"Half a dozen chicks," the shepherd says, pointing to a corrugated-iron henhouse with his rolled-up newspaper. "Family of goats."

"I won't need to see the poultry, but I should take a look at those goats."

"That'll be tricky, you see. They're wild, isn't it, up on the mountain."

Bell looks puzzled.

"To keep an eye on the sheep," the shepherd says, and when Bell's expression doesn't change goes on. "Goat can get down to a sweet patch of grass on a crag, or a ledge. Sheep can, too, but she won't be able to get out of a tight spot after. She'll graze the ledge and then starve there. Goat gets there first, removes the temptation, so to speak." A blush spreads on the shepherd's rough face at the end of this speech. He's embarrassed to have to explain it.

"I see," Bell says, nodding, and after a second, "Righto!" He heads briskly around the back of his van and opens the rear doors with a squeak. It's a very clean van, the shepherd sees as he follows, not like his own corroded, straw-lined heap, greasy with lanolin. He uses his knee to push the younger dog's nose aside. Bell pulls out a couple of aerosol cans and a small black device, like a boxy gun. "Geiger counter," he says, patting it. "Let's be having them, eh?"

They walk along the lower edge of the meadow to the flock, Bell admiring the high stone walls around them.

"Drystone," he says. "There's a dying art. You build them yourself?"

"My father and me. He used to call it a puzzle fitting all the stones together, wedging them right, so's you wouldn't need mortar. Like a big jigsaw."

"What about them?" Bell asks, pointing uphill to a much higher line of wall running along the ridge, encircling the mountain.

"Them's before my time," the shepherd says. "Medieval. Some say prehistoric. All I do is keep 'em up."

They move through the sheep, the flock spreading open before them as if it's been unzipped. Bell flicks on the device, waves it around like a magician's wand, passing it over the rump of each of a dozen or so sheep. It seethes with static, crackling and scratching like an ancient radio, the shepherd thinks. Bell studies the small white dial on the counter, the needle bouncing around like a live thing. He looks up at the shepherd now and then, and once even says, "What was that?" But the shepherd shakes his head. He hasn't said anything. He is standing back, watching the work, but not craning to see the reading on the gauge, until Bell waves him over and shows it to him as he passes it back and forth across one of the broken-mouth ewes. "The safety level is a thousand becquerels," he says, pointing to a mark in the middle of the counter. The needle strains to the right edge of the scale, and the machine makes a sound of tearing.

"Well, Mr.—"

"Hughes," the shepherd says. Then: "Gerry." Finally: "Gerry Glynllwyn." Glynllwyn being the name of the farm, and how he is known from the five other Hugheses in the village, the three other Geralds.

"Well, Gerry. I regret to inform you that your flock has ingested irradiated material, most likely from the Chernobyl plume, deposited here by precipitation, and are registering unacceptably high levels of radiation." It sounds as if he's reading a form.

"But they seem fine," the shepherd says. "They're not off their feed. I haven't seen anything out of the ordinary." He realizes he's tapping his rolled paper against his leg, and jams it in his pocket.

"The animals themselves are in no immediate danger," Bell says. He keeps his eye on the needle. "But I'll have to restrict their sale and movement. They're not fit for human consumption." He waits, but the shepherd seems impassive. "I've got some paper-work in the van. For you to fill out in case of compensation."

"Maybe the machine is wrong," the shepherd says. "If we can't see anything."

"But the radiation's invisible," Bell says, and oddly he's the one who sounds confused.

There's a pause. The shepherd studies the sky for a moment. The worst things that used to come out of it were the low-flying fighter jets from the base nearby, ripping overhead on their train-ing sorties. They'd put the flock into a panic, sending them rip-pling over the mountainside like a great white flag. He'd called the base half a dozen times to tell them to keep clear at lambing time; in the end he'd clambered onto the roof of the barn and painted, "Piss off, Biggles," in letters six feet high. That'd done the trick.

"I can help you with the forms if you like," Bell is saying.

"Thank you."

"But first I have to mark the animals." He pops the top off the orange aerosol and sprays a bright cross onto the back of the nearest sheep.

"So now we can see something," the shepherd says, over the hissing of the paint. "Now it's visible."

"In a manner of speaking," Bell says, reaching for another sheep.

"Give me the other can, and I'll help," the shepherd says, hold-ing out his hand, but Bell shakes his head. "Sorry. I have to be the one. Regulations. Besides, the other can is blue. Blue for clear. Orange for restricted. If you could just hold them for me, though?"

It takes them about an hour to move through the whole flock, sheep after sheep. At one point, Bell says that the flock might be able to purge the contaminants if pastured in areas unaffected by the fallout, like the lowlands. "And what do you think I'd be doing up here if I owned lowland pasture, or could afford to rent it?" the shepherd asks him. They work in silence after that. Finally, when the last ewe has been shrugged loose, the shepherd follows Bell back to his van.

"I make that forty-seven head," Bell says, filling in a form on a clipboard. "You're registered for nearly eighty."

"There's a dozen or so stray on the mountain."

A flicker of irritation passes over the man's face. "You'll have to call me again when any stragglers come in. And the rest?"

"The rest are gone. It's been a hard winter or two, and we had a busy fox this spring among the lambs."

"We?"

"Me and the flock," the shepherd says, smiling crookedly. He is one of five; a sister dead in infancy, a brother in the war, another of cancer six years ago. His surviving sister is a grandmother in Australia, although he hasn't seen her in thirty years. She writes him a card every Christmas. Last year she even called, invited him to visit. "Who knows," she said gaily, "maybe you'll fancy retiring here." The idea of that—more than the slight delay on the line, her hybrid accent, half-familiar but with an odd twang to it—made him realize how far apart they were.

"I'm sorry. I hope you get him," Bell says.

"Her. It were a vixen."

"I see." Bell looks down at the clipboard, starts to make checkmarks.

The shepherd watches him, turns away to cast an eye over the flock, turns back. He runs a hand down the lapel of his old suit jacket.

"Can I ask you what'll happen?" he asks carefully.

"It's hard to say. There'll be regular monitoring. The radioactive agents in the rain are iodine and cesium isotopes. It's peaty soil hereabouts, as you know, which means the water doesn't run off quick. So it gets absorbed by the grass, or the bracken or the heather, along with the contaminants, which are then ingested by the livestock."

"Then what?"

Bell sighs.

"There are a few scenarios. The radioactive material concentrates in the thyroid of the sheep, which as well as compromising the food chain means a chance of deformed lambs in the future. Then there's something called a toxic cycle where the radioactive material passed through the sheep's digestive tract, fertilizes new vegetation which is eaten by the lambs."

"But how long will it all last, like?"

"Well, iodine 131 decays in a matter of days and cesium 134 in around twenty-four months." Bell blinks. "But cesium 137 has a half-life of around thirty years."

It makes the shepherd think of his grandfather, who used to work in the slate quarry under the mountain, under their very feet, as a young fellow. He was a "danger man." He used to climb up a long, weaving ladder, sometimes two lashed together, fifty feet into the darkness of the galleries, to chisel loose any slates that might fall from the ceiling onto the men working below. "It was like chipping stars from the sky," he remembers his grandfather telling him. The slates were dislodged from the ceilings by a steady trickle of water from the mountain above. "Thousand-year-old rain," the old man called it. "That's how long it takes to work its way through the rock." His grandfather had been laid off during the great strike of '01 and had never gone back. Blacklisted by management, he'd used the last of his savings to buy the flock.

"You know about *cynefin*?" the shepherd asks now.

"Come again?"

"*Cynefin*. I'm sorry, I don't know the English for it. It's the flock's sense of place. What keeps them on any particular patch of the mountain in the winter. Like an invisible border. It's what makes it possible to farm up here at all, really." He begins hesitantly, but then he's speaking urgently, leaning into Bell.

"*Cy-nefin*," Bell says, making it sound like he's saying "Kevin" with a stutter. "I might have heard of it. 'Hefted' is what they call it in the Lakes, I think." He smiles awkwardly, glances at the knot of sheep over the shepherd's shoulder. "I always thought it was an old wives' tale—sheep having memories."

"Not the sheep, really," the shepherd says, ignoring that smile, making himself tell this, pressing out the words. "It's the flock, like, that remembers. The ewes teach it to the lambs. Only, if you put a new flock up there, they'd scatter across four counties. People say it goes back to medieval days when they had enough men to stay with them year-round. Over years and years, generations of sheep learned their ground." He has his rolled-up newspaper out of his pocket now, brandished, gesturing at the hillside.

"I'm not quite sure what you're asking," the other says, taking a half step back.

"So if a flock were destroyed or died out," the shepherd goes on, "the farm'd be done for, too." He looks down at his hands and sees how tight he's been gripping the paper, wringing it until it begins to tear. Bell slowly raises the clipboard between them, and the shepherd realizes the man has no answers.

Clouds, he sees dully, are massing above the mountain; it's coming on to rain again.

"If you'll just sign here?" Bell asks gently, and the shepherd takes the clipboard. "You know," Bell says, after a second. "About your foxes? There's some places bringing in a llama, or two. They're complementary with sheep, and there's a profitable market for the wool. But there's also some research that they reduce fox attacks." He laughs nervously. "Foxes think the llamas are massive sheep, you see. Scares the crap out of them!"

The shepherd looks up from the form for a long moment.

"Llamas, is it," he says, shaking his head. "There's progress for you."

Bell coughs, and the shepherd's pen finally scratches over the form. He passes the clipboard back, and Bell tears off a smudged pale-green copy and gives it to him, climbs back into his van. The engine starts first time.

"Just don't forget to mark any strays that come in and give us a call with a revised head count, all right?"

The shepherd nods.

He doesn't watch the van back out of the lane. Instead, he turns and studies the hillside: the mountain wall, curving away into the low cloud, and below it the flock dotted on the hillside, the crosses on their backs.

He thinks of the invisible ones, the rest of the flock that he gathered the day before with the dogs and guided into the disused quarry tunnels beneath the mountains. They're there now waiting for him, their white fleeces gray in the dim light, faint as starlight, sifting down the airshafts like dust. He tried to explain it, after all, he thinks. He'll go to them tonight—already he can hear the weird clacking percussion of loose slate underfoot, see his torch light running over their faces, their slotted eyes flashing back at him like a signal.

But first, he thinks, as the drizzle begins to fall, he needs to buy a blue spray can.

In the Garden

Andrew Byar began his experiment in the garden, going out in the dusky evenings after the help had dispersed for the day, after the cook had served the last meal and washed the china and departed to catch the final trolley, after the gardener had arranged the tools in a gleaming, orderly progression against the shed walls, had carried the remnants of the weeding to the mulch pile at the edge of the grounds, and had tended to the orchids hung like lanterns from the trellis—that was when Andrew Byar went outside, the house behind him lit like a great ship, his wife and grown sons moving through their evening rituals beyond the panes of glass.

It was June, the air fragrant with jasmine, honeysuckle, and mimosa. Catalpa blossoms burst like stars in the trees; their delicate custard scent infused the violet air. Andrew walked to the shed, stepping quickly, almost stealthily along the path, as if he were a thief and not the owner of these three verdant acres in the heart of Pittsburgh, high on a bluff overlooking the flatlands on the opposite shore of the Monongahela River. There, his steel plants roared all day and night, bright as beating hearts, glinting in the distance like piles of burnished coins.

At the shed door he turned on the flashlight and stepped into darkness rich with the scent of raw wood and linseed oil and fresh, damp earth. He made his way to the workbench. Beneath it, shoved in a corner, was a wooden crate once used to ship fresh persimmons from the sea coasts of Japan, now buried under blankets. Dust billowed in Byar's narrow beam of light, and the smells of mildew and oil flew up as he dragged the crate to the middle of the room. He slid the lid off and groped inside for the strongbox hidden beneath a pile of old magazines, limp and yellowed. The box, smooth steel, was wrapped carefully in layers of oily rags, which fell in a soft pile by the polished leather of his shoes. He opened the latch with a tiny, intricate key he took from the inner pocket of his coat.

A ten-ounce bottle, fashioned of brown glass, was cushioned in a cloud of cotton. Ubiquitous, it might have held iodine, or smelling salts. Andrew Byar balanced his flashlight on the bench. He took a test tube from his pocket and carefully poured a clear liquid from the bottle, filling the vial to a line marked near the top, then stoppering it with a cork. He put the brown glass bottle back into the box, nestled the box into the rags and beneath the wilting magazines, and slid the crate back to its position beneath the bench, the moldy blankets. Flashlight in one hand and the test tube in another, he went back outside, striding past the swimming pool and down the gravel path between the camellia bushes laden with rosy white flowers, until he came to the trellis where the orchids hung.

Here, he paused. From this clearing the house was visible only in pieces through the trees, magnificent elms and oaks and sycamores hundreds of years old, rare remnants of the virgin forests felled a century before to build the city. He stood watching for a moment, glimpsing the glassy light and shadowed brick amid the leaves, imagining his wife in her evening bath, plush towels on the floor of Italian marble and rose petals scattered on the water. Recently, her hair had begun to gray, and each week a stylist came to the house and left her gilded, as pale and ornately framed as a mirror. Still, in her expressions, her slowing movements, Andrew Byar faced his own age. His two sons were home from college for the summer, apprenticed to the steel factory, which he had built from nothing and through which he had made his fortune. They were indolent young men, handsome and spoiled, and he had no confidence in them. This summer they had brought friends, steady rivers of young men and women whose bright laughter flowed through the house, who studded the tennis courts with their flashing limbs and shouts, who draped themselves over benches, sofas, armchairs, who swam laps in the natural spring pool or splashed in the shallows or drank martinis at its edge. Andrew avoided them and slept poorly, waking from nightmares where his empire, built at such sacrifice and with such canny skill, constructed so painstakingly from the hours and sweat of his whole life, had been frittered into nothing as they played.

The test tube in his hand had warmed until it seemed to give off its own heat. Andrew held it up, trying to discern if a faint glow came from within, or if this was merely a trick of the scarce evening light. The single brown bottle hidden in his shed had cost more than his pool, more even than the private train carriage fitted out with velvet and gold in which he traveled to New York City once a month. Yet if this liquid was, as he believed, an elixir of life, then no expense was too much, no cost beyond consideration, even if it cost him the earth.

He took the cork from the test tube. Slowly, carefully, drop by drop, he poured the liquid evenly into the soil around the orchid.

He stood still before the trellis then, until the darkness was complete, until the crickets and frogs filled his head with a frenzied singing that seemed near madness. Then he slipped the empty tube into his pocket and went home.

In this way his evenings passed for one month, then another. By day he was, as usual, consumed by business. He drew up contracts in his office or strode along the catwalks over the burning furnaces, while below men worked, shadows shoveling and hefting and shaping long bars of steel. The heat from the red-hot metal pleased him, as did the intricate dance between machinery and men, and he looked forward, too, to the end of every week when the accountant brought the production figures to his office high above the plant, sliding them across the mahogany desk in a black leather folder edged with gold leaf. Andrew Byar, born poor in Scotland, was a self-made man, and proud of it. He believed in the power of his own personal will, and he believed in science. Pittsburgh in the 1920's was a pulsing city, powered by great machines and fabulous inventions, and if soot sometimes fell from the air like dark snow, if the rivers grew choked and black, then Andrew Byar believed that science would find solutions. Already electricity had displaced the dangerous hiss of gas, the awkward churning of steam; in decades to come the city would gleam, a bright metropolis, sunlight scattering and refracting from the mirrored surfaces of a million well-oiled moving parts.

All made, of course, from steel.

Byar had profited from his keen understanding of new technologies, as well as from his instincts for risk and innovation. He trusted people less completely, knowing as he did about human frailty and failure—how many men had died in his plant through a single careless action, after all? How many times had a widow appeared in his office, begging for money to feed her fatherless children? He gave it, always, taking care to explain each time how the accident might have been avoided. Thus wise in matters of human failure and culpability, he had given his gardener a camera with instructions to photograph the orchid in the garden every morning at precisely eight o'clock. Memory, with its unexpected currents, its tendency to favor hope over facts, was not something he would trust. Each day the gardener came into his study and put a manila envelope on his desk, and each day Andrew Byar dated this envelope and filed it in the oak drawer of his desk without opening it up.

At the end of the second month, when his family was in Europe, he locked the door to his study and took the sixty-one sealed envelopes from the drawer. Clear morning light poured through the windows which ran floor to ceiling along the wall behind him. He hung the photos one by one, in chronological order, against the opposite wall, securing each to the plaster with a bit of tape. By the time he reached the last, his hands were trembling. Still, he was methodical, careful, precise. Not until the final photo was hung did he step back to survey the whole.

What he saw astounded him. He had begun with an orchid whose flowers were sparse, a plant well past its prime. Yet, nourished by this experimental liquid, the plant had flourished so profusely that change was clearly visible from one photo to another. After only a single week the orchid had burst its pot; twice more in these two months it had done the same, and now it was as large as a bush. Blooms cascaded from stems grown so long that they draped themselves over one another, trailed against the ground. He went immediately to the garden, where the orchid hung from the center of the trellis, its blossoms living jewels. He touched their waxy white petals, their deep purple hearts, with awe. What had been ordinary had become something from another world, a place more fertile and profuse, a place of unending plenty.

All day he was in a state of euphoric agitation, distracted in his morning meetings, pacing the factory grounds and glancing at his watch, willing the slow hours to pass. At last, evening began to gather, and he went home. He dismissed all the help and sent his car for Beatrice. *Wear white*, he instructed in a note, folding the dense paper once, imagining her at her dressing table, the dark words discarded amid her bottles of perfume. She would be late, he knew. Spirited and capricious, she would take her time; perhaps she would not come at all. He had seen her first one morning at dawn, an errant, early-rising guest floating like a petal on the invisible and mysterious currents of the pool, her pale skin almost iridescent.

Dusk was softening the edges of the world. Impatient, unused to idleness, he arranged the setting carefully to pass the time, carrying a white wrought-iron table and chairs to the expanse of soft lawn. It was a night garden, bordered by low clouds of white alyssum. Moonflowers opened as Andrew worked, releasing their faint scents of lemon into the darkness. He hung the spectacular orchid from a low branch of a sycamore tree, each blossom like a candle in a chandelier. In a crystal bowl filled with water he placed white lilacs and camellia blossoms, so that the table seemed a part of the garden and yet appeared to float above it, too, to be suspended, hovering as bright and fleeting as a wish.

At last he heard her footsteps, rustling the gravel. And then he glimpsed her on the path, as pale and slender as the stem of plant. Her white dress had a diaphanous layer, making her both vibrant and undefined, amorphous. She wore a fitted hat, close as a caress against her skull.

"What is it?" she asked, laughing, her lips cool against his own. "I can't wait to know. What is your surprise?"

They sat at the table. Andrew Byar pulled an unlabeled bottle from the canvas bag on the grass, the old glass smooth and undulant in his hands.

"This wine," he said, "is two centuries years old. A case of it was discovered on the bottom of the sea, part of a shipwreck off the coast of France in 1718. For all those decades it lay beneath the waters, and when they brought it up it was still intact. Think of it, Beatrice—the grapes which made this wine grew in the world when the garden where we sit was nothing but wilderness."

Beatrice smiled, intrigued, he could tell, and curious. It was the same look she had given him when she climbed out of the pool at sunrise, her skin so pale against her lavender suit, water streaming from her limbs, and found him standing there, watching her and waiting.

The cork crumbled; he poured the wine and raised his glass to hers.

"To the lost past," he toasted. "And to our future."

The rare vintage tasted darkly of burnt oak; it was dry, not bitter, with a trace of cherry. *Marvelous*, Beatrice murmured. When their glasses were empty, Andrew reached into the canvas bag and pulled out another bottle, which he put on the table beside the first.

"This one has a label," Beatrice observed.

Andrew smiled. The night air was as warm as breath. "Yes," he said. "It's the most recent vintage from the same vineyard in France where the first wine was made." He turned the modern bottle, keeping his eyes on her face. "Of course, in another two hundred years, when this bottle is opened, almost everything that is living now will be dead."

"You puzzle me," she said, and looked away, and he remembered that despite her youth she was sensitive to death; she had lost her only brother to influenza.

"Yes," he said, "it is most depressing, I agree. But Beatrice, what if you could live to drink this wine?" He put the bottle down and took her hands. "What if, in two hundred years, we could sit in this garden again, just as we are now, and open this bottle together?"

She laughed, and her laughter struck his silence like waves and fell away.

"I don't understand you," she said.

He stood then, and pulled her up. He showed her the orchid which had been so withered, now profuse with life. The year was 1922, and the Curies had transformed plain earth into something rare and unimagined. A secret of the universe had been revealed, and a restless world dreamed of transformation. In drugstores everywhere were special toothpastes, hand creams, bath salts, liniments, chocolates, all laced with radium, promising miracles. In factories across the country, women painted luminous faces onto clocks, licking the tips of their brushes to keep a fine point, tasting a bitter metal from the heart of the dark universe. The era was affluent, and most people could afford to have a little radium, but only a man as rich as Andrew Byar could have all he wanted. *Radi Os.* He whispered the name of his elixir, running his fingertips over the vial in his pocket. When he told Beatrice what the bottle had cost, she gasped. And when he poured the drops into her second glass of wine and his, this wine from grapes vanished for two hundred summers, she drank.

Paradise lost, he thought leaning back in his chair. Pale flowers opened in the darkness, amid the rising sounds of insects, and the wine warmed his throat, hers.

Paradise lost, now found.

Andrew had called the car, it was waiting when Beatrice finally left the house, sitting quietly as a shadow by the gate. She walked, listening to the night sounds of crickets and wind in the leaves, and the harsh crunch of the stones beneath her pale satin shoes. Her eyes would not stay down, she looked up into the night sky with its endless wheeling, scattering stars. Her father had a telescope and had tried to teach her the constellations, taking her to the roof of their own great house and pointing out, with infinite patience, the belts and flames and streaming hair, the cups of stars brimming over with night-darkened sky. She had studied it to please him, but she could never see what he was so intent on showing her. Celestial navigation, he explained, a science of the air: whole fleets had traveled with only these stars for guides. Beatrice stared until her eyes ached and stars burned phosphorescent against her closed lids, but even then the patterns eluded her. Often, just as she felt on the verge of seeing the stars coalesce into a shape, they seemed to swell, spilling over into rivers, shattering like a handful of rice strewn across blacktop. Her father sighed and put the telescope away. He could not imagine that his only living child would not share his love and aptitude for science.

The driver had the window rolled down. His cigarette ember made a bright arc as he reached to start the engine. Beatrice paused to tell him she would walk—the night air was so lovely—then passed through the gate into the street. Her footsteps were solid and lonely on the city sidewalks. The vast grounds of the estate rose wild and tangled beside her; a soft breeze stirred the diaphanous wrap she wore across her shoulders. The night was so dark that the random stars seemed nearly within her reach. Beatrice flung her head back to gaze at them, joy cascading through her flesh. She felt like a star herself, pale and radiant, as if every one of her cells were burning bright, as if she gave off her own particular light into the universe.

This feeling was something new: perhaps, though not certainly, it was the consequence of Andrew's elixir. When he put the drops into her wine, she had stopped laughing out of respect, though privately she had remained amused. She had drunk out of curiosity and politeness, repeating the formal, nearly silent exchanges that held their passion like a vessel, but also being true to a vow she had made to herself. For Beatrice was involved in an experiment of her own, one that had only tangentially to do with Andrew Byar. The wine had tasted old, of worn oak with a trace of mold. She let it linger on her tongue, imagining those vanished grapes, but she had tasted nothing out of the ordinary, not even the tinge of salt from all those decades beneath the sea.

It was not until later, after they had finished the wine and were walking along the rock path through the white garden, that it began. Moths, luna and sphinx, skimmed through the shadows and lit on the moonflowers, lifting their slow wings. Near the house, a bed of white nasturtiums seemed to flicker and spark. Beatrice slipped off her shoes and waded into the pool, a natural spring shaped by stones. *You look like a water lily,* Andrew said, and she glanced down at her dress, its hem soaked now and darkening. She smiled and pressed her palm to his cheek. He caught her hand and kissed it, his lips against the shallow concave below her fingers, his breath in the palm of her hand. She felt it then for the first time, how her flesh, where it had been touched by his, seemed to pulse with light, transformed, but she blamed this sensation on the wine, the starry light, the strangeness of the moonstruck garden. They walked across the grass. She stumbled, and he caught her arm, and she felt it again: the splay of his fingers like rays of sun on her skin. Inside the house, it was no different. Light trailed from his fingertips and marked her flesh, light soared through her like a comet in his bed.

Now she turned onto the avenue of stately homes, the white wrap slipping from her shoulders, her hair falling loose down her back. It was an extraordinary night, the air soft and warm, a caress. She heard the car following her in the near distance, and as she passed through the familiar gates of her father's estate, less grand than Byar's but magnificent all the same, she turned and waved to the driver, who looked straight ahead at the empty road and pretended not to see her. Then, still smiling, she followed the tree-lined path to the back garden, where she sat on a bench by the pond. On the rooftop her father's telescopes stood in a line, and beyond them, the stars.

Beatrice was twenty years old and beautiful, and she had made herself this promise: she would never be used, she would always be free. She would follow her heart wherever it might take her, and in this way she would discover her own true understanding of the world. It was an experiment as daring as Andrew's, as full of uncertain hope, though to those who knew her she was merely wild, spoiled, a girl whose family had never recovered from the death of her older brother, that young man of great promise who had survived the war only to die of influenza eight months later in the room where he'd been born. Three years ago, this was. Beatrice had been seventeen, and when the doctor emerged from her brother's room to break the news, she had felt her world splinter, like glass cracked and held only tenuously in its former shape. Her mother had collapsed, weeping, and her father had bent his graying head, revealing a vulnerable place at the back of his neck, reddened by his collar. Beatrice, however, had not moved. She had not dared. What had been held together, logical and orderly, was suddenly unbound. Her brother, whom she had loved, who had taught her to ride a horse and sneak to the train tracks to flatten pennies when the engines roared past, this brother with his pale hair and paler blue eyes, was suddenly, mysteriously gone from the world. Why? she demanded, turning her fierce anger on the friends and relatives and clergy who came to visit in the days and weeks that followed, but they shook their heads and could offer no answer more complete than the natural order of the world, a pattern fixed in place, preordained, divine.

Beatrice had been a dutiful girl, receiving the world and the rules of her society as true and inevitable, just as one accepted the moon rising or the servant girl bringing clean clothes into her room at dawn. However, she could not accept this. Walking the paths of the estate at all hours of the day and night, remembering her brother's laughter and the touch of his hand and the way sunlight made his pale hair look white, she began to question everything.

She began to push the limits of her world, too, tentatively at first, then more urgently. She was steadfast against the hue and cry which resulted, utterly determined to step beyond the strictures she had known. But she was not cynical. More than ever, the world seemed full of mysteries she could hardly comprehend, and the visible fell like a veil between herself and something else, something glimpsed at unexpected moments—a white curtain rising from an open window, or leaf shadows playing on the tiled floor of her room—images that layered and gathered, inexplicable but powerful. Yet her intuitions could no longer be contained by the structures she had accepted all her life, and this discovery made her feel breathless, as if she stood on the edge of an abyss, even while the world around her went on much as it always had, knit back together by the ordinary day-to-day. *Don't you see,* she wanted to shout, at her father bent over endless figures of steel sales and her mother arranging flowers and the cook cutting a hundred biscuits out for tea. *Don't you see that everything has changed?*

Had they looked up, she would have explained that the rules were like a net: they could not hold the fleeting thing they sought to capture. But no one did look up, and Beatrice slowly understood that she must discover the truth of the world on her own. And so, she decided, she would. She would embrace every experience; she would discard all preconceptions; she would see every moment as an open door, and she would step through each one wide-eyed, without fear.

Thus, when she emerged from the pool, water glistening cool on her pale limbs, and saw Andrew Byar watching her, transfixed, she had smiled.

And thus on this night, when the leaves stirred behind the hydrangea bushes by her father's house and a figure emerged, tall, dressed in black, invisible except for his hands and face shining out to her like beacons, she smiled once more.

"I thought you were never coming," she said, tranquil.

"I waited here for hours," the young man complained, sitting down beside her, taking her hand. Light shot through her; she thought of Andrew Byar and his garden.

"Poor Roberto," she said.

He was a distant relative of her mother's, come from Italy for the summer. Ostensibly to study, but she knew her father was seeking someone suitable to take over the business when he died. He had never considered asking Beatrice to do so, something which had not troubled her until she perceived that the rules of the world were light and hollow, easily knocked aside. Idly, she wondered if her father's decision might change if he knew that she was going to live forever, and she laughed.

"It is not funny," Roberto said, speaking in a formal, lilting English that she loved. "All day I have been dreaming of this time with you, and then you do not come. It is insulting."

"I'm sorry," she said, and she was, though she was not regretful. "I was called away unexpectedly. There was no way to inform you."

"Called away to where?"

"It's not discussible," she said lightly. "It is my own affair entirely."

He did not answer. She felt his presence beside her, dark and churning. The old Beatrice would have hastened to soothe away his anger, but now she sat quietly, waiting with interest to see what would happen next.

"I am in love with you," he said, angry at having been forced into this admission, or perhaps at the feeling itself. "I don't want to lose even a moment of our time."

She put her hand to his cheek, as she had earlier with Andrew. Offended still, Roberto turned his face away. Beatrice let her hand fall to her lap, wondering for the first time if what Andrew had claimed might be true. She had not really considered it, what it might mean to be ageless, to live outside of time. To explore every facet of the world, to follow every passion to its depths, because she would not have to choose one over another.

"What do you think?" she asked Roberto. "Would you like to live forever?"

"I have done so already," he replied at once. "Each moment you are gone is an eternity to me."

Beatrice laughed then, delighted by the way all doors opened to new places. Impulsively she kissed Roberto, sliding her hand behind his neck and her tongue into his mouth, where it bloomed like a flower struck by light.

Summer grew rich and dense, and then, subtly, it began to wane. A few leaves drifted to the ground, and overnight the dogwoods turned flame red. In his garden the orchid still flowered profuse and opulent, and elsewhere, in his car, Andrew Byar splayed his long, hard fingers on the custom-built walnut desk. The city was a rush of lights beyond his open windows, and from a distance came the roar from the steel plants, humming night and day. Recently, he had ordered a new furnace, determined to best his competitors, richer and more famous than he. They were old men now, men whose time of building and creating would soon end.

His, he believed, would not.

For two months and five days he and Beatrice had been drinking the *Radi Os*. It had become a ritual, and as with any ritual there were rules, intricate ceremonies which had taken on their own life, and which must not be broken. Each week they met in the garden, even though his family had returned and sometimes moved, visible, beyond the panes of glass. The alyssum had grown brittle, and the moonflowers had wilted, and the magnificent orchid would soon be moved into the greenhouse in anticipation of an early frost. Capricious still, as beautiful and willful as ever, Beatrice nonetheless joined him at the table each week, watching seriously and silently as he placed the drops into her glass. Any wine would do by now, any sort of dress, but they each assumed the same position at the table as they had on that first night, and they knew without speaking that they must finish their drinks in a single swallow. Dusk, it must be, though dusk came earlier now.

Sometimes they went inside afterwards and sometimes Beatrice merely rose and disappeared into the shadows. The eager talk of their early days, the chattering comparisons of change—flesh that quickened, fingertips that trembled—had given way to a pensive silence. They touched less and less often as the new sensations grew; even the most casual union was almost more than they could bear. One kiss, and his lips hummed for hours. A brush of their fingertips, and his hands carried her warmth, her imprint, like a brand.

Like a brand. It was so. Before the experiment, Beatrice had been a flicker on the edge of his mind, a pleasure, a reward, laughter falling amid the flowers in his garden at the end of the day. It had pleased him that she was the daughter of a significant rival, that she was pliant and easy, slipping so carelessly into his bed, apparently removed from any of the strictures and concerns that governed other women. A wild child, a free spirit, and he had chosen her because of this. Strangely, however, now that they had been sealed together by this secret, now that he saw her regularly and might go on doing so for decades or even centuries to come, she never left his mind.

Indeed, he had become obsessed with her, with her indifference. Here, after all, was the rarest gift, and he had given it to her alone, to Beatrice. Not to his wife with her gilded hair, not to his indolent sons, not to anyone else but Beatrice. She had been surprised and pleased and curious; it was true that she came faithfully each week to meet him. Yet not once had she expressed joy or wonder at having been so chosen, and lately this had begun to trouble Andrew Byar. He had given her this gift: why, then, should she still withhold her heart? Yet Beatrice remained as she had always been, amused and curious, but strangely distant, as if her own life were a book she was reading, one she might put down at any moment in order to gaze out the window at the sky.

Andrew's expectations had been so fully disappointed that he found himself regretful of the future. What if, in the uncountable days that lay before them, he became completely disillusioned with her? What if his companion turned out to be a woman he despised? The orchid thrived, cascading gem-like blossoms; released from the prospect of death, however, Andrew Byar's feelings for Beatrice were withering into dust. He saw her now in the harshest light, and became critical of the tiniest habits of her being: the way a muscle flickered her cheeks when she stifled a yawn or a smile, the irritating motion of her throat as she drank, her persistence in murmuring the foolish slang of the day whenever she was moved or delighted by the world.

In a decade, he wondered, in a century, would her quirks move him to violence? A life sentence, he mused: the phrase had taken on new meaning.

Yet at the same time he could not get enough of her. More and more often he dispatched his driver to seek her out, and more and more often she was not to be found. Her aloofness made him brood, it made him angry. He would cut her off, he thought sometimes, awash in anger, sitting alone in his great office, trembling with this unfamiliar inability to accomplish what he wished. Science had been Andrew Byar's life, yet science had not prepared him for this. Not for the rage he felt upon learning she met others, in the garden of her father's estate or on the rooftop or in the cars of trains. Not for the longing and misery which welled up to replace the rage, a depthless yearning which was what had driven him, finally, out in his car to confront her on this night.

He pulled into the circular drive before her father's house. A maid, fluttering and startled when he asked for Beatrice, explained that she was in the roof garden. Andrew brushed away her attempts to have him sit and wait. He strode across the foyer, following his instincts up the wide, curved staircase to the second floor and the steeper one to the third, where he discovered the open door and the ladder that went to the roof. He climbed, emerging into the crisp night air. Urns of flowers and small trees had transformed the rooftop into a park. Benches and tables offered places to rest and view the glittering cityscape below. Beatrice stood with her head bent over a telescope, her hair cascading over her shoulders, as the silhouetted figure beside her pointed out the belt of Orion, the Big Dipper and the Little, the flowing tresses of the Coma Berenice. "Surely you can see them," he exclaimed. He was wearing a hat, and he gestured at the stars with a folded newspaper. "Why, they are as clear as if I had drawn them there myself."

"Let me look again," she soothed. Dark hair slipped across her cheek, and in that instant Andrew Byar's anger faded. He understood that he could never deny Beatrice, any more than he could deny himself. What had begun as science and desire had become something more, something as essential to him as life itself, so that seeing her in this intimacy with a stranger, involved in a world of which he knew nothing, made him catch his breath in pain.

At this the two looked up, startled, from their telescopes.

"Andrew!" Beatrice exclaimed. Her father—for it was her father, Jonathan Crane, with his shock of white hair falling over his eyes and an old man's spotted hands—took a single step and said, "Byar, what the devil are you doing here?"

"I came to talk to Beatrice."

"Uninvited," Beatrice said sharply.

Jonathan Crane looked swiftly from one to another, his spare white beard cutting the air.

"Well," he said. "Beatrice is right here, as you see. Whether she will speak to you, I cannot say. But in any case, you may be of some assistance to me, Byar. Come here, and have a look. Beatrice insists that there is no order in the sky. Tell her, if you would, that she is wrong."

"Perhaps not wrong, exactly," Byar demurred, crossing the roof. Beatrice was staring at him; he felt her gaze like the sting of a slap. "Perhaps she prefers the stars to remain unknown."

"Perhaps I see my own patterns," she replied. "Perhaps I seek new patterns altogether."

"The world is as it is," her father said. "Come, Byar, have a look."

Andrew leaned over the telescope, gazing up at a familiar sky. When he finally stood, the old man was studying him with a gaze both unremitting and intent, reminding him of the many meetings at which they had faced each other just so, opposed on issues of steel production or charitable trusts.

"Orion," Andrew said, for the order of the stars was clear to him, and he could not see the point in saying otherwise. "And the Big Dipper, hung from the North Star as if from a hook."

"There, you see, Beatrice?" her father said. "Even your secret lover can find the constellations."

Into the shocked silence which followed, the old man spoke again. "Yes, I know," he said. "All except for your intentions, Byar. Beatrice visits you, in secret, or so she presumes, every week. At those meetings you give her a glass of wine. Sometimes, she goes inside with you, and sometimes she does not. I am her father, and I am asking what your intentions are."

Andrew Byar stared at his old rival. How had he been discovered so completely? His next emotion, however, was pure fear. For he had understood, in that moment when he emerged onto the roof and saw Beatrice, that desire had its roots in the possibility of loss. He understood, too, that if Beatrice were not present to solidify his belief, to confirm his confidence like light confirms a shadow, then belief might disappear from him entirely.

"This is my own affair," Beatrice was protesting, her voice clear, but trembling with anger. "You do not own me, either one of you, and you have no right to be discussing me like this."

"But I want to answer," Andrew said. Carefully, he explained the experiment to her father.

Jonathan Crane whacked the folded paper against his palm.

"Ridiculous. Your ideas are nonsense."

They began to argue then, worrying the properties of radium as they had once exhausted the properties of steel. They argued with such ferocity and passion that they forgot Beatrice entirely. It was her father who noticed first that the quality of silence had changed; the rooftop with its intricate tile and urns of flowers was empty.

"You see how it is," he said gruffly, interrupting Byar. "She has gone. She chooses to ignore us both."

Beatrice was near enough, standing just beyond the doorway, to hear her father say this. She did not wait for Andrew to reply. How little they understood, she thought, descending the ladder and the flight of stairs to her rooms. How much they took for granted, and chose not to see. She had never made Andrew any promises; he had mistaken her silence for complicity, that was all. The experiment was no more her passion than were the distant and abstract patterns of the sky. Why be limited to seeing the stars as bulls and goats and scuttling crabs, when from another vantage point—from, say, the moon or Jupiter or Saturn—they might resemble something else entirely? Or beyond even that, within another way of perceiving, within a new framework of thought, a person might discover patterns beyond what her father or Andrew Byar or anyone else imagined. They did not, after all, have the slightest insight about the mysteries of her own heart. Why, then, should she trust their vision of the world?

Well, she would not. It did not take her long to pack a suitcase.

The house was silent. Roberto had proposed to her, and in the wake of her refusal he had in turn refused her father, turning his back on the steel trade and returning to Padua to study botany. *I am free of you now,* he had written on one terse postcard, and she had considered this for a moment before she wrote on the bottom, *Your freedom brings me joy,* and sent it back.

One suitcase, but it was heavy. She lugged it down the stairs and through the marble-floored foyer, grateful for the murmuring of the fountain, which masked her footsteps. Outside, Andrew's car was waiting. The driver started the engine the instant he saw her in the doorway. Well, why not? Beatrice thought, though she had intended to call a cab. Tonight she would accept a ride—yes, why not? The driver tossed his cigarette into the gravel and got out to put her bag in the back. Beatrice slid across the cool leather seat, folding her hands on the walnut desk, inhaling Andrew's peculiar scent: cologne and cigars and an underlying whiff of steel. The liquid in his little bottles was odorless, but the car was filled with the aromas of money and autumn air, close counterparts, somehow. *To the station,* she instructed, and the driver pulled away. She glanced back at the house, wondering if Andrew and her father were still on the roof, discussing the stars or the stock market or her own stubborn nature. No matter, really. She would take the first train, wherever it might go. She picked up Andrew's pen. Across the production figures, which he would see as soon as the car returned to fetch him, she wrote in bold black letters, *My freedom brings me joy.*

Beatrice traveled for nearly a year, to Boston and Chicago, New York and Philadelphia and Washington, D.C. Stories of her wildness rippled in her wake, how she drank too much and danced barefoot in the snow and took lovers with careless abandon. Scandalous photos appeared in the society pages: Beatrice with her slender arms around one neck or another, the delicate rise of her breasts visible beneath her risqué dresses. Beatrice dressed up like a man, dressed up like a bear, wearing a corona like a star. She was always laughing, but people noted that her wildness had made her thin, had lent a feverish quality to her eyes. They watched Andrew Byar slyly, too, commenting on how gaunt he'd grown, waning like a moon in her absence. Or perhaps it was the strikes, which had begun just after the new furnace arrived and three hundred workers were laid off in the name of progress. In bloody protest, whole production lines had shut down for weeks, rendering meaningless the neat projections across which Beatrice had scrawled her liberation.

On the verge of summer, the stories of Beatrice's escapades suddenly ceased. The photos stopped. Her father made discreet inquiries, only to discover that no one had seen Beatrice since a party at an estate in the far reaches of the Adirondacks a month earlier, where she had danced frantically, people said, frenetically and without ceasing. She was there, dancing, and then she was gone. Just like that, disappeared, though no one had thought too much about it at the time. Perhaps she had stepped out onto a terrace for a breath of air, perhaps she had gone for a stroll.

No one had seen her pause on the side of the swirling room and light a cigarette. Or they had seen her and had not noticed, for the party was wild and everyone was drinking, and in the kinetic mosaic of the evening Beatrice was only one more fragment of color. She drew the smoke in deeply, watching the flash of arms and ankles, the beaded dresses glinting. Then she slipped through the French doors onto the terrace, closing them behind her, so that the visual intensity of the party was separated from its noise, which came to her distantly now, muffled. She inhaled again, folding her bare arms against the night air. She had begun to smoke at some point, in Chicago, she thought it had been, where a young man had left his cigarettes on a table and she had slipped them into her purse. Chicago or Boston or New York: this was one discovery, that it really didn't matter. Whatever truth she'd been seeking, trying on the laughter and the costumes and the men, she simply had not found. One by one she'd discarded them, and now she stood here, at a party that was real, but also unreal, a place that was not her own. Her Pittsburgh life was lost as well, no more now than a dream. She had heard rumors of the strikes, of course, and through them rumors of Andrew. She had seen his photograph twice, and noted how he'd aged. Strangely, she found that she missed the meetings in the garden, so secret and exhilarating. She missed even Andrew and her father, for without their orderly views of the world to work against, to define her, the freedom she had gained had fallen flat. The room beyond the glass doors swayed and pulsed. Beatrice threw her cigarette, still smoldering, into the wet grass, and walked alone to the lake.

It was dark. Waves lapped at the shore. She slid her shoes off and waded to her ankles in the frigid water, so recently ice. In recent weeks the sensations of light had slowly left her, replaced now and then with mysterious shooting pains which came and went and finally came and stayed. In motion, she did not feel them, which was one reason she lived as she had. She squatted down and cupped the icy water in her hands, listening to the distant call of loons. A flash of white on the opposite shore caught her attention. She looked up, then held herself as still as the water, searching the line of trees.

Maybe it was nothing, or maybe nothing stranger than nasturtiums glinting sparks in the dusk of Andrew's garden. But it seemed to Beatrice that she glimpsed her brother, standing as naturally amid the trees as a deer, one hand in his pocket and his head tilted at an angle, the forest at his back. For a long time, until her legs ached and began to tremble with the exertion of stillness, she did not move. When she stood, he was gone. But she was convinced that he had been there, that she had glimpsed something vital through these trees. Barefoot, still, she left the lake and followed him.

It was a near-wilderness, and night. In the house, people laughed and sang and fell asleep on sofas even as the music played, ices slipping from their hands. Days passed before her disappearance was discovered. Two weeks before search parties were dispatched, and yet another ten days before Beatrice was found, not by anyone looking, but by a group of boys attempting to become Eagle Scouts. Thin as a leaf, her clothes torn and dirty, she was sitting on a rock by a stream. She did not seem at all surprised to see them. "Oh, hello," she said, standing and brushing dirt from her hands. "I've been wondering when somebody would come."

The boys clustered around her, astounded. To them she seemed like an enchanted creature, a deer that spoke, a shaft of light assuming human form. They were afraid at first, hesitant to offer her their arms. The unplanned hike back took most of a day, for the boys, inexperienced, were forced to stop often and consult their compasses. Also, Beatrice was weak. She walked slowly, and at first she walked in silence. After a few hours, though, she began to tell them stories, fantastic stories, of her weeks alone in the woods. Later they would argue over them, agreeing on the details but never the whole. She had eaten the earth, she claimed, she had broken open maple trees no bigger than her finger and drunk the rising sap. She had stood in a shockingly hard rain, water dripping from her fingertips, from her hair, and watched a herd of elk move across a clearing. She had been following her brother at first, sighting the glint of his hair one moment and the flash of a limb another, but in the end he had disappeared, and she had been left alone. This she did not tell the boys, fearing it would frighten them, as it had frightened her, to hear of the dark nights she'd spent, sleeping on moss or pine boughs, the nights so pure black that she couldn't tell, finally, if the darkness was coming from within her or without. As it was, she frightened them, anyway. Her arm was no more than a living bone beneath their hands as they helped her across streams and over fallen logs. They imagined a dark forest of the heart, the pulse of blood and weave of branches, and they let her go as soon as possible.

Beatrice saw the fear in their eyes; she heard them saying, later, that she had lost her mind. In the wake of this derision she grew silent, aware that she could never explain how solitude, so unfamiliar and so perilous, had altered her forever.

In his great house on the bluffs, Andrew read of her rescue. No longer well himself, he spent most days in his sunny office, going through his papers, or sitting in the solarium with his wife. He studied the brief story on the back page which chronicled Beatrice's emergence from the forest, leaves woven in her hair, dirt ground into her dress.

When she returned to Pittsburgh, he went to meet her at the station. She stepped from the train, dressed simply in a white silk skirt and a gray cashmere sweater. She was very thin. *She is dying,* he thought, which is what Beatrice thought, too, when she saw Andrew standing on the platform, as hunched and gray as a comma. Her heart swelled up with sadness, as well as with a sudden, inexplicable love. She knew as vividly as if she had seen it herself that the orchid was withered in the greenhouse, its flowers gone, its very leaves and stems marked with burns. She was twenty-one years old.

"I loved you," Andrew whispered as she passed him. "You must believe me, Beatrice, I chose you out of love."

"No," she said. She spoke evenly, for her fear and bitterness had faded during her weeks in the forest. "It was not love between us then, never enough love from either you or me. I was your experiment. And you were part of mine."

They did not speak again, though within months they were living in the same sanatorium. What they had observed in one another was terribly true: they were dying. Geiger counters clicked and chattered on their breath, voicing the disintegration of their cells. The slightest touch raised bruises, the color of pale lilacs against thunderclouds, on their arms. The families came, bearing flowers, wine, books, news, the small comforts of the day-to-day, and if they passed one another in the halls they averted their eyes: whatever connection had existed between Andrew and Beatrice was ignored, as if ignoring might erase it.

One afternoon, when everyone had left, Beatrice stood, filled with an insatiable restlessness. She must move. The staircase was grand, built of hickory and curving down to the main floor, where French doors opened onto the gardens. It took her half an hour to descend. Outside, the grass was warm, thick, springing up beneath her bare feet. She felt a wave of pure astonishment at its texture, as if each blade pressed separately and softly against her flesh.

No one was in sight; the sunlight was a warm hand, moving and returning. She thought of Andrew, how solemn he had been as he put the drops into their glasses, how deeply he had believed in—had depended on—the certainties of science. She had never shared his belief, but she had no regrets. It was not, as some argued, misguided love or self-sacrifice or the whimsical nature of a young girl's heart that had brought her to this moment. She had been no vessel for another's dreams, no casualty in Andrew's single-minded pursuit of scientific knowledge. It had been life she wanted, life she had embraced, no moment lost or left unexplored, no light or darkness left unseen.

Beatrice paused to rest on a ledge of stone. High up in the brick building, a curtain flickered in a window, lifting for an instant like a veil. *I create the universe,* she murmured, knowing it was in some strange sense true, for she understood now that the world was a shimmering place, shaped anew in every instant by the mystery of perception, each atom in constant if invisible motion. Except that suddenly for Beatrice the motion *was* visible. The earth beneath her feet felt as volatile as ocean waves, and the transitory beauty of the garden, the subtle shifts and alterations of even the boulders, left her breathless.

The wind lifted. Branches hummed, and then the stones began to groan, resonant and strange. All around her borders dissolved, spilling trees and flowers from their shapes; the air was stained with color. Within herself, beyond herself, there was this swirl and glitter: this was the wondrous and terrifying knowledge she had gained. Beauty, too, and even a coherence in the way her thoughts themselves were splintered, coming to her in layers and rushes: her brother's bright hair and the feel of a horse about to leap beneath her, her father's reddened neck and the scent of baking biscuits floating through the house on a rainy day. And Andrew's face in his luminous garden, so solemn and so full of hope. *The elixir of life,* he was saying, and now the stones were speaking, too, a chant reverberating through every cell of everything, living and inert, a sound so powerful that even her own body began to blur and lose its form, cascading into the unstill world like petals falling, like water shattering, like every minute particle of light.

Train to Chinko

So all right, thought Peterson, he was speaking English, and, all right, so the map was from America. Well, naturally. And so, all right, the names of towns were spelled differently here and pronounced differently. But come on, hadn't this country been open to tourism for at least ten years?

"C-h-i-n-k-o," said Peterson, pronouncing the name of the town very distinctly. "C-h-i-n-k-o. I want to take the train to C-h-i-n-k-o."

But the clerk standing behind the ticket counter at the railway station kept frowning. A second clerk, seated at a wooden desk behind the counter, watched.

"See," said Peterson, pointing at the map that he had placed on the counter upside down to him but right-side up for the clerk. "See? Here. This is where we are. Right here." Peterson showed exactly with his finger. "And over here, right here, this is the town I want to go. Chinko. C-h-i-n-k-o."

Still frowning, the first clerk took the map over to the second clerk sitting at the desk. They both studied the map and spoke in some incomprehensible language.

Then the second clerk said, "Cakovecza."

"Cakovecza!" said the first clerk.

The first clerk brought the map back to the counter, laid it out right-side up for him but upside down for Peterson, and pointed at the town that on the map said, upside down, "Chinko."

"Cakovecza," said the clerk.

"Cakovecza?" said Peterson.

The clerk took a piece of paper and printed a word on it and pushed the piece of paper across the counter to Peterson.

Peterson looked at the piece of paper. The word printed on it said: "Cakovecza."

The second clerk, the one seated at the wooden desk, had already inserted a blank ticket into the roller of a big, black type-writer, and had begun to type.

Peterson studied the word printed on the piece of paper. Well, yes, there was a certain resemblance between the two words, "Chinko" and "Cakovecza." Both started with a "C," for example. So perhaps it was possible that "Chinko" was the English spelling of "Cakovecza." On the other hand, maybe they weren't the same town at all. Maybe the clerks had made a mistake. An honest mistake. Perhaps he would get on the train and find himself going where he didn't want to go.

The second clerk spun the finished ticket out of the typewriter roller, placed the ticket on the desk in front of him, whacked it with several different stamps, took a pen, inserted something over the stamped parts of the ticket, and handed the ticket to the first clerk.

"*Zog!*" said the first clerk, carrying the finished ticket to the counter and pushing it towards Peterson.

"How much?" said Peterson.

"*Taroj,*" said the clerk.

He took another piece of paper, wrote something on it, and also pushed the paper over to Peterson.

Peterson had a look. The clerk had written "150,350." All right. But 150,350 what? Of course, 150,350 units of this country's basic currency. But Peterson had to admit that he had no idea what that basic unit was. He had asked about it in Munich. Oh, they'll take your euros, you can bet your life on that, he had been told.

So Peterson pulled a fifty-euro bill out of his wallet.

"Euros?" he said.

The clerk lifted the bill from Peterson's hand and took it over to the second clerk sitting at the desk. The second clerk pulled out the drawer of the desk, put the bill in there, took out some coins, gave the coins to the first clerk, who brought them over to Peterson.

Peterson looked at the strange coins in his hand. They certainly didn't look like they amounted to much money. That meant he had paid almost fifty euros for his ticket. That was about fifty dollars. Fifty dollars? To Chinko? Only to Chinko? Not even an hour's ride away?

Unless, of course, these clerks had gotten the two towns mixed up. In an honest mistake. Because that could explain it. Maybe it did cost around fifty dollars to get to Cakovecza. Maybe Cakovecza was a lot farther away than Chinko.

"Excuse me," said Peterson.

Both clerks stood at the desk looking at Peterson.

"I don't think...," he started, but gave it up. Probably both of them had survived the purges, and nothing that he could do now was going to change anything. So instead he pointed to the schedule board on the wall, then to his watch, and asked, "When?"

"*Zog!*" said the first clerk, who found another piece of paper, wrote out something, and pushed the piece of paper over to Peterson.

"Thanks very much," said Peterson.

He looked at the piece of paper, made out that train 4012 left at 16:26 from track two, put the piece of paper in his shirt pocket along with the ticket, folded up the map, and slipped it in his back pocket, extracted the long handle out of the top of the suitcase, and pulled the suitcase along behind him out of the ticket office and past the waiting room/café and towards the train tracks.

And saw a difficulty ahead of him.

If his train had been leaving on track one, it would have been all right. He simply would have pulled his suitcase through the door ahead of him and out onto the platform. But he saw that to get to tracks two and three he had to go down a stairway, then along an underground corridor which crossed under the tracks, and then undoubtedly up another stairway.

The problem was his suitcase. Getting it up and down that stairway. To be honest, he had overpacked. Up to now that hadn't mattered because with the handle pulled out all the way the suitcase was perfectly balanced, and as you walked along pulling it behind you, you just didn't feel it, the weight. Plus, he'd had porters to help him at the Munich and the Vienna train stations.

But now he saw that he himself was going to have to drag the suitcase down this one flight of stairs and up another.

Peterson edged his suitcase over to the staircase and clunked it down one step. Then another. And another. Until he reached the landing halfway down. Actually, thought Peterson, the impact of all that weight on the wheels might be too much. Probably he ought to carry the suitcase. So he pushed the extended handle in and gripped the regular handle. My God! He really *had* overpacked! He found he had to lean his body way over to one side to balance himself as he carried it down.

At least in the underground corridor he could extend the handle again and pull the suitcase along on its rollers. But naturally the corridor smelled of urine, and naturally there was a lot of graffiti on the walls. Peterson even saw a "Fuck you!" written in English. Perhaps, it occurred to him, that during the Communist times there hadn't been any of this, that is, not only the "Fuck you!" but the graffiti as well. Although, who knew? Maybe that sort of thing went on regardless of the government.

Peterson paused at the bottom of the stairway going up to tracks two and three and saw daylight up there. He looked back down the corridor past the "Fuck you!" to see if by any possible chance he'd missed an elevator. But, of course, he hadn't.

So, nothing for it. He pushed the extended handle down into the suitcase, grabbed the regular handle, braced his body, and lifted. Again, my God! Up one step, pause, up another, pause, then another. Had he put all that weight in there? Maybe later he could take some things out. Just leave stuff behind.

At the top of the stairway Peterson eased the suitcase down on the train platform and found himself between two waiting trains, one at track two and one at track three. The cars of both trains seemed antique, as if perhaps they were museum pieces put out here on display, the bodies of the cars very square and resting high off the wheels.

Peterson extracted the handle of the suitcase and began to pull the suitcase along between the two trains towards the departure boards. But now, even though he was up on the level again, the suitcase didn't follow along behind him as effortlessly as before. Well, that was because the surface of the train platform was old and cracked. Either that, or the wheels had been damaged by that clunking down the steps.

At the departure board for track two, he pulled out the ticket and the piece of paper from his shirt pocket. Yes, the number of the train on the departure board matched the number on the paper, 4012, and down the list of the town names, "Nagyada," "Dioskal," "Szapeth," and "Ikervar," he saw "Cakovecza," which also matched the name on his ticket. But no "Chinko." Unless, of course, "Cakovecza" and "Chinko" were the same town. Which was probably true.

Peterson turned to look down the train platform to see if there was another departure board and saw an apparition of a man approaching him. Well, the man wasn't an apparition, of course. He was real enough. It was just that he was dressed so outlandishly in a red and green uniform all covered with braids and epaulets and stripes, as if he had stepped out of a Gilbert and Sullivan operetta or was a holdover from the Austrian-Hungarian Empire. The man walked with a pronounced limp, almost dragging one foot, which caused his head to bob up and down. As he got closer Peterson could see that, in fact, he looked old enough to almost be a holdover from the Austrian-Hungarian Empire, the skin of his face gnarled, a large wart on his cheek, his eyes watery, and his ears standing out and away from under his peaked hat.

It was only when the man stopped right in front of Peterson that Peterson saw the whistle hung around his neck and the little round metal sign, red on one side and green on the other, that he carried in his hand.

The train master, Peterson now understood. This was the man who whistled the trains off.

"Excuse me," said Peterson. "Chinko?" Peterson pointed to the departure board and said still more distinctly, "C-h-i-n-k-o?"

"Tschesno?" said the man in a barely audible, reedy voice.

"C-h-i-n-k-o?" said Peterson again.

The man, without looking at the departure board and counting on the fingers of his hand, said, "Nagyada, Dioskal, Szapeth, Ikervar, Cakovecza."

"Cakovecza? So, this train goes to Cakovecza?"

The man focused his watery eyes on Peterson. "*Zog*. Cakovecza!"

"Thanks very much," said Peterson.

The old man's fingers found the bill of his cap, and he bowed slightly to Peterson.

Peterson made a slight bow in return, realizing at the same time that he hadn't learned anything. He already knew this train, the one on track two, went to Cakovecza. That was the name of the town on his ticket. The question was, were Cakovecza and Chinko the same town? Because if they weren't, why should he get on this train and go where he didn't want to go?

"Excuse me," said Peterson.

But the old man had already turned and was walking away, the one foot dragging, his head bobbing up and down.

Well, thought Peterson, undoubtedly Cakovecza and Chinko were the same town.

So he pulled his suitcase, its rollers not working all that well now, probably it was the uneven surface of the platform, up to the nearest car on track two, pushed in the extended handle of his suitcase, grabbed the regular handle, braced himself, and gave a heave. He just managed to get the suitcase up onto the floor of the car. Peterson climbed into the car next to the suitcase, drew the handle out, and began to pull the suitcase down the aisle of double-facing seats.

Peterson stopped in front of one of the pairs of facing seats, again pushed the extended handle of his suitcase in, and again grabbed the regular handle. But this time he couldn't get the suitcase all the way up to the luggage rack above him. It was just too heavy. So he guided it back down onto the seat.

But that was all right because as he looked around the car he saw he was the only passenger. So it didn't matter. His suitcase could just stay where it was. Even though it should have been up on the luggage rack.

Except that it was too heavy.

Nevertheless, since it was beside him, Peterson undid the latches and saw the lid pop up from the compression beneath it. The wonder was how he'd managed to get all that stuff in there. Not just all the clothing and the two extra pairs of shoes, but even his books and the folder containing all the draft manuscripts.

He looked at his watch and saw that he had another twenty-five minutes before the train left. So, why not? He opened the folder containing his draft manuscripts and pulled one of them out and arranged it on his lap. Yes, why not?

He had just started to read the first words of the first paragraph, "A systemic examination into the morphology of certain previously unobserved links...," when he heard a sound he couldn't quite believe. Music. A Dixieland band. "Sweet Georgia Brown." A Dixieland band? Here? In this town? In this country? Playing "Sweet Georgia Brown"?

He put the manuscript back down on top of the suitcase and crossed the aisle to the other side of the train and pulled down the window in order to hear the music better. To his surprise he saw that the platform over on track one was beginning to fill with revelers of some sort, people dressed as clowns and ghosts and goblins, a man with an enormous hat pretending to ride a horse and four or five people on different length stilts and absurdly long pants. Then—so he had been right—a Dixieland band, six men, each with a red blazer and a blue straw hat, the man with the sliding trombone leading the way and the banjo player bringing up the rear, marched right to the edge of track one. The trombone player swung his instrument this way and that, and the banjo player got down on his knees, ratcheting up "Sweet Georgia Brown." Behind the Dixieland band the people on stilts were reaching into bags at their sides and tossing out candy.

Then something else Peterson couldn't quite believe. A royal procession also crowded onto the platform, a fake king and queen and fake attendants, princes and princesses, dukes and duchesses, more men with coats of arms pretending to ride horses, more people on stilts, and finally priests in black robes and black hoods, the lead priest carrying a large, shiny golden cross.

"*Fasching.*" That word drifted into Peterson's mind. Hadn't he read about this festival somewhere? The middle of February? Carnival? A religious connection? Something to do with Lent? Thus the priests and the cross?

Whatever the celebration was about, it now seemed to be over, as if the railway station were the endpoint of the parade. The Dixieland band had stopped playing, the musicians were now beginning to put their instruments away, some of the royal personages and the clowns and ghosts were taking off their costumes, the men on stilts were slipping down against the walls, and some quite normal-looking person was going around with a coffee thermos and paper cups.

But what a pleasant development. Such a very nice thing to happen. Although Peterson was sorry that the Dixieland band had stopped playing. He had especially enjoyed that. Pulled at something inside of him. Deep out of the past. "Sweet Georgia Brown."

Many of the revelers, now carrying their costumes, were heading back through the doors into the train station, but also, Peterson saw, many had started to disappear down the stairway which led to tracks two and three. And sure enough, soon he could see the same stream of people reappearing. Half began to board his train, and half began to board the train on track three. Peterson crossed in front of his suitcase and sat down in his seat just as the first of the newcomers came down the aisle. In a matter of a minute or so, most of the seats were taken.

"Excuse, excuse," said a boy who belonged to a group of young people. They were holding their discarded costumes in their arms, and all had their faces painted with shiny red and blue and white paint. One of the girls wore a golden wig. "Excuse," the boy repeated.

Peterson indicated that it was certainly all right for them to sit beside him. He pushed down on the lid of the suitcase, finally getting the latches to lock, stepped out into the aisle, and was about to grab the handle when two of the boys took the suitcase and lifted it, seemingly effortlessly, up to the rack above the seats.

"Thanks very much," said Peterson.

"*Chjerszte!*" said one of the boys.

Four of these young people sat on the seat opposite Peterson, and two squeezed in beside him. One of the boys had a plastic hamper and began to take bottles of beer out of it, while one of the girls, the one sitting directly opposite Peterson, started taking off her golden wig.

Just at that moment Peterson noticed that the revelers in the train on the opposite side of the platform had pulled the windows of their cars down and were waving to the people in his train. Holding her wig in one hand, the girl sitting across from Peterson pulled their window down, and, since Peterson was the one sitting next to the window on his side, he stood up, leaned through it, and looked at the sea of hands reaching out from the other train. He especially looked at a group of girls in red blouses and red scarves, crowded around three windows in the car just opposite, who were making exaggerated operatic gestures of love and despair to the occupants of Peterson's car. One of these girls saw Peterson and began to blow him kisses. Not ordinary kisses, but slow kisses, out along her hand, the fingers of her hand fluttering after each kiss.

Peterson was just beginning to think of returning her kisses when the old man, the train master, the one with the gnarled face and outfitted in his ridiculous red and green uniform and dragging his foot as he walked, raised his round metal sign, and, to the jeers of all, blew his whistle. The train on track three eased forward and then stopped. The old man still kept his sign high in the air. More jeering from passengers at the windows of both trains, and the train on track three started up again.

"Excuse, excuse," said one of the boys sitting next to Peterson. The boy was offering Peterson a bottle of beer.

"Thanks," said Peterson, taking a bottle. The beer inside the bottle looked very dark.

"*Chjerszte!*" said the boy, holding up his bottle for a toast.

"*Chjerszte!*" said Peterson, trying to copy how the boy said the word and also holding up his bottle.

The other young people held up their bottles.

His manuscript! Peterson had just put the lip of the bottle to his mouth when he remembered his manuscript. Where was it? He had been reading it, something about unobserved links, and now it wasn't here. He started to look around, but just at that moment he heard a whistle right outside the train window and, when he looked, saw the old man in the red and green uniform holding up his round metal sign.

Peterson's train jerked forward, causing those in the aisles to reach out for the seat handles to steady themselves. The train went some yards down the track, then came to a halt. Peterson leaned out the window and looked back at the old man. He was still holding his round metal sign up in the air.

Another jerk, and the train started off again. The old man grew smaller and smaller back there on the train platform.

Peterson retracted his head back through the window, pulled the window down, and turned to the young people.

"*Chjerszte!*" he said, and brought the bottle of beer up to his lips and drank. And thought back to that girl floating kisses to him. Of course it had all been just in fun. Nothing serious.

"*Chjerszte!*" said several of the young people opposite him.

Peterson was just taking another swallow of his beer when he saw the conductor come down the aisle, checking tickets.

"Excuse me," said Peterson when the conductor got to his group. "Chinko? Does this train go to Chinko." The conductor took Peterson's ticket, looked at it, punched it, and moved on.

"Excuse," said the girl across from Peterson, the one who had been wearing the golden wig. "You were English?"

"Am I English?"

"*Zog!* Excuse. Only school English."

"I'm American," said Peterson.

"American!" said the girl.

"American!" said several of the other young people.

"I get uncle in Denver," said one of the boys.

"Ah, Denver!" said Peterson.

"California! She super beautiful?" said another of the boys.

"Very beautiful," said Peterson.

"Where you now go?" asked the girl.

"Chinko," said Peterson. When none of them responded to this, he repeated the name of the town slowly, as he had in the ticket office. "C-h-i-n-k-o."

"Chinko?" said one of the girls.

"Just a moment," said Peterson. He reached for his map in his back pants pocket and unfolded it. "See? Here. Chinko." He pointed with his finger.

The girl took the map, and all the young people on the seat opposite Peterson looked at the map and began to talk in their incomprehensible language.

"Or maybe Cakovecza," said Peterson.

"Cakovecza?" said the girl.

"Maybe," said Peterson.

"*Zog!* Cakovecza!" said the girl.

"Cakovecza!" said the boy.

They all smiled and handed the map back to Peterson.

"So," said Peterson, taking the map and folding it up again, "Chinko is the same as Cakovecza?" When they just looked at him, he added, "Or Cakovecza is the same as Chinko?"

At that moment the daylight went to night, and the air pressure pushed against Peterson's eardrums, and he realized the train had gone into a tunnel. All but two of the young people sitting with him got up and started collecting their costumes. The train began to slow even before it got out of the tunnel. When the daylight returned, Peterson saw that at least half the people in the car were getting up to leave.

"Goodbye," said the girl. She reached out and shook Peterson's hand. Then each of the young people in turn shook Peterson's hand, each saying goodbye.

As soon as the train stopped, Peterson pulled the window down, and as he had expected and hoped, the young people came down the platform to Peterson's window.

"Goodbye, American friend," said one of the boys, reaching for and shaking Peterson's hand again.

"I visit you in California," said another boy.

"It was much pleasure to meet you," said the girl.

"California!" said one of the boys.

"California!" said Peterson.

"*Zog!*" said the girl.

Peterson heard a whistle, the train jerked forward, pushing him against the rim of the window. All the young people waved, and Peterson waved back at them, and at the very end, when he almost couldn't see them anymore, he blew the girl a kiss. Whether she saw him doing that or not, Peterson couldn't tell. But now he was looking at the rest of the town as it slipped past. How dreary, he thought. All those small stone houses, the bare yards, the dirt streets. Surely those young people didn't have to live in a place like this.

And, anyway, too bad they had left the train. He had been having a good time with them. "*Chjerszte!*" and so forth. Whatever that word meant. And as the train picked up speed and Peterson pushed the window closed and sat down again, he saw that the two remaining young people, the boy and a girl sitting opposite him, were engaged in some kind of serious conversation. It was no longer important to them that he was an interesting American, a visitor to their country.

And, anyway, he found himself distracted by a woman who had just gotten on the train and was sitting in the next row of seats. She had deposited a number of plastic sacks around her and was in the process of going through each one of them, apparently moving objects out of one into another and then maybe into still another. Peterson could hear the rustling and rattling of plastic even above the sound of the train.

Suddenly Peterson remembered his manuscript. He had been reading it before all those young people got on the train. Where was it?

He was beginning to look under the seat when the conductor came down the aisle asking for the tickets of those who had just gotten on. The woman in the next row of seats up from Peterson rattled her plastic sacks and said something to the conductor.

"*Zajka?*" said the conductor.

The woman raised her voice, almost shouting at the conductor. Other people in the car turned to look at the woman.

"*Zajka!*" said the conductor.

Again the train went into a tunnel, the air pressure pushed on Peterson's eardrums, and most of the rest of the people in the car, including the two young people opposite him, the boy and the girl, began to get up and collect their costumes. Even the woman started to collect her plastic bags. Peterson guessed that she couldn't find her ticket, or didn't even have a ticket, and the conductor had told her she had to get off.

In fact, as soon as the train came out of the tunnel and began to slow down, the woman, in that language Peterson didn't understand at all, began to harangue the other passengers who had gotten up from their seats. When they ignored her, she turned to Peterson, her face now quite red.

"I'm sorry," said Peterson. "But I don't speak your language."

"*Smykalla!*" said the woman, shouting.

"I don't know your language."

"*Du bist ein fucker,*" said the woman, gripping all her plastic bags and moving down the aisle, the bags hitting the sides of the seats.

Again Peterson pulled the window next to him down, thinking that maybe the two young people would come along the platform and shake his hand and say things about California, or at least about America. But he saw them walking into the interior of the station without even looking back. Only the lady with all the plastic bags remained on the platform. She had found an old man in a red and green uniform and was shouting at him, waving her arms in all directions.

Peterson didn't believe it. This old man was the same old man Peterson had seen at the first train station. At least he wore the same outlandish Austrian-Hungarian operetta outfit. Had this old man come along with the train, maybe riding in the front car with the engineer?

But when the old man turned to raise his round metal sign and blow his whistle, Peterson saw it wasn't the same man, or, at least, probably wasn't the same man. Well, it couldn't have been the same man.

Although, admittedly, it was getting a little dark to see now. Partly that was because it was late in the afternoon and partly because they seemed to be in a mountain valley that shut out what was left of the sun.

The train started up with another jerk, began to slide by more stone houses, bare yards, and dirt roads. Peterson pushed the window back up and looked around his car. The lights to the car had come on, or had been on all the time and he had just not noticed it. As far as he could tell, all the happy people, the revelers, had gotten off by now and only a few people had gotten on. And they were dour-looking types, a woman with a headscarf, some kind of workman wearing rubber boots, and a man, probably at least partly blind, because he held a white cane next to him. Certainly no chance of a lively conversation here. No more talk about California. Or America. Outside the window, the valley had narrowed down, the mountain wall coming in quite close.

And Peterson remembered: his manuscript!

He stepped out into the aisle, kneeled down, and looked under the seat, and, thank God, saw the manuscript lying under the seat in front of him. He knelt down even farther, reached under the seat, retrieved it, sat down again. He started to read the opening paragraph again: "A systemic examination into the morphology of certain previously unobserved links..."

And stopped reading. Wasn't this the point where something interesting, something pleasant had happened? "Sweet Georgia Brown"? Something out of the past?

He looked out the window again. Perhaps he saw some snow-flakes slipping past. He wasn't sure. The air pressure changed, and Peterson assumed they were in another tunnel. And sure enough, even before the end of the tunnel, the train began to slow for the next station. Peterson put the manuscript down on the seat next to him and watched the man with the white cane get out of his seat and walk down the aisle.

At the station, two people got on, a girl of about twelve who wore a long, yellow plastic raincoat and a tall, well-built man with prematurely white hair. Since he wore a red-checked woolen shirt and mountain-type boots, Peterson decided that he was a woodsman. Probably wasn't. But that's what Peterson decided.

A whistle blew, the train started up with a jerk, passed the end of the platform, slowed, and came to a complete stop. Outside, back against the lights from the train station, Peterson could see the train master in one of those operetta-type uniforms walking in the opposite direction.

Peterson took the map out of his shirt pocket, unfolded it, stood up, and went over to the workman with the rubber boots.

"Chinko?" said Peterson, pointing first at the map and then at the front of the train.

The man studied the map.

"C-h-i-n-k-o," Peterson said again.

The man said something Peterson didn't understand.

"Is this train going to C-h-i-n-k-o?"

Again the man said something Peterson didn't understand.

The train started with a jerk, almost upsetting Peterson.

"Thanks so much," said Peterson, taking the map from the man and going back and sitting down in his seat just as the train went into another tunnel. After the tunnel Peterson leaned his face against the window and tried to see outside. But it was too dark. He thought that maybe he saw the side of a mountain. But he wasn't sure.

Suddenly Peterson found himself having to hold on to his seat to keep from sliding off it as he heard the screech and ringing of the wheels as the train strained to a stop.

Peterson eased back into his seat. Clearly that had been an emergency stop.

But as he looked over at the other passengers, the workman with the rubber boots, the girl in the plastic raincoat, and the man in the red-checked shirt, none of them, as far as he could tell, seemed to think anything had happened out of the ordinary.

Just then the conductor walked very quickly down the aisle in the opposite direction the train had been going and exited into the car behind. Even if he had known the language, which he didn't, of course, Peterson would have had trouble asking the conductor what was going on.

Peterson had no more than leaned his face up against the window again, trying to look out and see something, when the conductor walked quickly back up the aisle in the opposite direction as before. Why didn't someone else ask him? thought Peterson. One of the other passengers?

The train started moving again. But in reverse. The train was going backwards!

After maybe two minutes, the train stopped.

Again, Peterson looked at the other passengers in the car. They sat there as before.

A popping and whining. Then a man clearing his voice. It was the train's loudspeaker system. The man said something in a measured tone, then more popping, a wheezing, and the loudspeaker system went off.

Peterson saw the other passengers in the car get up and start to walk towards the front of the train.

"Excuse me," said Peterson to the workman with rubber boots.

The man motioned Peterson to follow him.

"Why? What's happening?" said Peterson, but the man had already gone through the door at the front end of the car.

Peterson reached up to the luggage rack, struggled his suitcase down to the floor, extended the handle, and began to pull it along the aisle. The door was a problem. Or rather, the doors. He could get the suitcase through the door of his car all right, but as he reached forward to get the rear door of the next car open as well, the first door closed on his suitcase, and when he reached back to open that door again, the door in front of him closed. He had to go through this process three times before he arrived at the final car, a kind of baggage car where he found the other passengers, not only the ones from his car but other cars as well, seated along the sides of the baggage car. There must have been twenty people in all. The conductor was standing at the front making a speech. Peterson parked his suitcase, took a seat at the end, and pretended to listen to the conductor. Well, he was listening to the conductor. It was just that he had no idea what he was saying.

"*Zog,*" said one of the passengers.

"*Zog,*" said another.

Peterson understood that the conductor was asking each passenger in turn a question. When the conductor asked Peterson the same question, whatever that was, he also replied, "*Zog.*"

People were standing and putting on their coats, and one passenger had already opened a side door and had stepped out into the night.

"Excuse," said Peterson, leaving his suitcase and going up to the conductor. "What's going on?"

"Boos," said the conductor. *"Boos."*

"Bus," said somebody else.

"Ah, bus!" said Peterson. "We're going to meet a bus?"

In any case, Peterson had no choice, because all the rest of the passengers had already stepped out of the side door into the night. He pushed the extended handle of his suitcase in, hauled the suitcase over to the door, swung out himself, grabbed the regular handle of the suitcase, and pulled the suitcase out and lowered it down onto the ground. Or gravel. Or cinders. Whatever was beneath his feet.

And tried to follow the other passengers as they walked along the length of the locomotive and then out ahead of the locomotive. Of course, here there was no question of pulling his suitcase. The gravel or cinders or whatever was beneath his feet was too rough for that. So he simply lugged it, leaning to one side, not quite believing again how heavy it was, all the time falling farther and farther behind the other passengers, until he couldn't see them anymore.

"Taroj!"

That was the conductor passing Peterson, his feet making crunching sounds on the gravel or cinders.

"Hello! Excuse!" said Peterson.

The conductor walked out ahead of Peterson until he, too, disappeared into the night.

Peterson wanted to keep going, knew he had to keep going, that he had no choice but to keep going, but his suitcase was too heavy. So he put it down. Just for a moment. For a small moment. Below him, off to one side, he thought he heard the rushing of a river.

As he was listening to the river, he also heard the crunching sounds of somebody walking towards him.

"Taroj."

It was the woodsman. The man with the prematurely white hair and the red-checked woolen shirt. Not that Peterson could see those features all that clearly now. But he still recognized the person as the woodsman.

"What's going on?" said Peterson.

The woodsman reached down, grabbed hold of Peterson's suitcase, and started back in the direction he had come from. Peterson almost had to hurry to keep up with the woodsman and not lose sight of him in the darkness.

Until he heard voices and saw the forms of people in front of him. The woodsman put Peterson's suitcase down, and Peterson realized that these people were, of course, the other passengers who had been on the train. Again, the conductor was making a speech, only this time several of the passengers were arguing with him.

"*Strujcka!*" said one of the passengers.

"*Rila!*" said the conductor.

"*Strujcka! Strujcka!*" said the passenger again.

"*Vlach!*" said the conductor. "*Vlach!*"

The conductor raised his fist at that passenger and then began to walk back along the tracks toward the train. He turned one more time, raised his fist again, and shouted, "*Vlach!*"

In the dim light Peterson had been able to make out that they were all standing on what appeared to be a dirt road crossing the tracks, and that the road disappeared into trees in each direction. The man who had been arguing with the conductor pointed up the dirt road in one direction.

Now Peterson saw that the passengers seemed to be splitting into two groups, the one group getting ready to follow the man who had been arguing with the conductor, and the other group getting ready to go the other way on the dirt road.

The woodsman came over and picked up Peterson's suitcase again.

"*Yudhy scutarja,*" he said.

"*Zog!*" said Peterson.

It turned out there were five of them in the woodsman's group. Peterson walked up at the head of the line, just behind the woodsman, who seemed to carry Peterson's suitcase with no effort at all. Once or twice Peterson turned around to see what had happened to the other fifteen or so passengers who had gone the other way, but already he couldn't see back even as far as the railway tracks. Below them he could now clearly hear the rushing sound of the river.

When they came to a bridge that crossed the river, the woodsman put Peterson's suitcase down and leaned up against the railing.

"*Yor hoxha,*" said one of the passengers next to the woodsman.

"*Scutarja*," replied the woodsman.

Then the woodsman picked up Peterson's suitcase again, and this time the road headed upwards away from the river. As they walked, its sound grew fainter and fainter, and when Peterson looked up above him he could see that the clouds were thinning and that the moon was trying to break through. He could even see the outlines of mountains back where they had come from. He wondered what the other passengers were doing over there and why they had decided to go towards the mountains.

And suddenly remembered the draft of his manuscript. The one he had been reading in the train. The one he had temporarily lost and found again under the seat. Something about missing links.

Oh, well, thought Peterson. Too bad. About his leaving that manuscript behind. Not that it was completely lost. Surely it was there in the train. So he could go back to look for it if he wanted to. Except he wasn't about to do that, of course. Not right now.

Ahead of him the woodsman swung Peterson's suitcase around to his other hand. Peterson watched the woodsman as he walked and again wondered how the woodsman could carry the suitcase so easily. He didn't even lean his body to one side as he walked. And they were now walking uphill, after all, and even though Peterson wasn't carrying anything, he was beginning to get out of breath. Think of all the weight in that suitcase.

Sometimes the moon came out from under the clouds and then went away again. The road twisted ahead of them always going up, and then, after a while, crossed a large field where there weren't any trees at all.

Suddenly, without any warning, as it were, all five of them were standing at the edge of a highway. A major highway, as far as Peterson could tell. No dirt road, but wide and paved with a broken yellow line going down its middle.

The woodsman put Peterson's suitcase down and looked up and down the highway. One of the other passengers came over and began to talk to the woodsman, and then the two other passengers came over and began to talk as well. In the tumble of words Peterson heard "*Strujcka*" repeated again and again. Then one of the men pointed down the highway, and a woman, who Peterson guessed was the man's wife, started walking in that direction. The man hurried up and joined her.

That left three of them, the woodsman, Peterson, and another man.

"*Taroj*," said the woodsman.

He picked up Peterson's suitcase and started walking up the highway in the opposite direction the man and his wife had gone. Peterson followed right behind the woodsman, and the other man followed along right behind Peterson.

Again, Peterson couldn't believe how easily the woodsman carried Peterson's suitcase. Not leaning his body at all. Still, Peterson thought of going up to the woodsman and explaining that since the highway was so smooth here, he, Peterson, could take over the suitcase and pull it along by its extended handle. On the other hand, he didn't know how he would explain this to the woodsman, and also maybe the wheels of the suitcase had been damaged.

So Peterson just kept walking.

In theory, he told himself, he should be concerned, perhaps even alarmed, about his present situation. Here he was walking along some highway in the middle of the mountains in a foreign country with two other people whom he didn't know and who couldn't speak a word of English. And God knew where they were taking him. Strujcka or where?

But that was in theory. For some reason Peterson wasn't alarmed. Not at all. He had the clear feeling that as long as he stayed with the woodsman, as long as he kept walking right behind him, as long as the two of them were together, everything would work out just fine.

Of course, there was also the matter of his manuscript. Again, in theory, his leaving it in the train should have disturbed him. But, for some reason, it didn't.

Ahead of them the surface of the highway reflected the moon's light and off to one side a valley, or really a canyon, sloped away, and Peterson thought he could still hear the faint sound of the river. Beyond the canyon he could see the hulking shape of mountains.

He wasn't quite sure how long they had been walking. Every once in a while the woodsman swung Peterson's suitcase to his other hand.

"*Cughir*," Peterson heard the woodsman say.

Peterson saw it, a little building off to the side of the road. But when they approached it, the woodsman putting down Peterson's suitcase, Peterson saw it wasn't a regular building at all, but some kind of shrine with an open arched roof and the figure of Jesus hanging from the cross, his face turned to one side.

The woodsman sat down on a log near the shrine, and following his example, Peterson found another log and sat down. But the other man didn't sit down. He went back out to the highway.

Peterson looked up at the moon hanging up in the sky, then at the figure of Jesus. Jesus' whole body pulled against the nails that held him to the cross, but his face, which was turned to the side, expressed no pain. Why? thought Peterson. Why no pain?

The other man came back from the highway and began to talk to the woodsman. Again Peterson heard the word *"Scutarja."* The man shook the woodsman's hand and then came over and shook Peterson's hand.

"Zog!" said Peterson.

With that, the man went out onto the highway and began to walk back in the direction they had come from.

Which left only Peterson and the woodsman.

"Taroj," said the woodsman, getting up.

"Taroj," said Peterson, also getting up.

The woodsman pointed at Peterson's suitcase and shook his head. He pointed up into the hill on the other side of the highway.

Peterson got the idea. They were going up into the hill. His suitcase had to be left here. It couldn't go any farther.

"Wait," said Peterson.

He went to his suitcase, laid it flat on the ground, and opened the latches, the lip springing up. Surely he ought to take something, he thought. Something. Anything. When he saw the folder containing his draft manuscripts, he thought, I'll take that, the folder.

He pushed at the lid of the suitcase, got the latches locked, and held the folder up to his chest. "Okay, okay?" he said.

"Zog!" said the woodsman.

They started walking along the highway again. At one point Peterson turned around and looked back along the highway, trying to remember this spot. So that when he came back he could find it again.

After about five minutes the woodsman stopped and studied the side of the hill, then pointed, and Peterson could make out the beginnings of a trail going up into the woods. Or thought he could make out the beginnings of a trail. The woodsman stepped across a ditch, grabbed a branch, and lifted himself up. He held out a hand, and Peterson, holding the folder with his manuscripts in one hand, held out his other hand and let the woodsman pull him up.

And it certainly was a real trail, because by the moonlight that filtered down between the trees, Peterson could see it extending in front of them.

They walked, Peterson right behind the woodsman, until the trail began to switch back and then back again, and back once more, the trail always going up. Although Peterson realized that in ordinary circumstances he ought to have been concerned about leaving his suitcase with all his things in it back down there on the highway beside the shrine, right now didn't seem like an ordinary circumstance.

Finally the trail leveled out.

"*Cughir,*" said the woodsman.

They had come to another shrine. In fact, it looked almost exactly like the shrine down below alongside the highway, except this one was smaller. But it had the same kind of arched roof and the same figure of Jesus hanging on the cross, his face turned to one side, again showing no pain.

The woodsman found a place to sit, this time on a stone. Peterson found a stone to sit on, too, and placed the folder with his manuscripts beside him. He could see the mountains beyond. Quite a beautiful sight, thought Peterson. He must remember this place. Return to it sometime.

The woodsman started signaling something to Peterson, holding out the fingers of both hands. He opened and closed his fingers three times. Then the woodsman pulled out his wallet, pointed to it, and opened and closed his hands three times again. Thirty. The woodsman was signaling "thirty."

Peterson pulled out his wallet, and the woodsman nodded.

So, Peterson thought, he wants thirty euros. In ordinary circumstances Peterson wouldn't have done this, but he pulled out a twenty and a ten and held them towards the woodsman. The woodsman got up, took them, and stuffed them into the front pocket of his pants.

"*Brancusi,*" said the woodsman, pointing up the trail.

Peterson got up to see a man approaching them, walking in long strides. He was tall and thin and carried some kind of walking stick, although it was really too long to be a walking stick.

"*Shkod!*" said the woodsman, shaking the new man's hands.

"*Shkod!*" said the new man.

The woodsman reached in his pocket, pulled out the thirty euros, and handed the two bills over to the new man. The new man held them up to the moonlight, then stuffed them in his pants pocket.

Then the woodsman came over and shook Peterson's hand, and Peterson understood that the woodsman was handing him over to the new man and that he, the woodsman, was turning back.

"Thanks so very much," said Peterson to the woodsman. "I can't tell you."

The woodsman touched his forehead with his fingers, bowed slightly, and started back down the trail even before Peterson could bow in return.

"*Taroj?*" said the new man to Peterson.

"*Taroj,*" said Peterson.

The new man, probably because he was taller and thinner, walked faster than the woodsman, pumping the stick beside him. At first, as the trail went uphill, it was hard for Peterson to keep up. Several times the man in front of him stopped and waited for Peterson.

"*Plov?*" asked the man the second time he stopped.

They had just started walking again when Peterson remembered his manuscript folder. Gone. Not in his one hand and not in the other. So where was it? Beside the rock, of course. He remembered putting it down beside him when he sat down on the rock at the last stop. After the woodsman had sat down on his rock. So the folder must still be there. Beside the rock.

But he wasn't going back for it. Maybe tomorrow, thought Peterson. When he came back for his suitcase. Then he could also come up the trail and get his folder. See that beautiful view again.

"*Cughir,*" said the man.

Peterson looked ahead and saw another shrine. Only this one

wasn't a building at all but a long wooden carving fixed against a tree. Again it displayed the body of Christ nailed to the cross, his head hanging to his side.

Peterson's new guide started opening and closing his hands five times.

This time Peterson understood immediately. He pulled out his wallet, looked inside, and saw in the moonlight that he only had one bill left, and that it was a fifty. He handed it over to the man.

The man leaned his stick up against the tree next to the shrine and held the bill up to the moonlight. Then he pulled the other euro bills out of his pants pocket, put the fifty with them, and shoved them back.

"*Brancusi,*" said the man, looking along the trail.

Peterson looked, too, and wasn't all that surprised to see still another man approach. Unlike his current guide, this man walked slowly, even dragging one of his feet a little, causing his head to bob. As he got closer, Peterson could see why he walked so slowly. He was very old. He also carried a stick, and Peterson could see that it was a real walking stick and he leaned on it as he walked.

And suddenly Peterson understood—and this didn't totally surprise him, either—that he knew this man, that he had seen him before: the train master at the station where Peterson had started his trip today. The man even had the same wart on the side of his cheek, and his ears stood out away from his head in the same way. Of course, he wasn't dressed in that uniform with all the braids and stripes. Rather, he wore an old suit coat and vest, a peaked cap, and rubber boots that almost went up to his knees.

"*Shkod!*" said the tall, thin man to the old man.

"*Shkod!*" rasped the old man.

The thin man reached in his trousers pocket and brought out the euro bills, all eighty euros' worth of them, as far as Peterson could tell, and handed them over to the old man. The old man passed the bills into a pocket of his vest without even looking at them.

"*Beyzo,*" rasped the old man and looked at Peterson. "*Taroj?*"

"*Taroj,*" said Peterson.

It was easy to follow the old man since he walked so slowly. Peterson even had plenty of time to look around. He and the old man seemed to be walking across an open field. The moon lit up everything, giving the grass around them a kind of silvery glow. A number of times Peterson looked over at the hulk of the mountains behind them and wondered what had happened to the group of train passengers who had gone that way. He was certainly glad he wasn't with them.

After a while the trail started downhill and then went into the woods. But it wasn't completely dark in the woods because the moonlight still filtered through the tops of the trees.

Suddenly, without any warning, as it were, the trail broke out into a clearing, and down below in the valley, a surprise: a walled town with turrets. Peterson could even make out the moat around the wall and the bridge over the moat to the towered gate. In the center of the town, of course, the church. It was lit up with floodlights, its steeple going up into the sky. And, or was he imagining it, weren't those the strains of "Sweet Georgia Brown" drifting up from below? A Dixieland band?

"Chinko," rasped the old man.

"What?"

"*Zog.* Chinko."

"Chinko!" said Peterson.

And now no doubt about it. Down there, somewhere in that town, probably next to the church, a Dixieland band was ratcheting up "Sweet Georgia Brown."

The old man lifted his fingers to the peak of his cap and made a slight bow. "*Tarog,*" he said.

"*Tarog,*" answered Peterson, returning the bow.

The old man started back up the trail, dragging the one foot behind him. Just as he was about to reenter the woods, Peterson called out, "California!"

The old man stopped and held up his stick.

Then he went into the woods.

And then Peterson was alone. But that was all right. Being alone. Because he saw the trail. Just follow it. Down the hill. Along the moat. Cross the bridge. Enter the gate. Go to where he had always wanted to go.

ELIZABETH L. HODGES

The Firebird

"You shouldn't play with fire." Lena leans over Ivan's shoulder and blows out the votive candle over which he is passing his index finger back and forth. She jiggles her arm nervously, and the silver bracelet slides beneath her sleeve. She looks around her. Everywhere there is plenty. The people are fat. How can some have so much and others so little? The sun is low in the sky outside the airport lounge's long windows. There's still enough light to catch on Lena's earring as it tucks in and out of her platinum hair. The reflection flickers on Ivan's face; his pale eyes move from the wisp of candle smoke to Lena's hair. One strand would light a room. Would illuminate one's way.

The room is dark as night although outside the sun shines on the bare branches encased in ice. Princess Elena sleeps under eider down quilts, behind thick brocade drapes, and dreams about violets blooming in the snow.

In her dream, she walks through the fields in fur-lined boots, in a fur hat, her hands in a fur muff. She picks her way through the blossoms with cheeks flushed by the cold, no, with excitement, no, by love. She is walking toward her love. She can't see him, but he waits for her at the edge of the field, at the edge of the forest.

A white wolf leads her journey through the field. He speaks to her, saying, "Follow me. You'll be glad." When he turns to look at her, his pale eyes are older than her grandmother's, the oldest eyes she knows. They are kind as her mother's—the queen's—the kindest eyes she knows. They are strong as her father's—the king's—the strongest eyes she knows. His paws are graceful as they rise, hang limp in the air, and softly fall. Where they land, violets appear—a delicate path leading to the forest, to an unknown love.

Inside, it is dark as night; outside the sun shines.

Lena turns her head and looks at Ivan sideways.

"So, do you think I'm done for?" she asks in Russian.

Ivan looks straight ahead, as if he's looking to see someone he knows in this strange airport, in this strange land. "What do I know?" he answers.

"You know your brother." She spits the words at him in English.

"Nyet," he replies, still looking at no one, still forcing his eyes nowhere.

"Why didn't he just send me tickets?" She pauses. "You *know*."

She looks down at her hands, her hair covering her face. Lena feels like crying. Her fingers are laced, slowly extending and retracting. She is thinking ahead. Her mind races beyond the flight with its constant offer of cold champagne, warm nuts, hot towels, ice cream. Her thoughts fly faster than the speed of light, much faster than the plane with its enormous wings lifting through the air. She is beyond her dreams, the tiny, white pill, the groggy wakening to the voice in her ear announcing. She is past the landing, the crush of people on the stairs, behind the red line, across it, the thud of the stamp, the non-smiling face behind the glass. There she is. She sees herself standing beside the perfume stall, staring at the door beyond nothing to declare. It is dark. Dread waits in the shadows. It blocks her path. She can't think past the Moscow airport carousel spinning with so many futures except her own.

Prince Ivan watches from behind the boulder as the white wolf comes closer and closer. The prince has been walking, lost in circles for hours, his horse having been torn to bits by the wolf as it stood drinking from a forest pool while Ivan slept in a nearby tree, tied to the branches to keep from falling. The shrieks woke him. In his dreams, he blindly slashed out at what he couldn't see.

Now he peers at the pale eyes in the dying light. He rests his hand on the bloodied saddle and bridle beside him. He thinks of his horse nuzzling his face just yesterday, the warm breath down his collar against the cold. His poor horse. Bits of horse flesh still cling to the white coat skulking toward him. He holds the hilt of his sword tight in his left hand. His arm freezes in midair. The wolf looks at him and smiles.

The wolf speaks. "I want to make amends."

* * *

Ivan touches her arm.

"It's time to go."

She looks up at him quickly and nods.

"I'm going to the bathroom first." She fumbles with her backpack.

"Be back in five minutes." He looks into her eyes. She won't run. He almost wishes she would. Lena nods again. He watches her out of the corner of his eye trained on *Sports Illustrated*. She disappears down a hallway.

In the bathroom, Lena stares at the mirror without recognizing the face in front of her. Her heart is broken.

Ivan sees her as soon as she reappears. He rises and rolls the magazine in his hands. She notices him at the last minute, just as he's close enough to take her arm. They have only one carry-on between them—her backpack. He needs no weapon and has not been in America long enough to require even a duffel bag.

He bends slightly and says into her ear, "He didn't send tickets because you wouldn't have come." She shrugs in acknowledgement.

He hesitates before he speaks again. He shouldn't be talking.

"He'll probably beat you." He states this as a fact; he offers it to her.

"How many times?" she asks bitterly.

"As many times as he wants," Ivan says simply.

"If I had a choice between being a whore in America or your brother Ivanovich's whore, I'd choose America." She says this to the front of her coat. He can barely hear her.

"You don't," he says.

The wolf runs over mountains and swims rivers with the prince on his back. He trudges through snow and ice. Ivan clings to the wolf's back and burrows his face in the white coat. He doesn't know where he is going or for what purpose. He is trusting a wolf who killed his horse. He is tired and wants to sleep, but dares not for fear of falling. Finally, the wolf slows, and then stops. Ivan rolls in exhaustion from his back.

Hours later, he wakes to the wolf licking his face. Ivan looks around. They are in a courtyard. There are fruit trees and waterfalls. It is the courtyard of a palace. Ivan walks toward the tile ter-

race. Hanging from one of the archways is a golden cage. In the cage, there is a magnificent bird with feathers ablaze with a golden sheen. Its eyes shine like jewels. Ivan looks at the sky and is surprised to see stars. It is night, but the courtyard shines with the plumage as if it were day.

"Set it free," the wolf says.

Ivan looks at the wolf.

"Set it free," the wolf repeats.

Ivan closes his eyes and leans back in his seat. Lena has already fallen asleep, having taken a pill with her tea and water and orange.

He remembers how she loves oranges. When they were little together, after her parents were killed, for Christmas they would sometimes have oranges. Her face lit up, her golden hair, the juice running down her chin—Ivan gave her his orange more than once just to bathe in the aura of her. Not so with his brother. He teased her even then. He sighs and opens his eyes.

She has no other relatives, no one except for his brother and him. And his brother wants her, has always wanted her. In the little closet of a bed-sitter they shared, they were lucky to be off the streets, except those times when the boys' mother came back with a client; then they waited in the front doorway and huddled to keep from freezing.

Ivan switches through the channels of movies. It could be worse. She is just another broad who ran to New York with all the money she could get her hands on. Yet even as he looks at her in the darkened plane, her hair is like a halo around her head, her ribs through her sweater, a breathing cage for her heart.

Ivan wasn't lying when he told Lena his brother would beat her. He would beat her before he killed her. Ivan felt his eyes burn.

In her dreams, Princess Elena is coming closer and closer to the edge of the wood. But instead of becoming clearer, the figure is moving farther into the darkness. She can only see the flash of a white tail, a pale light, and runs not to lose it.

This is unlike her. She never leaves the castle. She believes the ogre has a spell on her, making it so to step one foot outside is impossible. And here she is, following a white wolf that peers over his shoulder to make sure she doesn't lag behind. Just as the ogre's spell held her captive, the white wolf's spell sets her free. She follows close as she can, her outstretched hands holding the luminescent violets she's picked along the way.

As she goes deeper and deeper in the forest, she drops them, one by one. She doesn't know any longer who is the captor and who is the captive. Now, she can only see the wolf in flickers, fireflies against the black and dark green. But she can hear him, like the wind, rustling along the forest floor. She walks softly, dropping her violets, as if she were in prayer. The faces of the saints flash through her thoughts, and then all goes dark. Elena moans. She closes her eyes. Is she dead or alive? Through her lids she senses light. Slowly, she opens her eyes. Her white wolf is there with a young man, one hand on the wolf's neck, the other holding a feather that glows like the full moon in February.

Ivan nudges Lena awake.

"We'll be in Amsterdam in half an hour."

Lena straightens in her chair and rings for the steward.

"Voda," she says in a raspy voice. "Sok."

The steward quickly returns with bottled water and juice and just as quickly moves away.

Ivan leans over so closely his lips are touching her hair.

"I'm only going to say this once. Here is your passport and ticket. Here is $10,000 American. When we land, get off. You know what to do. I don't want to see you again. Ever."

She looks at his eyes. She has never really looked at them before. They are pale like a wolf's. She remembers a saying, "Never look a wolf in the eye." She touches his cheek. It is the first time he has ever been touched with love. It is the first time she has ever touched anyone with tenderness.

"You can't do this." It is the only thing she can think to say. "Come with me," she adds.

"I have no choice," he says ironically, knowing that it's true, even though he could walk off the plane with her. "I'll say you gave me the slip."

"He won't believe you."

"No, he won't."

Lena signals for the steward again.

"Vodka," she says.

Ivan looks out the window. In fifteen minutes, she'll be gone. He won't look for her again. The hole in his chest will be there forever. The bullet that Ivanovich will put through it will be nothing. It will only melt the frozen edges. It's the moment he's been waiting for all his life.

Double Whammy

Lucy calls Greg up as soon as she gets to her office. She was the one who had to run, as soon as the teacher conference was over, who took off out of there like a bat out of hell, heading for her car, leaving Greg to walk more leisurely home, no doubt stopping on the way for a pricey cup of coffee. That's the academic life for you; he'll run into half the neighborhood out for a stroll or sipping in the coffeehouse. Lucy herself drove dangerously right across town and then lucked into a perfect parking place at the hospital, the occasional bright benefit of coming late to work, when you get a spot right next to the building, a spot some night-shift nurse maybe occupied at one a.m., and has now vacated neatly in time for your tardy arrival.

A fast drive and a lucky parking spot mean that Lucy is right on time for her ten o'clock appointment, and then to further her sense that God is giving her the break she sorely needs, it turns out that the social worker has called and the Williams twins are not in fact coming in for their asthma compliance checks today, and she basically has an hour free. So she kicks her office door shut, sinks down in her chair, slips out of her shoes, and dials Greg at home.

"Howdy there, Paw," she says, and he starts to laugh.

"Gee, Maw," he says back, "guess you'n me have done gotten our hillbilly asses mixed up with some mighty high-steppin' folks."

"Back on the farm, we thought folks was dressed nice if'n they didn't have their long johns on outside their overalls," Lucy says, but she knows the joke is over.

"What an unbelievable self-righteous sugarcoated poisonous bitch!"

"Jesus Christ," Lucy says, signaling agreement.

The first-grade teacher sat across the little round table from them, all three of them too big for the first-grade chairs, of course. She looked, as she always looks, as they have only ever seen her look, competent and patient. She wears slacks and a sweater, and she usually has on a piece of fun jewelry, a cow made out of beads and sequins, or a necklace that looks like painted Tinkertoys. Her name is Mrs. Gallow, and Lucy finds these pieces of jewelry remind her of the bright smocks and scrub jackets printed with cartoon characters that nurses sometimes wear to make children think they don't carry needles. Greg has been calling her Old Gallows all year, strictly in the privacy of his own home, of course.

And this is the woman to whom they send their sweet, strange Freddy each and every weekday morning. Actually, their sweet, strange Freddy likes her fine, as much as he ever likes—or notices—an adult female other than his mother or his grandmother, which is to say, if you ask him how he likes the class, he'll politely tell you fine, and if you ask him if he has a nice teacher, he'll politely tell you yes, and if you ask him what her name is, he can now, three months into the year, usually remember it, and Lucy thinks he could probably pick her out of a police lineup. And surely, if the earth opened and swallowed up Mrs. Gallow, Freddy would put down his baseball cards long enough to ask anxiously who was going to be the teacher tomorrow, since change of any kind makes Freddy a little nervous. Well, maybe he wouldn't actually put *down* the cards, but he might pause in laying them out.

It's not that Lucy and Greg were expecting a completely smooth parent-teacher conference. Those are what they have with their daughter Isabel's teachers, always and forever, as Greg says, as long as the sun shall shine and the grass shall grow, and the Great White Father rules in Washington. Freddy's kindergarten teacher last year, an almost insanely good-natured, guitar-playing young woman named Sandy Sullivan (Greg called *her* Sister Bertrille) had folded up her habitual smile once or twice to tell them that some of Freddy's habits might seem, well, a little bit peculiar to some of the other kids, though of course everyone loved him, and gosh, you could just tell he was *so* smart. But Freddy has, they hope, gotten a little less strange and a little less scared, and in any case, here in first grade, surely the fact that he can read like a grown-up and do math like at least a fourth-grader must count for something. Lucy, who lost the coin toss and sat through Open Classroom night, remembers one long chain of reassurances for all the parents whose children still weren't reading. Everyone will read by the end of the year, everyone always does, Mrs. Gallow assured the parents over and over, and Lucy, who knew exactly how Greg would suggest that Old Gallows achieves those perfect results (a pack of slavering wild dogs to whom the non-readers are thrown in May), sat through the whole evening with the complacent smile of the mother whose son was home, right now, reading *Harry Potter and the Goblet of Fire* for the third time.

And yes, indeed, Mrs. Gallow had only kind words for Freddy's reading skills. Something about the woman, every time she says "Freddy," you imagine her putting a "Little" in front of it. She just has that kind of smarm in her voice.

"Clearly [Little] Freddy has wonderful reading skills," she said, but with very lukewarm enthusiasm. Clearly, Lucy thought, Old Gallows was more in her element talking to the parents of the children who had reading problems. "He's a very strong reader, and of course we try to encourage that."

No you don't, thought Lucy, you have him reading *Frog and Toad* with the other good readers, you have no idea at all what he's interested in, or what goes on in his brain. For which we should perhaps be thankful. Freddy's reading career is being shaped completely by his older sister; at school, he says, they mostly read baby books. Freddy likes baby books, mind you; he needs *One Fish, Two Fish, Red Fish, Blue Fish* read aloud at least twice every night—once on the couch before he has his bath, and once when he is in his bed, with his blankets and his decks of cards all properly arranged—with the result that every member of the family knows it by heart. Before that it was *Madeline and the Bad Hat,* and before that it was *Horton Hears a Who.* Lucy is happiest with *One Fish, Two Fish,* which seems to her, as she reads the familiar rhymes night after night, to be full of great and pungent wisdom to be applied in daily life.

"She doesn't get him at all, does she?" Greg asks. "She sees him every day, and she hasn't got the faintest idea who he is. It's kind of sad, really."

"It's probably lucky for us," Lucy says. "She wouldn't like what she saw."

She feels safe, is the funny thing. Safe and right where she belongs, here in her tiny and not at all cozy office, which she has never bothered to decorate in any way. Connected by phone to Greg, who is home in his office in their house.

This is no good, this is not right. My feet stick out of bed all night.
And when I pull them in, oh dear! My head sticks out of bed up here!

In the picture, the sad-faced, fuzzy-edged beast sticks his legs out through two holes cut in the board at the bottom of his bed—then on the next page, his feet are in the bed, but his woebegone head protrudes through a hole in the headboard.

Oh, they tried with Mrs. Gallow. They told her what a wonderful year Freddy was having in her wonderful classroom. In fact, when they first came in, prompt to the minute, another matched set of parents ushered out into the hallway, Greg praised the classroom so lavishly that Lucy worried it might be too much. The murals! The Our Book Forest display of all the different books they've read! Those wonderful African bark paintings they've been making! They tried hard to make her like them, because they believe, of course, these two overeducated advanced-degree types, that if she doesn't like them, she will take it out on Freddy, who is pretty completely in her power. And of Freddy they are highly protective, always worrying that the world will fall in on him, and he will discover the terrible truth: that he sticks out in all directions.

Mrs. Gallow gave Freddy his due: Reads well. Good at math. Much better now about not interrupting at circle time. She pointed to a large sign: Our Classroom Rules—Help Make 1-G a Great Place to Learn and Share. And Greg and Lucy sat there and nodded appreciatively at her bland and all-purpose remarks about their child, and admired the math quiz sheet she showed them on which Freddy's awkward wavering numerals expressed the exact correct answer fifteen times out of fifteen.

She saved it for a kicker. They were winding up, thanking her for her time and for giving Freddy such a wonderful year. They thought they were safe and free: no big problems, no concerns, no questions. There *is* one thing, she said.

Lucy braced. She can remember bracing, physically, her feet flat against the classroom floor, her shoulders suddenly tight. She did not look directly at Greg.

"Freddy comes to school, well..." Mrs. Gallow paused, as if it was almost too awful to be said. Then she made herself do her duty. "Freddy comes to school looking as if he has slept in his clothes. I mean, it's one thing to wear sweatpants, I know some of the boys *do* wear sweatpants to school—but they should be neat, and there shouldn't be any holes. And the T-shirts are just always so wrinkled, and sometimes there are stains, or spilled food."

Lucy, almost holding her breath, cut her eyes sideways quickly at Greg. He was carefully not looking at her. Greg, she noticed, had done Mrs. Gallow the courtesy of putting on a jacket. Under the jacket, though, he wore a brown cotton T-shirt which had definitely seen better days. In fact, Lucy could see clearly, the edge of the neck was fraying in a slightly moth-eaten scalloping, and there was a halo of tiny pinprick holes around the seam which joined the neckband to the shirt. Great. She straightened even more in her tiny awkward chair.

"I'm not saying this to make him feel bad. But you know, sooner or later the other children will start to notice this, so we might as well start now to get Freddy looking right."

Thank you so much, Mrs. Gallow. We'll get on it right away. How good of you to clue us in. What a great-looking classroom. They bobbed and nodded and bowed. Thank you for your time. And out the door they went, to be replaced, immediately, by the next parental dynamic duo, who were poised for their moment, out in the hall.

Greg said two things as they hurried out of the building, Lucy moving fast to get to her car and get to the hospital in time for the Williams twins. First was, You know it would be as much as your fucking life was worth to come for a fucking parent-teacher conference with only one fucking parent in this fucking school. Lucy wanted to hush him—all Freddy needed was to have his parents expelled from the building for obscenity. Second was, as they were already outside and heading for the car, Greg swung on her and said, For Christ's sake, he's a little boy! He has food on him because he's a messy eater! Don't we want them to play outside? If they play outside they get dirty, or their clothes get torn, and that's what it's like for little boys!

"Goodbye, honey," Lucy said, and kissed him, and then, key already out and poised, she was inside her car. Leaned out the window, though, and called to him, though she doesn't know if he heard it, "Check out that T-shirt you're wearing!"

What a great project for the whole family, she and Greg whisper back and forth that evening: First we'll iron Freddy's T-shirts. Then we'll fold them so tenderly into perfect rectangles. Oh, and maybe one of us should run out and buy starch—needless to say, there is no starch in the house, except for the pasta on the kitchen table. Isabel has finished eating the one exact portion of rigatoni that she allows herself, and is peeling a clementine with fastidious fingertips. Freddy himself has half a plateful left, but he has drifted dreamily away from eating, and instead he is arranging his rigatoni into careful furrows. A noodle shoots off his plate and onto his lap, and Isabel gives him a look of disgust. Yes, Isabel and Old Gallows might easily find some common ground.

And what about this business of not sending Freddy to school in sweatpants? What fun for everyone, looking for some pants that aren't sweatpants. Once there were some jeans, but Freddy hasn't worn them in months, and they are not easily findable. And anyway, for Christ's sake, Freddy has trouble with snaps and zippers. Hey, how about we just let him wear his sweatpants and leave him alone, okay?

After the kids are in bed, Lucy thinks, she and Greg will pursue the joke far enough to have clean and ironed and neatly folded clothes waiting for tomorrow. So okay, so it's stupid, but it's doable and they'll do it and they'll be done.

But you can never draw a single safe breath when your name is out there on the fifth-grade phone tree. Oh, you can run, but you can't hide.

Jesse Baxter's mother, the terminally over-involved Bianca Baxter, calls them to say, were they aware there had been an incident in the fifth grade and the school was taking it very, very seriously and there would be a meeting for all fifth-grade parents the next day at three?

"An incident?" Lucy's brain ranges generously: a sexual molestation, a racial epithet written on the wall, a gun found in someone's backpack. And at the same time a squeak of protest from her very bowels: I went in late this morning because of the fucking parent-teacher conference, how can I take tomorrow afternoon off for a meeting?

"The school is taking it very seriously," Bianca Baxter intones, yet a second time.

"What kind of incident?"

"I don't know all the details. I think Ms. Lederer is going to go over those at the meeting tomorrow. I really feel she's excellent in a crisis, don't you?"

Lucy tries to imagine Ms. Lederer in a crisis. What can Bianca be thinking of? The capital campaign falls short? Someone sees a mouse in the woodworking studio? Ms. Lederer is a personage, all right, but who the hell has ever seen her in a crisis?

"What's the crisis, Bianca?" Lucy asks patiently. Then, craftily, "I'm going to have to call the next family on the phone tree, and I'm sure they're going to ask." Thinking, Where the hell is the phone tree, or will Isabel possibly remember who came next after us, or should I just confess and ask this hellhound herself who I'm supposed to call?

"Oh, don't worry about that, Lucy. I know you guys are awfully busy, so I just went ahead and called the Rogers myself, earlier this afternoon. So that's all taken care of. I thought I'd wait and call you later because I know how busy your schedule is."

"One of us will try to make the meeting," Lucy says wearily. "But if you don't have any idea at all of what's going on, I should get off the phone and call Abby's mother, because she's pretty plugged in, and she might have some idea." Take that, you bright-winged avatar of death and destruction!

"Well, I'll tell you what I know," Bianca says. "There was an incident where some girls were tormenting another girl."

"So?" Lucy can't help it. These girls have been happily torment-ing one another since pre-K. It gives them a reason to get up in the morning.

"Epithets were used," Bianca says, lowering her voice.

"Racial epithets?"

"No, not that," Bianca says with clear relief. "Not quite as bad as that, but almost. Ms. Lederer called them socioeconomic epi-thets. The school is taking this very seriously."

From there to here, from here to there,
Funny things are everywhere.

Freddy hates the jeans, which Lucy has so triumphantly unearthed from a pile of dead and unclaimed laundry. Freddy cannot zip the zipper or snap the snap at the top of the zipper. He isn't strong enough, he says. The zipper keeps slipping out of his hands. The snap doesn't work right. He says he has never seen these pants before, even though Lucy feels sure that he must have worn them. Freddy is so thin that he doesn't really outgrow his pants, they just gradually get too short, but the jeans have rolled cuffs and could go for years. No, Freddy says. I want my sweatpants. I won't wear these awful stupid pants to school. Other kids wear jeans, Lucy says, reduced to the lowest level. But I don't, says Freddy, in no doubt whatsoever. And then finally, clearly, as she goes on suggesting it, just wear them for a day, Freddy says to her, If I wear them, I won't be able to go to the bathroom. I won't be able to get them open. I'll pee on myself.

Well, yes, there's that. Lucy imagines Mrs. Gallow, her righteous, concerned phone call. Okay, Freddy. Game, set, and match. Sweatpants it is, elastic waists forever, thus saith the Lord, thus say we all.

So Greg will go. He has to. He expresses himself eloquently about losing the afternoon, one of his precious at-home afternoons, when he teaches in the morning and then zips back home, puts on one of those suspect T-shirts, and works on his book. But Lucy has patients scheduled, and she did take the morning off for the parent-teacher conference, and although they do subject one another to a short episode in the long-running drama of my work is just as important to me as yours is to you even though I do some of it at home, Greg will go. It isn't even too long a fight, because Lucy has strategized it right; she gets the stuff about the parent meeting in there right at the beginning, and she can tell Greg wants to hear more. So all the time he is petulantly demanding to know whether she really has patients, whether she can't end her day a little early instead of asking him to end his, and didn't she go racing in this morning and find the patients had canceled after all, Greg is really wanting to finish the argument, and get back to the question of socioeconomic epithets. They can't ask Isabel, Lucy warns him; Bianca Baxter said it was not to be discussed with the kids until tomorrow. Well, they might have bent that rule, but Isabel has taken the occasion of her parents' argument to get herself virtuously into bed, and is sleeping what may be the fake but ostentatious sleep of those whose homework was done hours ago, whose trim folders are already neatly packed into the backpack for tomorrow.

So by the time they go to bed, they're friends again, united in the face of what Greg calls the prep-school double whammy: two compulsory school events in two days, one for each child.

"What do you think they said?" Greg asks. They are lying together in the middle of their bed, a good sign that the day is ending well. Greg's arm is splayed out across the bed, and Lucy pillows her neck on exactly the right comfortable part of his bicep. She lets herself think about starting to stroke his stomach, right around his belly button, where there is a soft tuft of hair. It's a weeknight, but it's not too late, and don't people need a little reward in between ironing their six-year-old's T-shirts and trotting off to the compulsory parent meeting to discuss the fifth-grade socioeconomic epithet emergency?

"My dad's richer than your dad," Lucy sings softly, to that old, old teasing tune. Her hand finds the little tuft of hair.

"How come your parents take you to that cut-rate ski resort every winter? Why don't you own a condo in Vail like all the rest of us?" But his voice is shifting slightly, thickening, and he folds his arm back over her, pulling her close.

Lucy feels righteously glad that the next afternoon is, in fact, incredibly busy. She has sat through an interminable lunchtime meeting about ICD-9 billing codes and reimbursement and productivity, every doctor's least favorite subjects and easily the tenth such meeting this year, and the meeting ran over a little because one of her colleagues got very angry about how it was easily the tenth such meeting this year, and started ranting at the new Special Billing Codes Consultant, who no doubt charged the hospital royally for the extra twenty minutes he spent listening to the rant. And that meant that all the afternoon patients got backed up, because by the time everyone got back to clinic and got down to work, they were almost forty minutes behind, and it turned out to be one of those afternoons when everyone who is scheduled shows up, and some of them bring their cousins.

So she spares a thought for poor old Greg, but it is a virtuous I-couldn't-possibly-have-gone thought, as she finishes removing the sutures from a well-healed laceration above Katika Lashore's right eye. This is maybe Katika's sixth or seventh injury requiring stitches; she's three now, and the first four or five injuries were part of what got her taken out of her bio mother's home and placed in foster care, although there were plenty of other issues as well, like the fact that she had never had any immunizations and she was fifteen months old. But whatever foster home you place her in, Katika will find something sharp to butt her forehead against, or a creative way to fall off a little tricycle and slice her leg on the edge of a chain-link fence.

Katika, who is sealed neatly into a papoose, a massive Velcro cocoon, toddler-sized, for holding small children down and still, is screaming like the proverbial banshee, but she stops the moment Lucy straightens up, her back aching slightly from the effort of holding her arms and hands so tightly tensed, snipping and pulling on those tiny electric-blue nylon knots that contrast so effectively with Katika's dark skin. The nurse releases Katika from the papoose, and she is immediately upright on the exam table, standing on the open papoose, and no doubt contemplating a swan dive off onto the floor. Her foster mother, moving fast, gathers her up and provides her with a massive lollipop, ready to hand in her purse.

And how remarkable it is, when you stop and think about it, that you can stitch children's skin up and see it heal, close over and grow together, as if the broken glass or the table edge or the chain-link fence had been a minor disruption.

"It was completely insane," Greg tells her. "Lunatic."

"Retarded," contributes Isabel, and is immediately shushed by both her parents. You can't use that word, not ever. Do you want us to have to sit through another compulsory parent meeting with a special consultant on working through ability-related epithets? Anti-disability slurs? Do you want us to have to sit through two hours of learning that some people are slower mentally and some people are quicker mentally and both ways are good? Have a care, Isabel, show a little mercy to your parents.

And after all that, nobody even knows exactly what was said and done. Isabel comes closest to knowing, of course, because the fifth grade has been buzzing. And the actual culprits, Kate Dykstra and Michelle Blumenthal, are known, and are walking around the school with red-rimmed eyes and a certain aura of drama-queen untouchable evil, having spent the last two days in multiple meetings and what Isabel calls lamebrained therapy sessions, with teachers and counselors and with their victim, Vanessa Hubbell. Isabel, of course, can keep all this straight without any trouble at all, keeps much more complicated things straight all the time. It's her clueless parents who keep mixing it up and saying Michelle when they mean Vanessa.

But even Isabel does not know exactly what Kate and Michelle *said* to Vanessa, except that it was about her family not having very much money and her clothes not being very nice and her dad only being a carpenter. In fact, George Hubbell is a very much in demand cabinetmaker, who probably charges enough every time he redoes one of Vanessa's classmate's kitchens to pay her way through till twelfth grade quite comfortably, thank you very much. In fact, Lucy and Greg, who could never ever afford a renovation on his fine-woods-custom-built terms, have in the past joked that for George Hubbell, the school tuition is a business expense; it's how he meets his clients. But there is no question that he drives a van with his name written on it, and he doesn't wear a suit. And if it comes to that, neither does Greg wear a suit, though academic drag is so well-understood in these parts, including its high-prestige-low-rent implications, that perhaps even the slower fifth-grade girls get the picture.

Anyway, Kate and Michelle made Vanessa cry. Which is nothing very new or surprising, if you ask Isabel; last month Kate and Michelle made three other people cry, but no one else went running to Miss Rexall, the school counselor, who just happened to have recently returned from an independent school counselor retreat (bet that was a treat of a retreat, Greg commented) at which a whole afternoon session had focused on socioeconomic epithets, led by these wonderful consultants, who were the same ones she brought in today to lead one compulsory assembly for the fifth graders, and one for their parents.

"Un. Fucking. Believable. We had to sit through a fucking PowerPoint presentation about different ways that people can make other people feel bad. Personal epithets. Racial epithets. Ethnic epithets. Socioeconomic epithets."

"It's a rough world."

"And then this I-don't-even-know-what-to-call-her woman puts us through this insane discussion, calling on people left and right, about how we all *feel* about there being some socioeconomic discrepancies in the school, and how we're going to help our kids handle that."

"Just so you know, Iz, *we* are the socioeconomic discrepancy in your school," Lucy announces to her daughter, who is happily perched on a kitchen chair watching them pull dinner together, happy to be part of their aristocracy of disgust on a brief break from her own. "You happen to go to a school which costs a great deal of money, and some of the families there are very, very rich, and some are only very rich, and then there are people like us, and we're perfectly comfortable and highly privileged, and don't you ever forget it, but by the standards of your school, we are probably down at the bottom. So you, Isabel, are the socioeconomic discrepancy."

"It's like describing the black children as the diversity," Greg tells her, helpfully. "It's called euphemism."

"Oh," says Isabel, worldly wise and weary, "it's just their usual PC stuff, that's all."

"This woman," Greg says, covering the tomato sauce and turning from the stove to face them, "I thought she was kidding, I honestly did at first. She had a fucking flip chart, and she was writing down what people said about ways to help children think about socioeconomic discrepancy here at Master Race Academy. And people are saying things like, *Well, be honest,* so she writes down HONESTY. How much do you think she got paid for this performance?"

Lucy thinks of the hospital billing consultant; word is he's pulling in a cool ten thousand a week.

Automatically, she and Greg both turn towards Isabel and start, "You can't call it—"

"Master Race Academy, I know, I never do. How much *did* she get paid?"

"We're in the wrong businesses," Lucy says. "That's why we're the socioeconomic discrepancy."

"You think you guys had it bad?" Isabel asks. Without anyone suggesting it, she has started setting the table, on their side and part of the team. "*We* had to go around the room and say what we thought went with being part of different socioeconomic groups. And she wrote it all down on one of those flip charts, too."

"What do you mean?"

"Oh, you know. Like there are blue-collar people who don't wear jackets and ties and they don't make much money and they drink beer."

Lucy and Greg regard their daughter. She is folding the paper napkins into swans, one for each place setting. When Isabel sets a table, she sets a table. She looks up to see them staring.

"Don't ask me. It was what we had to do. We wrote down what we thought were all the assumptions and prejudices about different socioeconomic groups, and then she led this discussion about how all of them were equally good in their different ways and we should never make anyone feel bad about which one they belong to."

"You mean," Lucy says cautiously, "never tease someone because her parents happen to be very wealthy?"

"That's what Andy Constantine said," says Isabel, who almost never mentions a boy, and who has mentioned this particular boy before. "He asked if she thought it was just as bad to make fun of people for being rich as for being poor, and she said yes, it was, because people couldn't help what they were and it was just as good to be one way as another."

"And what did you guys all think of that?" asks Lucy in a neutral tone, to head off the tirade she can see coming from Greg's direction. Yes, indeed, is this why we pay these insane tuition bills, so they can babble this incoherent meaningless crapola at our children? Just as good to be one way as another. The socialist millennium has come, and its name is Mason-Rickover Country Day.

"We all thought it was completely and totally re— I mean, lame. Sorry. It was lame. It was just the way they always do this stuff, where you have to process it and process it when all the time you know that Michelle and Kate were just being Michelle and Kate. I mean, they probably said that stuff because Vanessa is even skinnier than they are, because usually they go around asking people if they want their waists measured."

"You do understand that all of this is total crap?" Greg says. "All your stuff about blue-collar people drinking beer—those are stupid clichés. Social class in this country, and socioeconomic status, is much more complicated than that—and much more interesting." It's a little bit his lecturing voice, and Isabel likes it. The table is beautifully laid, napkin swans and the good water glasses and four matching plates—the only four left, as it happens, from their old set, but Isabel dug through the dish closet and found them all.

"Like Vanessa's father," Lucy adds. "You can be a carpenter who is an extremely talented and highly-paid worker, like he is—an artisan, and incidentally, a person who makes lots of money and who doesn't have enough time to do the work for all the people that want him. That doesn't mean that it was okay for Michelle and Kate to say those things—it would have been wrong to say them if Vanessa's family were poor, and wrong to say them if Vanessa's family was rich. Michelle and Kate are rude and stupid and mean—but you already knew that."

Isabel grins at them both: indeed she did. "I bet," she says, "that Vanessa's family has more than four matching plates."

Greg nods. "In their inlaid teak and ebony cabinets," he says.

Look what we found in the park in the dark.
We will take him home. We will call him Clark.
He will live at our house. He will grow and grow.
Will our mother like this? We don't know.

Lucy's favorite page. A little boy and a little girl carry an enormous round flask filled with turquoise water, and floating happily in the water is a Dr. Seuss creature, much bigger than either of the children. His flippers wave languidly in the water, the two horns at either side of his mouth turn upwards in a friendly kind of way, and his topknot is downright perky. The children are clearly moving fast, hurrying to show him to their mother. It always makes Lucy smile, and when she turns to that page, Freddy always checks her face.

Lucy sits on the couch, with Freddy curled up beside her. His T-shirt, which really did start the day washed, ironed, and folded, now bears extensive evidence of the tomato sauce from dinner. Probably, buried under those stains, there are stains from lunch, or dirt from recess, or paint from art class. Why shouldn't he accumulate a little road dust as he goes through his day, doing his best? Why can't the school get a consultant in to teach the teachers not to use appearance-related epithets?

She stopped on the way home and bought him one pair of elastic-waist chinos. They may be a little too short, but they're the biggest size she could find with an elastic waist. She had to cut the price tags off before Freddy would try them on, because he's scared of those little white plastic strings that hold tags on to clothes. And then, since she'd already cut the price tags off, she went ahead and cut off the label, since labels always bother Freddy. Anything to encourage him to try the pants on and like them.

And he did pull them on. And they looked, to be honest, terrible on him, silly high-water-mark pants bunched around his too-skinny waist. Or maybe it was the way he stood in them, tense and miserable, wanting his sweatpants or his pajamas. Freddy does not take easily to any innovation. And then Lucy, looking at him in his misery—over what, after all, over nothing—had one of those bad moments of wondering just how strange Freddy really is, and just what life will hold for him. Mrs. Gallow, after all, must be only the beginning. Put your sweatpants back on, sweetie, she told him. Let's read *One Fish, Two Fish*. Children heal over, she tells herself. Think of Katika Lashore, and the way she heals up after tearing her skin open.

But okay. She will get Freddy into bed, and then she will go iron a T-shirt for tomorrow. She will iron a T-shirt and the one pair of sweatpants which has no holes whatsoever, and put them on a hanger in the kitchen, and Greg will come in and see it and crack up. Poor boy, you're going to have to learn to struggle with those snaps and zippers. Can't stay a hillbilly forever, not at Master Race Academy.

Isabel is still hovering close, very unusual. Sat with them in the kitchen before dinner, set the table, and now she is sitting right across the room in the big armchair, pretending to read the Cleopatra volume of a girls' book series called *The Royal Diaries* (which Greg keeps saying he hopes will issue a volume on Isabella herself, and how she launched Columbus and did in the Jews. *Isabella and the Inquisition*, he has suggested it should be called). Is it possible that Isabel is actually somewhat shaken by what is going on in her school? Certainly they seem to be fomenting a certain hysteria, processing and reprocessing and never ever leaving things alone, which is how they always do it. That school counselor is a notorious menace. Miss Rexall. She lives to make a small private meanness into a large public trauma for all concerned.

"Come sit with us," Lucy says to her daughter. Who closes her book and crosses to join them on the couch, sitting on Lucy's other side and actually leaning very slightly against her mother. Tense and tight and controlled she is, but she is leaning. Lucy turns a page of *One Fish, Two Fish,* moving slowly and gently so as not to frighten anyone. Then she turns back a couple of pages and reads them her very favorite page once again. She is fond of the picture of the children bringing home the strange and large whiskered monster, Clark: look what we found in the park in the dark. They carry him in his big round balloon-like tank. He will live at our house, he will grow and grow, will our mother like this, we don't know! She loves it just for its trueness to the spirit of childish determination and trouble, for its sly manic certainty about what Mother will actually think. But over time, reading this story again and again, she has come to wonder whether in fact Freddy himself is Clark, whether Isabel is Clark, whether in fact Clark is just the child who comes out of the dark to live at your house and grow and grow.

Precision Marching at the Orphanage, 1890

We have a grandfather somewhere. We don't know where—I mean, we kiddos don't. Not anymore.

Mostly we remember him at the low house by the lake. Grousing at the black flies, stinking up Nature with the smell of his burning charcoal-and-plum pipe tobacco. A stout figure, like an orator in some senate, he liked to stand.

He went to stand and smoke under the white pines that leaned overhead all in one direction, like people straining to hear in a crowd. Grandmother, we knew, was buried beneath a large pink stone laid square in the ground. Letters were carved in it— ALBERTA WHITE FOX, 1888–1944. We used to laugh at her name, even though she was our grandmother. We'd never met her, so we didn't feel guilty. She was living under the stone at the lake long before we came along.

But we knew our grandfather fairly well. Well enough to be reluctant about kissing his hairy old face, his whiskers and wrinkles. We considered it indicative of lazy personal habits, that an unflattering yellow streaked the white beard raveling down into corkscrew spikes. As if he'd stained his own facial hair with tobacco runnings. But we were used to him, and his presents, and his whiskey, and his Bible, his whiplash way of throwing down the cards if he'd drawn a winning hand.

When he wasn't at the lake, he was off with Aunt Myrtle or Aunt Tessa or Aunt Pamela Pearl. "Taking a recreation this winter with Aunt Pamela Pearl"—he'd shake his unlit pipe at our parents—"don't you worry a thing about me. I've got the money, and she's got the mischief."

Sometimes there'd be a postcard. From Havana or New Orleans or the track at Saratoga. Gaming tables in Monte Carlo, one of us seems to recall. A note on fine stationery from a Mayfair hotel, describing Royal Ascot.

"Where does our grandfather live?" one of us asked once— because we were starting to be old enough to remember him year-round, not only when presents arrived, or when summer advertised itself, hot and promising, on the horizon of some sultry spring day.

"He's a man of the world," said our parents. "He doesn't live anyplace you can write to."

Well, we knew we'd see him at the lake, sooner or later. Slashing at the weeds with a golf club, he'd stick around until he made sure that we were settled in. That we remembered him. He loitered while we paid him due attention, and once we began to ignore him, he seemed relieved. He'd rent a car and visit some friends in Canada. "Going to play hooky. Too many bugs around the lake for an old man like me," he'd say.

And he'd return by the end of the summer, in time for farewells. "To smack you into good behavior for one more year," he'd insist, kissing us goodbye.

"How're you keeping, Alberta?" He'd stand on her pink stone, rub his shoes on it as if it were a welcome mat. "Alberta and me, we go way back," he bellowed at our parents once. "She stood by me; why shouldn't I stand by her? Or on her once in a while? Isn't that what family is for?"

But this past June when we got to the lake and unloaded the automobile and spread our boxes and suitcases and fishing gear and food all over the camp, our grandfather wasn't waiting for us.

"He won't be coming this year," said our father.

The truth leaned away from us, no less the truth for that. We hadn't liked our grandfather; we missed him, anyway. He had been a necessary obstacle to the joy of summer at the lake, a dour sentry to be placated with politeness. The task of greeting his smelly old bearded scowl had been a rite of passage. "Is he dead?" said the youngest of us, and ran to check the pink stone to see if ALBERTA WHITE FOX had rolled over to make room for our grandfather.

"No. He's found another aunt to escort around."

By now we'd learned that these aunts were not grafted onto the family tree in any respectable way.

The summer ended this year with a sweltering storm from the north. August heat leaning backwards against September chill. What a display: lightning, like discharge off a flywheel, thunder coming so fast it seemed to fall flat on the house. The lake was a panic of waves pushing in several directions. We packed up the car, bled the pipes, lowered the sashes, set traps for the mice. In the slashing downpour, as we pulled out of the driveway, our grandfather's absence made the camp seem lost, unrecoverable, as if the thunder carried shadows with it. We drove away, scared of the array of weather, both outside the car and in it.

It was our last departure. The camp burned down, not in that storm but through arson by local troublemakers a couple of weeks later. Grandfather sold the land and, for all we knew, ALBERTA WHITE FOX along with it. This Christmas we didn't get a postcard from some distant resort. We got an old browning photograph, printed on stiff stock. It was addressed to us kiddos.

On the back, in old-fashioned writing: PRECISION MARCHING AT THE ORPHANAGE, 1890.

And in our grandfather's quivery hand: *That's me, third from the left in the last row. I started out life as an orphan and understand I'm to end it that way too. I don't remember much of those days except we didn't have games at the lake as you've had. I don't understand much of these days either, come to that. But kindness did a good job of filling up the middle years. Be kind if you can, kiddos.*

"The nerve," said our parents, unable for an instant to catch themselves. The rest went unsaid, loudly.

Before it disappeared, we pored over the photograph. On shallow risers stood six rows of boys, four to a row. They all wore smart white caps with black brims, white shirts tucked into short black trousers, high black shoes with higher black socks, above which white knees showed vulnerably. Our grandfather could have been any one of those boys. There wasn't even the smallest smudge of recognizable family expression on the *third from the left, last row*. He was standing, as much at attention as a small boy can.

The boys made a stiff little army, ranked beside an equally anonymous proctor. The outlines of the trees at the end of the lawn were in sharper focus than the blurred edges of the orphans—we could make out birches leaning, an elm, a couple of rhododendrons squatting below. The focus so sharp we could count the petals on the rhododendrons one by one.

We'll see our grandfather again, we think. We hope we can recognize him when it happens. In the meantime we sometimes pretend we're orphans. To see how it feels. It's not such a hard game to learn.

Child Widow

"Quick weddings and short marriages are all I know," I admitted in my interview at June's Brides, "but I love lace, and I'm capable of telling white lies to brides' mothers. I was a psych minor, so I know everything is harder than it looks." I got the job.

And for the next few years, June's Brides and I took advantage of the convergence of a high divorce rate and a stock market that allowed the brides of Westchester County to spend more on their second and third weddings than their parents did on the first. Our designs were custom knockoffs, and because we made it fun to shop at June's—only the month was named June, but we all pretended we were—we attracted business from the city, too, taking advantage of our great location across the street from the Bronxville station just twelve minutes by train from Grand Central. With the Junior Bush administration's economic downturn, I got downsized, however, so I decided to mark my thirtieth birthday by retracing my steps to figure out how—starting with my two marriages—I went wrong.

My ticket was on the Ghana Airways direct flight to Accra, and though I knew to underpack, at the last minute I brought along a carton of lace samples to give away. My first stay in Ghana was as a Peace Corps volunteer, but because I left in such a hurry I'd brought back nothing more than my husband's body and no simple answer to the question of what happened to him. Married less than a year, I was still a child bride when I became a child widow in the minute Martin's motorcycle slid out from under him. Marrying soon again, but this time to someone I'd known since second grade, I just as quickly became one more divorced woman than Manhattan seemed to have use for.

"Is this your first visit to Ghana?" The passenger next to me was enjoying his Scotch while I sipped a Star beer, thinking it would work on me like a madeleine, which it didn't.

"I was last there six years ago."

"Peace Corps," he guessed. He looked about my father's age.

"It's that obvious?" He was right, though. I was wearing Eileen Fisher's wrinkled linen, which made me look slept-in, the way American travelers travel.

He smiled. "I still remember the first group that came to Ghana in 1961. They sang our new national anthem, in Twi, on arriving at the airport."

That photo was Exhibit A of our Peace Corps training, including how dressy they looked in their skirts and trousers. "It was broadcast throughout Ghana, we were told."

"I heard it on the radio, and, like all the best public relations, I never forgot it. And then of course your last president brought his family to visit. I saw that on television." He was crowding me now, having relaxed into my half of the narrow armrest, and let his beefy knee fall in my direction.

"President Clinton in *kente* cloth," I said, "was when I saw I had to come back." As I said this, I discovered how true it was. "And here I am."

"In transit," he corrected me as he ripped open his envelope of peanuts and funneled them into his mouth.

At the airport I'd noticed the flight attendants in their crew clusters, and I'd observed that KLM's uniforms were the color of their uniformly blue eyes, while Ghana Airways wore the midnight brown of theirs. To the extent that this was a marketing concept, I guess you could say it worked, at least as an effective reminder that by flying with a foreign airline, the trip begins immediately. As we boarded I'd noticed that, almost without exception, this Ghana Airways manifest was on its way home.

"You have a new president," I said neutrally.

"It was about time," he answered, equally matter-of-factly. His voice was soft but deep.

I decided to say, "But, for a change, yours was democratically elected. Unlike my own."

And now he laughed. "We noticed that." Hesitating before continuing, he then added, "We're wondering whether or not you Americans will still send yourselves around the world to monitor fair elections."

So now I laughed.

After the meal he slept with his knees pressed against the seat in front, boxing me in. With his watch set ahead, I could see it was evening, local time. I'd brought an anthology of Ghanaian poetry, but since it was in the overhead compartment I had nothing to read. There was no view, this high, not counting the dense white on white of the earth's atmosphere.

Martin had stayed on for a second Peace Corps term, so that by the time I got there he was already an expert. He was overly per-suasive, by which I mean that I, too, was capable of love at first sight—loving Ghana immediately, if not Martin, who seemed pushy—but in the end Martin also won me over, by proposing. Because Martin got word that his parents were divorcing after twenty-nine years, he convinced me to allow him to compensate. He taught in a secondary school upcountry, and although I'd been assigned to a village nearer to Accra, he'd decided I ought to be transferred. Cleverly, he arranged for me to visit him in Kumasi in the few weeks between the end of the harmattan winds and beginning of the rainy season. The city's seven hills had their way with me, too, but Martin seduced me with his knowledge of the female body—more sophisticated than internal exams—and the palm wine that grew on me with repeated applications. The motorcycle also helped.

Surprisingly, Martin was a cautious driver. He made us wear helmets that were so big they looked more suitable for outer space than life only five degrees from the equator. He never drove at night, to avoid collisions with roaming animals, and he always kept his eyes on the road. The only chance he ever took was in allowing me to press my body against his and slip my hands down the front of his pants.

"Tell me again," he'd say every time I told him I was happy.

"Again," I'd tease.

"Tell me again and again."

"Again and again."

That these were our last words to each other made me feel less guilty than if I'd been in a hurry and refused to play it for the two-hundredth time. Was there anything else that I might have noticed about that final encounter? The young policeman was ready to investigate me with his notebook and pen, but all I could say was, "Nothing."

Martin had one brother who lived with their mother in New

Hampshire, but I didn't dare call in case she answered the phone and I had to say, "You don't know me, but I was married to your former son." The U.S. Ambassador was away that week on what I later learned was a golf getaway to Bermuda, but someone else figured out how to send semi-official sympathy to the family. Of course Washington took care of all costs, including a coffin that was simple by Ghanaian standards, a plain gold-painted box with no carving on it. There was no autopsy required, since an eyewitness reported seeing nothing unusual in the moments before the motorcycle left the road. Because Martin's parents couldn't agree on a proper funeral, there wasn't what you could call a fitting tribute to a young man who, as his mother admitted the only time we met, had always been something of a stranger. Martin's younger brother said he knew Marty would love the coffin, though, which was when I learned Martin had that nickname, and which explained why he'd asked me not to call him that again, please.

Because the death was ruled "Accidental" there was a bit of insurance money I signed over to his mother once I saw how little she had. This seemed fine with her since I guess she didn't feel she was to blame, the way I did. I made copies of the pictures I'd taken of Martin in the year I'd known him, but she said he looked too different, in his *adinkra* cloth, from what she chose to remember. I didn't tell her *adinkra* is the word for farewell.

The eerie gray-green fluorescent streetlights made Accra look otherworldly as we circled before landing, but once in the terminal I recognized the chaos. Pressed from all sides for help I didn't need with my luggage, I was suddenly unsure why I'd come. I had no need for added proof of my own insecurity, but I asked myself anyway what I hoped to learn—to change—with my return to Ghana. Adaptively, the answer to this question could automatically become the new purpose of the trip.

The white light of the terminal extended onto the sidewalk outside. Flight crews from the various foreign carriers immediately vanished into vans to four-star hotels where they could change out of their uniforms and quench their thirsts with beverages imported from their own countries of origin. Ricocheting voices were a mix of tribal languages older than English, rising up in a cloud of sound absorbed by the dark sky whose gold stars looked closer to the earth here. The evening air was cool, fragrant with the sweet toxicity of diesel exhaust.

I knew better than to rent a car in Accra, and although the Peace Corps taught me to use local transport, after the long flight I decided to spare myself that ultimate crowding experience. A woman who balanced on her head a tray of stacked loaves of what looked like white bread pointed over her shoulder when I asked, "Taxi?"

My hotel was a one-star—hot water and fan—that called itself The Riviera Beach for its good location. As advertised, its "sea-facing" bar caught the evening breeze, and I easily remembered I was being welcomed when the desk clerk said, "*Akwaaba!*" The shower was shared, but because there were so few guests it was an upgrade to a private bath at no extra charge, he said gently. The water was lukewarm, in fact, but nothing could have felt better. With the exception of Martin.

He haunted my second marriage, or so Jesse complained, by having had the unfair advantage of being a complete stranger. Jesse and I remembered each other from the era before acne medication transformed adolescence, back when other city kids our age would kill each other for gold necklaces and sneakers. Our private school world was semi-precious in this regard, but our parents never knew the half of what we did in their apartments when they went out and we pretended to study. Like me, Jesse was the child of academics, but he traded up with his first marriage to the daughter of a corporate honcho, whose money wasn't sufficient to bribe her into pretending to be heterosexual. Jesse blamed himself for being a boring sexual partner, and since he was, it was difficult to argue. We decided we were each other's consolation prizes, but neither was that enough to make our marriage work. We haven't stayed in touch the way we might if we'd never married, but because Jesse writes our class notes in the Friends School Bulletin, I know that the three children he has with his third wife fulfill his only real ambition. He proved how happy he's become by bringing all four of them to a recent reunion, making it obvious how little I have going for me compared to what I once had, twice.

* * *

The cliché lesson to live as if you'll die tomorrow was my inheritance, and I spent it. My commitments never lasted longer than my interests, including on my twenty-ninth birthday when I woke up next to a man whose last name I couldn't recall having asked him the night before. The job at June's Brides was all about putting all of your eggs into one basket—repeatedly—so it wasn't any wonder that my own attention wandered from one customer to the next. I noticed this, but I wasn't ready to quit until the day I got laid off, when, yet again, I had the advantage and the disadvantage of the freedom to start over. This was when I traded in the cliché of living as if you'll die tomorrow for its opposite—as if you'll live forever—and saw how much harder it would be to put together a deliberate life.

If Martin had been Ghanaian, his brother could have married me—even without children, I'd have had some value—as a way of keeping my third of the estate in the family. It would be less easy to postpone adulthood here, where I could be a grandmother at my age. This wasn't hard to imagine, either, because Martin had already assumed I'd extend my Peace Corps service, like him, for at least one more term. That I'd left immediately after he died would have been understandable to anyone, but that I'd had no impulse to return would have been a mystery to Martin. Was I fleeing? The entire time?

My bus ticket to Kumasi cost less than fifty cents an hour at the rate it took to get there. I had a seat by an open window, so, unlike the other passengers whose hair grew close to the scalp, mine flew like a pinwheel. Every time the bus slowed, pubescent girls approached from the side of the road balancing on their heads shallow basins holding knotted sandwich-size plastic bags of cool water—"Iiiiiisss-wata!"—I didn't dare to drink. From the bus station a taxi took me a short way to Orchids Guesthouse, where I lay on the bed under the ceiling fan for the best twenty minutes of that day. In the morning, after a square of pale toast and tart citrus jam, I was ready to travel the road where Martin's motorcycle took him with it—or vice versa—at the place where now there was a little building and six women sitting at their sewing machines to work vibrant batiks into fitted dresses with short full sleeves and long straight skirts. The sign on the rusty corrugated metal roof said BRIDAL'S.

Martin and I lived in a cement-block house adjacent to the secondary school where he'd taught, but first I knew I had to present myself at the Chief's compound to pay my respects with gifts of cash and a good bottle of schnapps for libation. I'd decided that the carton I'd carried on the plane was for the Queenmother, who favored lace for her curtains and tablecloths. Though it had been six years since we'd seen each other, it was reasonable to assume that my life was the most changed. But it seemed not, when I was immediately surrounded by girls whose young mothers had been girls on my last visit.

The Queenmother invited me to sit in her parlor, where I'd spent the afternoon and evening of Martin's death, but now it was crowded with a boxy furniture set upholstered in a deep mahogany synthetic plush. Women gathered in her courtyard with the excuse of bringing Nana Abena a few warm eggs or okra pods from garden plots closer than the fields they also cultivated. They came shyly, but soon the carton was opened and its contents distributed, displayed against the brown fabric so the patterns were more obvious. When one woman draped a panel around her shoulders and another at her waist, a full-length mirror with broken corners was fetched and propped at an angle. And soon they all wore white, while they pointed to their reflected images and kept saying two words I didn't understand. How could I guess—when I imagined them pretending to be brides—they were saying *white* is the color for *widows*.

Next they shouted out their surprise at how easy it was to imagine their husbands dropping dead. The Queenmother was the only one not to indulge, and she said the others were just pretending. "Because they know I'm a widow?" Nowhere else in the world, but here, would I be known as a widow rather than a divorced woman.

"No, no," Nana Abena said, "since although of course they know you *were* a widow, they assume remarriage. They simply take pleasure, looking in the glass, in playing at make-believe, as I think you call it."

Because, here, the brides wear traditional dress for rituals that matter, this dress-up play wasn't about fairy-tale weddings where commoners pretend to be princesses marrying their princes. Here, to wear white was the opposite of belonging to a man. For this interval between marriage and remarriage—here was the reason for their outright laughter—it became possible to wear a non-color.

At June's Brides we always wore black, as if, for the effect, we could represent the men in their rented tuxedos. Like most women I know I prefer to look smaller than I am—I avoid white—and, though I couldn't admit this when I worked there, my two wedding dresses weren't just "off-white" but *way* off-white. The Queenmother would remember that Martin and I wore the *kente* cloths he'd commissioned, and the next time, as I told her, my dress was gray—silver, Jesse called it, always looking for that lining—because I was used goods.

"There is no such thing in Ghana," the Queenmother scolded, "as you remember from your short time here." Her assumption was that this time I intended to stay longer.

"They look happy," I deflected, watching them admire each other. It went without saying that, against their uniformly dark skin, the lace couldn't have looked better.

The bus trip back from Kumasi to Accra was shorter than the way up, but it was sufficient to convince me to drop by the Ghana Airways office to pay the penalty for changing my plane ticket from later in the week to sometime in the future. Then I stopped off at the Peace Corps office, which had remained in the same location. On the bus I'd realized I hoped it was an option for me to complete my interrupted term.

"Please, one moment," I was told by the young man at the front desk.

I knew my own way to the upstairs corner office, but since I was only asking to make an appointment for the next day, it surprised me to be taken right up. The taxi driver was happy to wait, since, as he'd already told me, I was his first paying customer of the day.

Other than the newer computer on the desk in the hallway, nothing seemed changed. There was a laminated set of instructions for personal e-mail, but the random issues of *Time* and *Newsweek* were still stamped DO NOT BORROW. The official photograph of the newly elected president, J. A. Kufuor, had replaced Flight Lieutenant J. J. Rawlings after his twenty years in strict power. But it was the same picture frame hung above eye level on a wall not recently re-whitewashed.

"Welcome," said the American woman who came from behind the closed door. "You caught me just as I'm leaving, but come in, anyway." She indicated that I was to sit, but she remained standing. "For Côte d'Ivoire." From her pronunciation of Ivory Coast I was meant to see she spoke French. I was to understand she'd been a volunteer herself from the framed snapshot on her desk, showing her in a rural health clinic. Contrary to the Ghanaian way of exchanging formalities before getting down to business, I was expected to explain myself this efficiently.

It was shocking how little time it took to tell Martin's story. My Peace Corps portion was short, too. "I left Ghana early," I decided to say, "and now that I'm back, I don't want to leave prematurely again."

"I'm gone ten or more days," she said, squinting at me with provisional suspicion, "and I suppose your visa's about to expire." The puff of air she expelled conveyed she had to deal with visas more than she liked.

"I'd need to renew it, but not immediately."

"In the meantime?"

I knew this was a test as well. If I said I'd go back to New York in order to put my affairs in order, she'd know not to bother with me. This is why I said, "On my way out, I could e-mail a friend about subletting my apartment."

Now she seemed to see she hadn't asked me anything about my life since Martin's death, so she did.

"Well," I said, "I remarried, but mostly to understand why I'd married Martin in the first place. And after that second marriage ended, I found my way to a shop called June's Brides, probably for the same reason. At the moment, I'm unmarried and unemployed."

Her look conveyed sympathy and disapproval. Not much older than me, she wore large gold hoop earrings and wrapped her hair, like a gift, in the same green and black Akosombo batik as the fitted blouse and skirt she wore with Chaco sandals from someplace like Eastern Mountain Sports. Her skin color was also a blend. In a polite voice she asked, "And would you say you understand why?"

"Not yet." Then I told her, "I *can* tell you why I joined the Peace Corps, though, and why I've come back here. Unfinished business."

"Your own?"

"That, too, but I was thinking of the world's."

At The Riviera Beach, when I told the desk clerk I'd need a room for two weeks, it was as if I'd single-handedly erased the hotel's budget deficit. I was provided a top sheet without having to request one, and the ceiling fan seemed to work on all three speeds. The afternoon sun was still high above the horizon, but it was clear that from this window I would have an unobstructed view of a Gulf of Guinea sunset.

Already, the sun spread its wealth, turning the water gold. This land continued to be mined for the precious mineral that lured foreign exploitation throughout Ghana's fierce history. Because Peace Corps volunteers are descended from those same colonizers, our mandate was to give more than we got. This was why I mistrusted the feeling I had in my chest, a fist-like clamp releasing its hold. Was it possible to seize power without taking anything from anybody?

From here the coastal road continued to the harbor at Tema, then north to the Akosombo township village I'd abandoned to join Martin in Kumasi. At the time, nobody questioned my abrupt departure, but it was also true that I hadn't been asked to account for my arrival, either. Once again it appeared that my immediate future was being radically reconfigured without any specific plan. This harshly exhilarating feeling seemed familiar to me, with a difference. Now I felt as free as sunlight.

"What would you like to do when you leave the Peace Corps?" was the one phony part of the application process, which is why I can't recall what I answered the first time. Since the Peace Corps was designed as transformative, I now know it's a trick question, but the truth is that not even a psych *major* could have predicted my spending three years in a bridal boutique. Martin told me he could never go back home to New Hampshire, where anarchy passed itself off as rugged individualism. Here, he said, the greater good required collaboration, which was why he wanted me to pledge myself to him—to this—for "whatever forever" we were to have. If this was a clue that Martin's time was limited, I obviously missed it.

My intake interview the first time had lasted an hour, whereas this afternoon it took seven or eight minutes. When I said my motivation was the world's unfinished business, I saw I had her attention, so I suggested to her that, while she was out of the country, I'd design a project she could fund or not fund. "I might be out of a job," I told her, "but I'm not out of work."

She supplied, "I understand your need to finish what you began," and then she asked, "but what do you hope to find?"

"The person I might once have become."

Filling my chest with a deep breath I held on to, I made myself focus on the bright surface of the Gulf, sparing my eyes the harsh reality of a direct look at the dense fiery sun. It shocked me to realize how few people would need to know I'd be remaining here for an indefinable duration—how few knew I'd left home, for that matter—which was what allowed me to weep for the impulsive boy who never turned twenty-six, and for the girl he married.

He always asked, "Tell me again," and "Tell me again and again," and I'd answer, "Again," and "Again and again." That last time it would have been simpler for me to tell Martin, "I'm not in the mood," instead of "Good idea!" I only wish I'd been more reckless about birth control, so that the seed he'd planted in me that last morning might have had a chance to grow. This might have been his intention, to the extent that he had one.

I felt unsteady on my feet, so I focused again on the brightly fractured water surface. Martin's impetuous love, I saw, had the power to stay alive within me, if I only let it. Turning thirty, I could toss the rest of my twenties overboard—not like an anchor—like a fish.

Witness

Jackie Flynn just turned eleven, but he has already spent plenty of time inside the Knickerbocker, a dark smoky barroom where men with rulers in their back pockets drink beer and stare at a soundless TV. Whenever his father goes out to do what he calls "moonlighting," Jackie's mother insists that Jackie accompany him. She tells Jackie to keep his father out of trouble, and although he's not sure exactly what she's talking about, Jackie always nods his head. When he was little, he simply watched his father work, but soon Jackie was fetching tools and measuring pipe and following his father into the bar when the work was done. By now Jackie knows the name of every song on the bullet-shaped jukebox; he knows that the extra can of sawdust for shuffleboard is stored high on a shelf in the rank-smelling men's room. He has hit the cue ball across the empty pool table often enough to memorize every imperfection in the faded green felt.

Jackie's still too young to legally sit at the bar, so he always occupies the same wobbly Formica table, where he drinks Cokes and studies the men as they toss crumpled bills on the bar to claim their territory. The Knickerbocker is not a safe place. At least once a month, Jackie's father has a fight. Frank Flynn is fearless, and Jackie longs to be like that, to act without thinking. He wants to know what these men know, but they conspire against him; no one ever lets him follow the crowd outside to watch the fight. Jackie's father always comes back first, and although he's winded and wild-looking, a band of disciples slap his back and buy him drinks. Jackie never knows what caused the fight, but he recognizes victory. He's always too far away to hear anything, so he waits and watches, memorizing poses and gestures, and he dreams of the day he will take his place at the bar.

Tonight, Jackie is helping his father fix a leaky drain pipe, and it is the first time he has ever been behind the bar. The owner of the Knickerbocker, Marty Sullivan, a powerful yet genial man with thinning red hair, stands on a raised floor of thin wooden slats that bend and squeak when he takes a step. Jackie's father hands Jackie a wrench and tells him to unscrew the sink trap. Behind him, on slick mahogany shelves, stand rows of gleaming bottles, each of which, Jackie is certain, is filled with a magical liquid that must be sweeter than he can imagine. He's so thrilled to be helping his father that he doesn't even bother to sweep aside the layers of dust and crumpled pretzels before he shimmies under the sink and wedges the jaws of the battered wrench around a rusty slip-nut. Once the sink is disconnected, Jackie follows his father to the basement, where rows of beer kegs line one wall. Frank Flynn balances on top of the kegs and struggles to separate two filthy pipes. Jackie stands below him, aiming a flashlight upward, stomping his feet to keep from freezing in the cold musty cellar.

"Will you hold the goddamn light steady," Frank shouts down. "I can't see what the hell I'm doing up here."

Jackie refocuses the beam toward the ceiling through a haze of dust and leans against a steel column; he wonders if it's true that liquor makes you feel no pain.

Frank grunts as he wrestles a mutilated pipe from behind an oak beam, then tosses it to the floor, where it clanks against the concrete. Blue and yellow sparks are flying.

"I thought that sucker was never going to come apart." Frank jumps down and fishes a cigarette out of his shirt pocket. He strikes a match repeatedly, but it won't light. "Do me a favor, will you?" Frank hands the matchbook to Jackie. "My hands are wet."

Jackie tugs off a match and lights it. As he holds the match out, Frank sticks his chin forward and cups his hands around the flame. The cigarette has red fingerprints on it.

"Dad?" Jackie asks. "What's a good reason to fight somebody?"

His father raises his eyebrows to look at Jackie and blows out the match. Then he takes a long puff and grins.

"Somebody giving you trouble? A big kid?"

Jackie is too embarrassed to admit that he has no idea what to do if another kid were to threaten him. He has never been in a fight, has never felt the desire to hurt anyone. He doesn't know whether this is simply because he has no enemies, or if he is a coward.

"Let me show you something." Frank stands closer and puts his hands on Jackie's shoulders. "If you're fighting with somebody bigger than you, get in close." Frank crouches down and raises his fists in front of his face; he moves in even closer to Jackie and begins to jab. His dark hair hangs across his forehead, shading his blue eyes. "You get in close, and they won't be able to touch you. Work on the stomach and always keep your hands up."

Frank is ducking and weaving as he swings. Jackie takes a step back. "You've got to keep your hands up," Frank repeats, swiping at Jackie's face. Jackie retreats farther, slipping behind the column. "Come on. Where are you going?" Frank tosses his cigarette on the floor. "I'm trying to teach you something here."

"But that's not what I mean," Jackie says, a little louder than he intends. "I mean, when is it the right time to fight?"

His father tilts his head and stares, bewildered. "That's what I'm trying to show you," he insists. "Get in there and hit him." A rust-coated fist darts past Jackie's ear, and he can't help flinching. "Never give anyone a chance to think."

After they finish up in the basement, Marty reaches into the register and slips Jackie a soggy five-dollar bill. "You do good work." Marty pats him on the back. Then, as Frank comes up from the basement, Marty leans closer. "Don't tell your old man. He'll think he's not charging me enough."

Jackie nods, then squats down and begins to pick up the tools that are scattered on the floor. While Marty settles up with Frank, Jackie spies two half-filled shot glasses among the dirty mugs. He hesitates only slightly before he grabs the closest glass and gulps it as fast as he can. His throat is sizzling, and he breaks into a coughing fit he can't control. Marty and Frank gaze over, concerned.

"I'm fine," Jackie assures them. "Dust." Jackie figures he must have chosen the wrong glass. He is convinced the other one will taste like maple syrup. The moment the men turn away, Jackie snatches the second glass. He can tell by the smell that it is something brutal, nothing like syrup, but he downs it, anyway. This time he manages to keep from coughing, but his insides are searing. As he squeezes past Marty and Frank, he's sure his face is red; his ears feel so hot they must be glowing. He ducks under the gate at the end of the bar and lugs the toolbox out to the parking lot.

In the glove compartment of his father's old Ford, Jackie finds a piece of Wrigley's Spearmint and unwraps it. He flips on the overhead light to check the time on the dashboard clock. Eleven forty-five. The only way he ever gets to stay up this late is when his father has a job to do. If he'd been home tonight, he'd have been in bed for two and a half hours already. He climbs out of the car and surveys the sky. There is a full moon on the horizon which turns the air a deep blue. Jackie tries to find the Little Dipper, but his vision blurs, and he feels dizzy. He settles against the car, and without knowing why, he lets out a hoot. He's sure it takes more than two drinks to get drunk, but something is different inside him. He feels older. More daring. He turns and studies the Knickerbocker. Smoky-blue neon signs flicker behind the plate-glass windows; streetlights tint the white clapboards a powdery yellow. He studies his reflection in the car window, then heads back inside to claim his table by the jukebox.

Jackie's father is still at the bar, along with Bill Laskowski, whose wife is always wearing her nurse's uniform when she comes to drag him home. Stan Gordon, the owner of Stan's Hardware, is playing pool with Sharkey Davis, who never smiles and is unable to hold any job for more than a week, but who is currently working for Stan at the hardware store, mixing paint and making keys.

Stan howls like a dog as Sharkey sinks the eight ball. Then he slams his pool cue on the table in disgust and hands Sharkey five dollars.

Sharkey throws up his hands. "Next victim?" he says, scanning the bar.

Nobody answers him, and then he spies Jackie. "How about you, kid? Got any money?"

Jackie hesitates long enough to look to his father for some sort of sign. He interprets Frank Flynn's casual shrug as permission and pulls out his five-dollar bill.

Sharkey looks to Jackie's father. "This kid a hustler, Frank?"

"There's one way to find out."

Jackie grabs a cue from a pine hutch and rubs blue chalk on the tip while Sharkey starts racking up the balls.

The men are all watching as Jackie settles his left wrist on the felt and takes his stance. Until now, he's only hit the cue ball around the empty table, but he's watched the men play, he knows what to do. He pulls the stick back slowly and lets it fly. Striped and solid-colored balls click against each other, but not one falls into a pocket.

It's after midnight when Sharkey is down to the eight ball, his final shot, while Jackie hasn't managed to sink a single ball. Jackie figures he keeps missing because it's so late, because he's tired; everything seems hazy, and the cue ball refuses to go where he aims it. As he focuses across the table, Sharkey moves next to him and leans in close.

"Don't blow it," Sharkey says. "There's a lot of green in between."

"Come on, Sharkey," Stan calls from the bar. "Let the kid shoot."

"We're not at work now, Stanley. So mind your own fucking business. I'm only giving the kid some advice. It doesn't bother him. Does it, kid?"

"Doesn't bother me," Jackie insists, although his mouth is as dry as dirt and his insides feel knotted. He barely grazed the cue ball, and it rolls about three inches.

Sharkey effortlessly sinks the eight, then winces as the cue ball drops in as well.

"Scratch on the eight!" Stan Gordon clutches his throat as though he's being strangled. "Choked under the pressure."

Sharkey tosses five one-dollar bills on the table, then heads into the men's room.

"Go ahead, pick it up. You won, the money's yours." Stan raises his glass in a toast, and even though he knows that his victory was nothing more than luck, Jackie can't keep from grinning.

Marty fills a beer mug with Coke and waves Jackie over.

"Here you go," he says to Jackie, holding the mug high. "You can sit up here." Marty slaps the chrome stool next to Frank Flynn.

It does not matter that Jackie's feet dangle limply when he spins around on the stool; he grabs a handful of pretzels from a rough wooden bowl as if he belongs there. "Want to play?" he asks his father, tipping his head toward the pool table.

"Don't go getting all high and mighty now," Frank Flynn says. "You were lucky is all."

Before Jackie can decide whether his father is teasing or not, the men's room door swings open, then slams shut with a series of slaps. Sharkey Davis fumbles with his fly for a moment and heads for the far end of the bar, next to Stan. "Where's my drink?" he demands.

Marty pours him a shot, but when he reaches for one of the bills on the bar, Sharkey puts one hand over the money; he glares at Jackie. "The winner usually buys the next round."

Jackie stops spinning, embarrassed by not knowing all the rules. As he quickly reaches into his pants pocket, his stomach refuses to stop turning.

"You keep your money, kid," Stan Gordon says. "It's on me. It's worth it just to see somebody beat Sharkey."

Before Marty can take Stan's money, Sharkey is in Stan's face. "He didn't beat me." He gives Stan a shove. "I lost. There's a difference."

Frank Flynn pulls his expensive dentures out and slaps them on the bar, ready for anything, ready to jump right in, but before he gets off his stool, Marty vaults right over the bar and grabs Sharkey, locking his arms behind his back. "Come on, pal. You've had enough for tonight. I think it's time to head on home." He steers Sharkey toward the door and kicks it open. Sharkey tries to wrestle free, but Marty's holding tight. The two men go outside, and the door closes behind them.

Jackie watches through the glass as Marty lets Sharkey go. Sharkey seems to want to argue, but Marty turns and comes back inside. As he walks past, he pats Jackie on the back. "The guy's an idiot, kid. Don't pay attention to him." Marty ducks behind the bar and clicks the remote to change the channel. Jackie's father replaces his teeth, no fights tonight. The men sip their drinks and study the television sports announcer as if nothing happened. When Jackie looks back at the door, Sharkey is gone. Maybe nothing did happen. Maybe he imagined the whole thing.

Ten minutes later, the phone rings. As Marty picks it up, Frank Flynn signals and whispers, "I just left." Jackie has heard this plenty of times before, has enjoyed the bond that sharing this secret lie with his father gives him. But this time it's not Jackie's mother.

Marty hangs up and announces that Sharkey's wife says he just grabbed a carving knife; he's on his way back.

Marty goes to the front door. He snaps the lock and turns off the lights. "He must really have a load on. Everybody just sit tight. He'll figure we're closed and give up."

Frank Flynn gives Jackie a nudge and stands up. "Come on," he says. "It's getting late, and I'm not about to sit around hiding in the dark. Let's get going."

"But he's coming back with a knife. Didn't you hear?"

"He's got no beef with me."

"You sure you don't want to just stay here until it blows over?" Marty asks, but he's already slipping the key into the lock. Everybody knows that if there is anyone more stubborn than Sharkey, it's Frank Flynn.

"He's got a knife," Jackie repeats. But Frank walks out into the night, and Jackie has no choice but to follow him.

Jackie sees the dull yellow dome light glowing inside the car and knows he is in serious trouble. Starting the car is always tentative, but he left the light on and the battery is sure to be dead. As his father tries to start the engine, Jackie can feel his heart beat. When the motor refuses to turn over, Frank finally gives up and opens his door. Jackie is ready to dash back into the safety of the bar. But his father is heading in the other direction, across the street, toward home. A car speeds past, and through the glare of headlights, Jackie spies Sharkey walking up the road. He hurries after his father; he's set to run, but once they cross the street, Frank stops by the woods that line the road.

Sharkey has reached the bar and is peering into the darkened windows. "Open up the goddamned door," he shouts, rattling the glass.

"Let's go, Dad," Jackie pleads. They should be hurrying, but Frank is busy peeing into the bushes.

"I want to see what he does when he can't get in." Frank pulls his zipper up and steps out, into the pool of a streetlight. What the men say about his father is right—no fear—but if this is a good thing, Jackie doesn't see why or how.

Sharkey squints in the glare. "Who's over there?"

Frank Flynn steps onto the street. Jackie can't believe it. "Don't," Jackie pleads. "Let's run."

His father grins. "Relax. He's not after me. I'm just going to tell him to go home and sleep it off."

The two men meet in the middle of the street, and Frank puts a hand on Sharkey's shoulder. Sharkey pulls away, and the blade he's carrying throws a white flash into the night. He swings the knife again, and Jackie's father jumps back.

"Take it easy, Sharkey. You've got the wrong guy here. You don't want to fight me."

"You're not so tough," Sharkey taunts, jabbing the knife out.

Frank swerves to his right, and the blade slashes across the front of his flannel shirt. "Shit," he says, surprised. "What the hell are you fighting me for? I thought you were mad at Stan."

Sharkey shoots the knife out again. "Well, I can't find that chickenshit asshole. And you're right here." He swings the knife once more and catches Frank in the arm.

Frank doesn't seem to notice the blood that splatters his work boots. He takes a step back. "Big man," he says. "Pretty tough with a fucking knife in your hand."

The men circle each other, moving from the center of the street to the curb. They are only ten feet away from Jackie when Frank turns both palms upward and beckons to Sharkey. "Come on," he says, "drop the knife, and I'll fight you like a man."

Sharkey grins and tosses the knife behind him. It clangs against the blacktop and skids to a stop so close to Jackie he can make out nicks on the cutting edge. Jackie knows he should grab the knife; he should get in there fast, but his feet will not move; he needs time to think. Can he get the knife? What if he does? Because of a game of pool, because he left the car light on, this is happening. They would stop if he got the knife. They would see how ridiculous the whole thing is; there's nothing to fight about. While Jackie tries to will himself to move, Frank lurches forward, his right fist pulled back. Instantly, Sharkey whirls back and scoops up the knife. He swings in wide arcs. Anything could happen, except the thing that does. Frank shoots out both hands, grabs the blade of the knife, and yanks it from Sharkey. Frank hurls the knife behind him, then charges, catching Sharkey with a right that sends him sprawling. The moment Sharkey hits the ground, Frank jumps on top of him. He continues to throw punches long after Sharkey is unconscious, he kicks him in the head, again and again until Jackie can no longer watch. Even though this is what he's always wanted to see, Jackie does not study the way his father moves without deliberation. He does not examine the technique because he knows now he will never use it.

A police car pulls up, and two officers drag Jackie's father off; they're about to arrest him when Marty appears and tells them they've got the wrong guy. Frank's hands are dripping blood, and his shirt hangs in thin ribbons across his chest. When one police officer sees the wounds, he calls to his partner, "We better get an ambulance."

Frank looks down at his hands and seems surprised by the blood. "Shit," he says. "I'm not going to any hospital. Those damn doctors will keep me up all night, and I've got work in the morning."

While the police handcuff Sharkey and drag him to the squad car, Marty wraps Frank's hands in a bar towel, then leads him back into the Knickerbocker. Jackie follows, then goes straight to his table and watches the men at the bar. Marty heads to the back room to hunt for some bandages.

"Some night, huh?" he says to Jackie. "You okay, kid?"

"Sure," Jackie says.

"Come on over with us." Marty nods toward the bar. "I'll sneak you a little drink. It'll calm your nerves."

A circle of neon flickers in the window, that blue that always makes Jackie think of summer. "That's okay," he says. "I'm not supposed to be there."

I Am Not Your Mother

Before they had ever lived in the house, somebody's useless cow had sickened and died in the shed next door. The shaggy rope that tethered her still lay in a corner, so when Sonia figured out that her older sister, Goldie, was having to do with a boy, she got up in the night, disentangled the rope, and tied Goldie to a leg of their bed.

Goldie never sneaked out at night. The town was dark even during the day. Wooden sheds, shops, and houses leaned into one another, creating attenuated triangles of shadow that met and crossed and made further overlapping triangles: layers of deeper shadow. It wasn't hard for Goldie to meet the boy—who was tall and chubby, with a laugh that flung droplets onto her cheeks and made her ears tingle—during what was known as day.

In the morning, Goldie's leg jerked sideways when she turned to put her feet on the floor, and she laughed at her sister's trick, then untied the rope and tied up Sonia, who was still sleeping. The rope's rough fibers had hurt Sonia's fingers. When she felt Goldie's touch on her ankle, in her sleep, her sore hand went to her mouth. Sonia, at fourteen, still sucked her thumb.

Goldie became pregnant. Their parents were frightened. Nothing like this had happened in either of their families before. They hadn't known about the tall boy—who had gone to America. (Everyone wanted to leave if possible.) The parents never spoke of Goldie's big belly, but at last Aunt Leah, the mother's sister, came to see them. "Reuben and I have money for the ship," she said. "Give us the baby." Leah and Reuben had no children. Goldie screamed in childbirth and for days after, bleeding in the bed, but the baby, a girl, was taken the day of her birth. Goldie's breasts were hot. They felt as if they were about to explode. "Suck me, suck me," she cried to Sonia at night.

Aunt Leah was religious. She went to the ritual bath; when she married, she'd cut off her hair, and now wore a dusty wig. Goldie cried, "She'll shave my baby's head!" Sonia was impressed that her sister could imagine the bald baby they'd barely seen (whose ineffective kicks and arm-swats Sonia couldn't forget) as a grown girl with hair, getting married. Maybe in New York life would be different, Sonia told Goldie.

Aunt Leah, Uncle Reuben, and the baby, Rebecca (who was theirs, they told people), emigrated promptly. Goldie recovered quickly from childbirth, but she looked voluptuous from then on. A man who worked on the roads married her, though Sonia disliked him. He talked loudly in the presence of their still-frightened parents, but going to America was easy for him. He couldn't imagine things the rest of them feared, and didn't understand how faraway and wide the ocean was. Everyone had letters from relatives about the horrors of the passage, the trials of Ellis Island—but he didn't believe. Goldie, who could read a little, tried to show him a map in a schoolbook, but he tore out the page, saying, "Nothing like that." Sonia couldn't read but had some respect for print. She was shocked, but her angry brother-in-law, whose name was Aaron, was making a point: his experience—simpler than other people's—never did resemble what people who spoke in detail described, not to mention the subtleties reportedly found in books. In a moment he uncrumpled the map. "All right, we'll go to that place," he said, waving at half of North America.

They followed a cousin of his to Chicago. Goldie had mixed feelings. She would never have been permitted to tell Rebecca the truth. Aaron knew about the laughing boy and the baby, but didn't believe in them, either. In Chicago, nothing turned out as Goldie expected it to; Aaron's habit of doubt felt reasonable. Hardest was losing her daughter, but now Goldie was also separated from her parents and from Sonia, who couldn't even write a letter. Goldie remembered Sonia's shy mouth on her breasts in the middle of the night, her sister's tongue mastering the unfamiliar technique, her teeth held back but just grazing the nipple, giving relief and a terrible pleasure. When Goldie had a baby boy, the old secret made her laugh and cry when he nursed.

She reared her boy, then three more, with spurts of pleasure at the time of the holidays—which she celebrated primarily with food—or when she'd hear indirectly of her sister. Best of all for Aaron and Goldie was sex, which was excellent, but second best was going out. They went to band concerts and parades, vaude-ville and the Yiddish theater, then films. They ate out before any-one they knew. Aaron made a reasonable amount of money, not working on the roads here but selling fruit off a pushcart and later in a store. Goldie sometimes watched her husband when he didn't see her, across the street from his pushcart or outside his store, observing him with a customer. His big mouth opened wide when he spoke, and sometimes she thought she could hear his loud voice—dismissing, denying, doubting—even when she should have been out of earshot.

Sonia married a man who whispered respectfully to her parents. They couldn't always hear him, but they liked him. She soon had a girl and a boy. When her husband, Joseph, left for America alone, he announced his plans in such hushed conferences that nobody was surprised when he did what he said he'd do: he secured a job in New York and after two years sent money for his wife's passage, his children's, and his in-laws'. His own parents were dead. But Sonia's mother had something wrong with her eyes and was afraid she'd be turned back at Ellis Island. Saying goodbye at the train, Sonia and her parents pretended that their only important task was to make sure the children were warm enough. Their grand-mother wrapped them in so many shawls, wiping her eyes with the corners, that the children could scarcely move.

On the trip to New York, Sonia thought only of her mother and father, whom she'd never see again. She was afraid she wouldn't find Goldie, and she couldn't remember why she cared about Joseph, but he met her in New York and had not lost his distinc-tive smell or sound; he had a quizzical way of speaking, as if he found himself a bit foolish, and in turn found that discovery amusing. The babies who were no longer babies made him shake his head in silence. When they were settled, Joseph wrote letters to Goldie for Sonia. The second summer, Goldie and Aaron and—by then—three boys came overnight on the train to visit. Sonia had had another daughter.

One day when Joseph was at work and Aaron was engrossed in a game of pinochle taking place in the street—not shouting, for once—the sisters and their children called on Aunt Leah, who lived at the end of a trolley ride. Goldie trembled when Leah's sturdy daughter kissed her gravely. Rebecca took little interest in the cousin from Chicago and her boys, but asked to hold Sonia's baby. Aunt Leah was quiet, and they quickly returned on the trolley to Sonia's house, not talking, busying themselves with the children. The next night, Aaron insisted that the women leave the children with a neighbor, and they all went to a boisterous performance at the theater. The actors' shouts, their stylized and exaggerated gestures, seemed to calm Aaron. Otherwise he was constantly restless; Sonia didn't know what he wanted and that made her feel like a bad hostess. She wondered what it was like to be Aaron, and got far enough to sense his relief when something was vacant, when nothing was inscribed on an object or a moment, so he didn't have to deny whatever others discerned in it.

Rebecca knew Sonia as a cousin, and Sonia's children—the boy, Morris, and, eventually, five sisters (Clara, Sophie, Sylvia, Bobbie, Minnie)—as slightly more distant cousins. At nine Rebecca scolded Cousin Sonia for insufficient attention to the Passover restrictions, and Sonia spoke sharply, then touched Rebecca's arm apologetically. Rebecca began taking the trolley herself to help Sonia with the children. She took good care of them, but was too strict about keeping them clean and quiet. She had unruly curly hair and a neat little nose rather like Reuben's, not that her father ever looked up from the Talmud to notice her. Cousin Rebecca didn't laugh, Morris and the girls complained. They sat her down and played her their favorite of a pile of records that their father had brought home one night, along with a Victrola: it was called "No News but What Killed the Dog," and told a story Rebecca found sad, though the others shrieked with laughter.

Rebecca finished high school and found a job typing. It was a Jewish company, and they gave her Saturday off, or she wouldn't have done it. Sonia's children didn't see her as often once she was working, but sometimes she'd come on Sundays. "Can I help, Cousin Sonia?" Rebecca would say, walking into the preparation of a meal or the bathing of small children. She said it so often that "Can I help, Cousin Sonia?" became a household joke, and the girls said it to one another whenever anybody picked up a dishrag or a paring knife.

Sonia had never learned to read—Sylvia tried to teach her, but Sonia's eyes became red and watery, and the project was abandoned—but the children read Goldie's letters out loud to her, and she dictated replies. Sonia mentioned Rebecca only occasionally in her letters, not wanting to make her children wonder or make Goldie sad. Rebecca stared when Sonia's girls talked about Aunt Chicago, as they called Goldie: Aunt Chicago ate in restaurants, went to plays, and wrote letters containing sentences about the bedroom.

One day Sophie screamed because she'd read ahead in a letter from Goldie to her mother. Sonia screamed, too, before she even knew what had happened. Aaron had disappeared: one day he had taken his shoes to the shoemaker's for new heels, and had never returned. The shoemaker said he didn't remember Goldie's husband or his shoes, and that was that. Goldie's oldest son had been talking about quitting school and going to work. Now he did so, and Goldie took a job in a dress factory.

Sonia pictured her brother-in-law, in shoes run down at the heel, walking into nothing—finding, at last, some fragment of life where for some reason nobody told him about what he couldn't believe in. "It's a disease," she told her family. "He can't remember where he lives. The police will bring him home when they figure it out."

Goldie wrote, "At last it's quiet around here, but I miss you-know-what."

Joseph sent Goldie money. He had worked in a furniture store for years, and now he was part-owner.

Several years after Rebecca graduated from high school, a friend married and quit her job, a *good* job: selling and keeping the books in a store that sold musical instruments and sheet music. The friend told the two bosses (who never yelled, she said) about Rebecca, who was hired after an interview, even though they were not Jewish and she said she wouldn't work on Saturdays. "I understand," said Mr. Hardy, the younger boss, nodding respectfully.

The store was called Stevens and Hardy. Mr. Stevens was an elderly man who could repair any musical instrument, while polite Mr. Hardy, who knew little about music, talked to customers. He was a widower in his forties, with two daughters. The third week Rebecca worked in the store, she was straightening the racks of music in the evening, after Mr. Stevens had left and they'd closed, when she was suddenly gripped around the legs. She looked down, alarmed. A little girl whose hair needed combing had seized Rebecca's skirt and was hiding her face in it.

"What's wrong?" Rebecca said.

"Mama died." Mama had not just died, but that was what was wrong. The little girl, Mr. Hardy's younger daughter, Charlotte, was playing a private game with Rebecca or her skirt. At the moment she was not grieving. Nonetheless, Rebecca bent compassionately and touched the child's hair, figuring out who she was.

A tall woman appeared. "I'm sorry, miss," she said. "Charlotte, get up."

Charlotte stayed where she was. The woman was Mr. Hardy's sister. She and Rebecca spoke politely, and then Mr. Hardy came out and introduced them.

The girl still knelt at Rebecca's feet, still with Rebecca's hand on her hair. Facing the child's father and aunt—two well-dressed, blond, self-confident Americans, descendants of George Washington, for all Rebecca knew—Rebecca felt for a moment like a participant in an unfamiliar religious rite such as she imagined took place at a church she passed (all but averting her eyes) on her way to work.

"Get up, Charlotte," said Mr. Hardy. Charlotte stood at last, flushed and laughing, and Rebecca's feeling passed. Rebecca swept the floor while Mr. Hardy replaced the trumpets and saxophones that customers had examined in the course of the day, and rechecked lists he'd made, as he did every night—sitting in his tiny office with the door open, singing jazz melodies extremely softly and slowly. When everyone left that evening, Mr. Hardy's sister and Charlotte went out first. Mr. Hardy held the door for Rebecca so as to lock it behind her, and he turned and looked at her in a way that seemed expectant. "Your daughter is pretty," Rebecca said.

Mr. Hardy's cheeks reddened, and then—standing in his coat, holding his hat at his side—he changed suddenly. He seemed to grow slightly shorter and wider; his limbs seemed rounder. It was as if a clever mechanical model of a human being had been replaced by a live person, inevitably less precisely assembled. Mr.

Hardy was a gentile, but when he grasped the brass doorknob, Rebecca realized, it felt round and hard to him, exactly as it did to her. She suddenly pictured his arm, under his coat and shirt, full of tangled veins. "How did your wife die, Mr. Hardy?" Rebecca said. "If it's all right to ask."

"It's all right," he said. "She had a ruptured appendix."

"I'm sorry."

"Thank you."

A few weeks later, after Rebecca had found herself having occasional strange thoughts about Mr. Hardy—not just about the veins on his arm but other parts of his body—he invited her to come for a walk. It was spring, and still light when they closed the store. They walked to a German bakery, where they drank tea and ate coffee cake. Rebecca, who brought her lunch in a bag, didn't object. The bakery wasn't kosher, but Mr. Hardy was such a conscientious person that she knew he didn't understand, and she didn't want to make him feel bad. The walk was repeated.

Her parents didn't ask why Rebecca came home from work later and less hungry. Everything about the music store baffled them; there was no point in inquiring. But Rebecca was surprised at how readily she ate at the bakery, just because poor Mr. Hardy was a widower, a man to be pitied—as if the kosher laws had an exception for tea with the grieving. She asked him questions about his daughters, about his own life. Rebecca was well-behaved, but not shy. At last, on a day when she was particularly enjoying Mr. Hardy, enjoying the look of his neck coming out of his shirt collar, she blurted out, "I'm not supposed to eat at a place like this."

"Even though it's not pork?"

"Yes."

"Your parents mind? Why didn't you tell me?"

"They don't know."

Timothy Hardy was not accustomed to concealing his behavior or feeling ashamed of it. He'd assumed she understood he was courting her, and that her parents would, too. Before asking Rebecca to walk, he'd decided he probably would marry her. He planned to give up pork and to accompany her to the Jewish church on Saturdays. He thought her parents would be doubtful at first—he was not Jewish, he had been married, he had children—but they would be reassured when they realized what an upright and serious-minded son-in-law he'd be.

Rebecca had liked Timothy Hardy's seriousness from the start. He reminded her a little of Cousin Sonia's husband, Joseph, who'd parcel out a small chicken with scrupulous fairness to his many children, making ironic, self-deprecating comments, sometimes inaudible except for their tone. Timothy Hardy was not ironic. Irony alarmed him because he couldn't endure the risk of being misunderstood, yet Rebecca had misunderstood him completely. She had not guessed he wanted to marry her. Rebecca didn't know gentiles could marry Jews.

"Tell them," Timothy Hardy now began to urge her, though he still didn't mention marriage. "Tell your mother I've asked you to drink tea. Let me visit her."

"What will you talk about?"

"I'll tell her I'd like to take you to a concert. She'll see that I'm not young, but that isn't so bad."

"I don't think I can do that," said Rebecca. She tried to imagine her mother, who was engaged these weeks in embroidering a Torah cover for the shul, putting down her work and rising to greet Timothy Hardy. It wasn't just that Leah would object to him. She would be as alarmed by his interest in her daughter as if Rebecca reported that the streetcar or the lamppost on the corner wanted to visit her at home.

Mr. Hardy stopped asking her to take walks. He'd spoken of his mother, now dead, with a warmth Rebecca envied, and she knew he wouldn't allow himself to lead a young person into disobedience to her parents. "Whenever I went to see my mother," Timothy had confided one afternoon, "she'd insist she had known just when I'd get there. At last I went to visit her at six in the morning, and she said, 'Well, Timothy, I am surprised to see you!'" After that story he blinked several times, smiling hard, his dimples showing and his mustache looking stretched. Rebecca understood how daring—how loving—it had been for him to go so far as to play a trick.

After taking some walks by herself in a different direction, Rebecca knew that she loved Timothy Hardy, and that he'd given her up because she was too cowardly to tell her mother about him. If she was in love, she thought she ought to be brave enough to tell Leah, even though she was now sure that Timothy Hardy would never take her for a walk or to a concert or anywhere. When she looked at her broad face in the mirror, with heavy curls falling over her forehead—the alert face of someone about to follow instructions carefully—she was astonished to discover that it could be the face of someone in love. She thought she'd like to die saving the lives of Timothy Hardy's children.

One evening, Leah was alone, embroidering near the window, when Rebecca came back from visiting her cousins. The day was fading, and it was time to stop and light the lamp, but Leah had kept working, making neat silvery lines and loops, soothed and enchanted by her own skill. When Rebecca came in, Leah smiled apologetically. "I should have more light," she acknowledged. Leah's eyesight wasn't as good as it had been.

It was unusual for Leah to sound apologetic or tentative. She was a firm, vigorous person who followed the elaborate dictates of her religion precisely, picturing herself as a small but muscular horse pulling a sledge. Leah had had a deeply pious father, and now she had a deeply pious husband. She was grateful to both of them, feeling obscurely that if they hadn't taught her to be quite so scrupulous, something bad would have been freed in her. Her father and husband didn't seem to experience something Leah had known from childhood, a slightly exhilarating, slightly nauseating awareness that truths might also be false. Sometimes a compelling, hateful picture appeared uncontrollably in Leah's mind: the embroidered Torah cover, for example, smeared with feces. Leah knew how to keep her head down when that happened, whisper a prayer, and keep embroidering. She'd brought up her daughter carefully.

Rebecca lit the lamp. Her mother looked up and smiled, and Rebecca thought that Leah looked surprisingly young at that moment, with her double chin and the bags under her eyes momentarily in shadow. A look of query passed over Leah's face, and it was almost as if she'd invited her daughter's confidence, and so Rebecca, still in her coat, slid into a chair, rather than seating herself properly, and said, "Mama, I think I love Mr. Hardy."

"I think" was a lie, Rebecca's bow to convention, her effort to sound as she thought she should. She had always been so good that she'd had no practice speaking of hard subjects. Everything she'd said up to now had been something she knew her parents wanted to hear.

Leah looked up, so startled she thought for an instant that she must have imagined rather than heard her daughter's words, and her hand went to her mouth. "Sha!" she said involuntarily, though nobody could hear them.

"But I do."

Rebecca suddenly grinned at her mother like a baby, and her wide face glowed. Leah's hands prickled. She saw herself sitting in her chair, the Torah cover in her lap, as if she were someone else: she had a sensation of disconnection from herself, which she'd had only once before, when someone told her that her father was dead. She said, "He won't..."

"He did. I think he's changed his mind, so there's nothing to worry about, but I want to tell him I love him, just so he'll know. He's a good man, Mama. Sometimes when we walk together, he says just what I'm thinking. It's as if he's Jewish."

"Shhh." Leah shook her head hard. It was beyond consideration. They would have to hold a funeral. "You must stop talking like this." It was her fault. Leah should have thought about men. She should have pointed Rebecca toward a man at shul, or spoken to a friend. In Europe it would have been simple. "Rebecca," she said, "would you bring me a glass of water?"

Rebecca hurried out, still in her coat, and brought it, stretching her arm and the glass of water toward her mother when she was still halfway across the room. Leah started to rise and accept the glass, but its surface was slippery, or Rebecca, with new recklessness, let go too soon. The glass did not fall for a moment. Somehow it seemed to rise, and the water—Rebecca had filled it too full—rose in a circle as well, as if a heavy fish had dived, making a wave that broke over the hands and arms of Rebecca and her mother, and the Torah cover that was still in Leah's other hand. For a moment the water resembled feeling, pure and intense. Then it was just water, and the conversation ended with mopping, broken glass, apologies, and consultations about damp embroidery.

Just after the front door of the store had been locked the next evening, Rebecca stood in front of Timothy Hardy's desk as if she wanted to request permission to buy ink for the ledger. He looked at her over the rims of his glasses. "I would like to tell you that I love you," said Rebecca. "I know you don't want to take me walking anymore, and of course we couldn't... I told my mother—"

Timothy sprang up, letting his glasses fall to the desk and slide onto the floor. He seized her by the shoulders. "Marry me," he said. "I will become a Jew."

"You can't."

"I mean I'll convert."

"I don't think..."

"Your mother will change her mind when I convert."

She shook her head tearfully. He kissed her.

Timothy went to a synagogue he'd noticed on the Lower East Side. He knew enough to go on Saturday, but he couldn't read the Hebrew letters saying what time the service began. He thought ten a.m. would be fine, and when he arrived he saw men coming out and going in, so he walked in behind them and sat down. All around him, men were swaying and murmuring, stopping to converse, swaying and murmuring again. Eventually the scrolls in their silk cover were brought out, and Timothy was amazed to see something lavish and colorful in this drab setting. The service went on for hours. When it was over, Timothy approached the rabbi, hat in hand. "Excuse me," he said, "I would like to become Jewish." He wondered if the rabbi spoke English.

"Put on your hat," the rabbi said, and Timothy took that as a dismissal, apologized, and left. Maybe he could find a different synagogue.

Rebecca noticed that her mother looked frightened for weeks after their conversation, and she worried that she'd damaged Leah's health with her surprising admission. She didn't mention Mr. Hardy again. When they were alone in the store, she and Timothy planned their life. She couldn't resist these conversations. She would care for his children, and they'd have more. "Maybe you'd better come see the furniture," he said. "You might not like Lucy's taste." Lucy was his dead wife.

"We're keeping Lucy's furniture," said Rebecca, sounding like her mother.

"You are the bride."

"Bride shmide." She'd found her true work and wanted to get

busy. She'd learn to laugh so Timothy and his daughters could laugh. Her cousins could teach her jokes. She'd get them to explain what was so funny about that record, "No News but What Killed the Dog," which consisted of a recital of disasters.

One evening Timothy told her that the rabbi who was preparing him to become Jewish, after discouraging him several times, had explained an unexpected next step. It was necessary for Timothy to be circumcised. He looked at Rebecca with love and some embarrassment, and she slowly took in what he was saying. Rebecca had allowed herself, for a few seconds at a time, alone in her bed, to consider that Timothy had a penis, but now it was as if lights had been turned on in a room that should be dark. Staring into Timothy's face, Rebecca acquired a rapid education. Her father must have a penis, too, as well as Cousin Joseph and his son, Morris. When they were little Jewish babies, their little penises had been cut. She had been to a bris more than once. She knew all about mohels and what they did, but she had never allowed herself to think the thoughts she thought now, that baby boys grew into men, that their penises grew, too, that men who were not Jewish had different penises, that a different penis hung at this moment in Timothy's trousers. Involuntarily she glanced down, and then she glanced down frankly. "It will hurt."

"They do something..."

"When are you going to do it?"

"Next week. There's a man who does it."

"A mohel."

"Yes."

There would be a sharp knife, slender and very bright. "Shall I come with you?"

"If you would walk to the building with me..."

"And wait?"

He hesitated. It was late fall, and Timothy was wearing thick trousers. He stood firmly on his two big legs, which he tended to separate a little. His tweed jacket was thick, too. It seemed to her that his clothing was fur; he was naked in the way an animal is. Rebecca knew she wanted to do something, but at first she didn't know what. Then she pulled her broadcloth blouse free of her skirt. As she pushed it up toward her neck, she knew the gesture was clumsy, that she must look more foolish than alluring, with crushed cloth bunched under her chin. Holding the sturdy material in place, she tried to push aside her slip, which came up high on her chest, with a brassiere under it. Rebecca's breasts were large, and she wore underwear with good support. She took Timothy's hand, which trembled, and drew it under her clothes. He pushed the cloth aside, leaned over her, found and released her breast, and put his mouth on it. He seemed to be crying. "Walk there with me, but then go away," he said.

"But won't you need someone, later?" Her voice had a sob in it, because of the pleasure of his touch on her breast.

"Jews are used to trouble," Timothy said. He was making a joke, the second of his life.

She loved his joke. "Are you really Jewish?" she said.

He stepped back from her and held out his hands, turning them as if the answer was written on them, maybe on his palms, maybe on the backs of his hands. *Shema Yisrael...,*" he began, and though the vowels were flat, Rebecca recognized what he was saying. Her cheeks grew warm, and she straightened her clothes.

All night—shamed, throbbing—Timothy was enraged with himself and with all Jews. He wondered if a cruel trick had been played on him, and if years from now he might discover that circumcision was rare among Jews, and that the rabbi had put him through such an experience as punishment for desiring one of their women. First his wife had died, and now, when he had miraculously fallen in love again, this hideously ludicrous requirement had been placed upon him. A religion that required him to expose himself, that required blood and pain... They gave him whiskey, but it just caused a headache. In bed, he tried not to think of his view of the knife, just before the job had been done, despite the mohel's courteous effort to place his black-clothed self between Timothy and the table where it lay. Now his penis felt as large as a melon. If it were infected, he would die and be buried a Jew, to the consternation of his Protestant relatives. Timothy began to pray in Hebrew. Then he prayed in English, to Jesus, the Jew he'd betrayed. As the pain lessened a little, as he began to think he might want to touch his penis to someone else's body again, he imagined the future, in which he and Rebecca would endure derision and shame. Timothy and Rebecca, the well-behaved. That was what they had in common, good behavior and the discovery that it meant nothing: it originated in no excellence, afforded no ease or safety.

Timothy wanted to be present when Rebecca told her parents that he had become a Jew, but she refused. Three days after his conversion, she helped her mother cook supper, though her hands shook and she dropped the potatoes. "Stir," Leah said, and Rebecca stirred the soup and skimmed the fat. It was Shabbos. Rebecca waited until her father came into the dining room, then until her mother had spoken the blessing and lit the candles. She still couldn't speak. Once she did, there would be no more eating, and there was no reason to waste the food and leave everyone hungry.

When the plates were almost empty, she put down her fork. "Mama, Papa, I have to tell you something," she said.

Her mother drew her hand to her mouth so abruptly that Rebecca knew she had thought incessantly of their last conversation. Rebecca said, "Mr. Hardy wants to marry me." Her father sat back quickly; obviously Leah hadn't told him. "He has become a Jew," Rebecca continued. Then she started to cry. "Because he loves me. He . . . he went to the mohel. He was cut."

Her father stared. "You didn't tell me?" he said. "Rebecca?"

It hadn't occurred to her how he'd feel. He didn't look angry, as she had expected. He pushed his chair back, looking pinched and fearful, as if he'd been exiled. She'd never seen her father look that way.

Leah had kept her hand on her mouth, and now she bit it and pulled it away quickly and then put it on the table. Rebecca could see tooth marks. "Rebecca," said Leah quietly, her voice unsteady, "I am not your mother."

In a rush, Rebecca heard the mumbled story of Goldie the difficult and shameless, who she thought must somehow remind Leah of Timothy—but that wasn't the point. It became clear why Papa, by now, was backing his chair toward the window. The knob at the top of the chair made a star-crack in the glass that nobody noticed until next morning, by which time Rebecca, who'd cried all night, no longer thought of it as her window, or in any sense her responsibility. Yet she felt for the poor broken pane a nostalgia that made her weep some more. For calamity had not made Leah's speech extravagant and hyperbolical. Leah was not Rebecca's mother.

She was not Rebecca's mother, Reuben was not her father, but they loved her like parents. They didn't hold a funeral because Rebecca wasn't their daughter and, by means of some chicanery, she was not marrying a gentile. Leah continued embroidering Torah covers and following the laws, but sitting in her chair in the late afternoons, she felt as if the sides of her house had fallen away from the roof, that the furniture around her had slid down slides made by the fallen walls, that the wind blew on her without obstacle.

Sonia's children were amazed, full of whooping and obstreperousness. Rebecca was their first cousin, and Sonia, who seemed incapable of secrecy but had known all along, was Rebecca's aunt. After the first hard night, Rebecca had taken the trolley, Shabbos or not, to her cousins' house. "Mama says she's not my mama."

Sonia started and sucked in her breath. "Aunt Chicago is your mama."

Nobody remembered Goldie very well. "Aunt Chicago whose husband walked out."

"That Aaron, the rat."

Five years earlier, when Aaron had left, Rebecca had been dismayed to think of a cousin who couldn't keep track of her husband. "She wasn't married when she had me?"

"She was a girl. What did she know?"

Rebecca got on a bus and went to Chicago, where she located her mother in a tenement that seemed from the outside much like the one where she'd grown up, but was different inside. Rebecca had not thought to telephone Goldie; she'd simply taken the address from Sonia, packed a bag, had a tearful, stubborn conversation at the store with Timothy, and set forth. When Aunt Chicago—who had long gray-brown hair that she hadn't yet braided that morning—opened the door in her bathrobe, a dog pressed past her, wagging her tail and barking. Goldie and Rebecca looked at each other, listening to the dog. Finally Goldie said, "Who?"

"Rebecca."

"From Aunt Leah?"

"She told me."

"They wouldn't let me say anything," said Goldie, before she began to scream so loudly that the neighbors, not knowing whether they heard joy or anguish, came running. Suddenly Rebecca belonged to twenty people and a dog she had never known about: half-brothers, friends. The rejoicing involved food, dancing, drink, talk, shouts. Goldie said, "I lost that worthless Aaron, but I got my baby back." When Rebecca told her about Timothy, Goldie asked, "What if he can't still do it, from the cutting?"

"It's healing."

"Thank God."

Goldie and the boys needed her as much as Timothy and his girls, but nobody could imagine moving. Changing a religion was one thing, leaving New York or Chicago something else. Rebecca and Goldie wrote letters from then on, and shouted on the telephone. When Aaron had been gone seven years, Goldie had him declared dead. She married a widowed neighbor, a man who was gentle with her. In the end everyone moved to Florida and ran in and out of each other's apartments, but that wasn't until the fifties or sixties, when they began to grow old. Goldie had been so young when Rebecca was born that they grew old together. Timothy was the oldest, but he outlived them all, weeping and praying in a Florida synagogue in his old age, when he looked more Jewish. People asked him what his name was changed from. He thanked God for the happiness he'd had in his life. He and Rebecca, Goldie and her second husband, would all go dancing at a big hotel in Miami Beach. Rebecca always looked like a demure young girl, even as she grew gray, but she learned lightheartedness. At the wedding of one of Goldie's sons, she walked to the microphone in a slinky green satin dress and wished her half-brother "every kind of happiness, including with no clothes on." It was Rebecca's closest approximation to a dirty joke. But nothing Rebecca did could be dirty, Timothy thought, remembering—as he drove a big white convertible to the synagogue in the Florida sun—the way she had offered him her breast that first time, drawing his hand under her clothes. How happy he'd been, then and later, bending his head and pressing it into her neck, putting his mouth on Rebecca's breasts.

JILL McCORKLE

Intervention

The intervention is not Marilyn's idea, but it might as well be. She is the one who has talked too much. And she has agreed to go along with it, nodding and murmuring an all right into the receiver while Sid dozes in front of the evening news. They love watching the news. Things are so horrible all over the world that it makes them feel lucky just to be alive. Sid is sixty-five. He is retired. He is disappearing before her very eyes.

"Okay, Mom?" She jumps with her daughter's voice, once again filled with the noise at the other end of the phone—a house full of children, a television blasting, whines about homework—all those noises you complain about for years only to wake one day and realize you would sell your soul to go back for another chance to do it right.

"Yes, yes," she says.

"Is he drinking right now?"

Marilyn has never heard the term "intervention" before her daughter, Sally, introduces it and showers her with a pile of literature. Sally's husband has a master's in social work and considers himself an expert on this topic, as well as many others. Most of Sally's sentences begin with "Rusty says," to the point that Sid long ago made up a little spoof about "Rusty says," turning it into a game like Simon Says. "Rusty says put your hands on your head," Sid said the first time, once the newly married couple was out of earshot. "Rusty says put your head up your ass." Marilyn howled with laughter, just as she always did and always has. Sid can always make her laugh. Usually she laughs longer and harder. A stranger would have assumed that she was the one slinging back the vodka. Twenty years earlier, and the stranger would have been right.

Sally and Rusty have now been married for a dozen years— three kids and two Volvos and several major vacations (that were

128

so educational they couldn't have been any fun) behind them—
and still, Marilyn and Sid cannot look each other in the eye while
Rusty is talking without breaking into giggles like a couple of
junior high school students. And Marilyn knows junior high
behavior; she taught language arts for many years. She is not
shocked when a boy wears the crotch of his pants down around
his knees, and she knows that Sean Combs has gone from that
perfectly normal name to Sean Puffy Combs to Puff Daddy to P.
Diddy. She knows that the kids make a big circle at dances so that
the ones in the center can do their grinding without getting in
trouble, and she has learned that there are many perfectly good
words that you cannot use in front of humans who are being
powered by hormonal surges. She once asked her class: How will
you ever get ahead? only to have them all—even the most pristine
honor roll girls—collapse in hysterics. Just last year—her final
one—she had learned never to ask if they had hooked up with so-
and-so, learning quickly that this no longer meant locating a person but having sex. She could not hear the term now without
laughing. She told Sid it reminded her of the time two dogs got
stuck in the act just outside her classroom window. The children
were out of control, especially when the assistant principal
stepped out there armed with a garden hose, which didn't faze the
lust-crazed dogs in the slightest. When the female—a scrawny
shepherd mix—finally took off running, the male—who was
quite a bit smaller—was stuck and forced to hop along behind
her like a jackrabbit. "His thang is stuck," one of the girls yelled
and broke out in a dance, prompting others to do the same.

"Sounds like me," Sid said that night when they were lying
there in the dark. "I'll follow you anywhere."

Now, as Sid dozes, she goes and pulls out the envelope of information about "family intervention." She never should have told
Sally that she had concerns, never should have mentioned that
there were times when she watched Sid pull out of the driveway
only to catch herself imagining that this could be the last time she
ever saw him.

"Why do you think that?" Sally asked, suddenly attentive and
leaning forward in her chair. Up until that minute, Marilyn had
felt invisible while Sally rattled on and on about drapes and chairs

and her book group and Rusty's accolades. "Was he visibly drunk? Why do you let him drive when he's that way?"

"He's never visibly drunk," Marilyn said then, knowing that she had made a terrible mistake. They were at the mall, one of those forced outings that Sally had read was important. Probably an article Rusty read first called something like: "Spend time with your parents so you won't feel guilty when you slap them in a urine-smelling old-folks' home." Rusty's parents are already in such a place; they share a room and eat three meals on room trays while they watch television all day. Rusty says they're ecstatic. They have so much to tell that they are living for the next time Rusty and Sally and the kids come to visit.

"I pray to God I never have to rely on such," Sid said when she relayed this bit of conversation. She didn't tell him the other parts of the conversation at the mall, how even when she tried to turn the topic to shoes and how it seemed to her that either shoes had gotten smaller or girls had gotten bigger (nine was the average size for most of her willowy eighth-grade girls), Sally bit into the subject like a pit bull.

"How much does he drink in a day?" Sally asked. "You must know. I mean, *you* are the one who takes out the garbage and does the shopping."

"He helps me."

"A fifth?"

"Sid loves to go to the Super Stop & Shop. They have a book section and everything."

"Rusty has seen this coming for years." Sally leaned forward and gripped Marilyn's arm. Sally's hands were perfectly manicured with pale pink nails and a great big diamond. "He asked me if Dad had a problem before we ever got married." She gripped tighter. "Do you know that? That's a dozen years."

"I wonder if the Oriental folks have caused this change in the shoe sizes?" Marilyn pulled away and glanced over at Lady's Foot Locker as if to make a point. She knows that "Oriental" is not the thing to say. She knows to say "Asian," and though Sally thinks that she and Rusty are the ones who teach her all of these things, the truth is that she learned it all from her students. She knew to say Hispanic and then Latino, probably before Rusty did, because she sometimes watches the MTV channel so that she's up on what is happening in the world and thus in the lives of children at the junior high. Shocking things, yes, but also important. Sid has always believed that it is better to be educated even if what is true makes you uncomfortable or depressed. Truth is, she can understand why some of these youngsters want to say motherfucker this and that all the time. Where *are* their mommas, after all; and where are their daddies? Rusty needs to watch MTV. He needs to watch that and *Survivor* and all the other reality shows. He's got children, and unless he completely rubs off on them they will be normal enough to want to know what's happening out there in the world.

"Asian," Sally whispered. "You really need to just throw out that word Oriental unless you're talking about lamps and carpets. I know what you're doing, too."

"What about queer? I hear that word is okay again."

"You have to deal with Dad's problem," Sally said.

"I hear that even the Homo sapiens use that word, but it might be the kind of thing that only one who is a member can use, kind of like—"

"Will you stop it?" Sally interrupted and banged her hand on the table.

"Like the 'n' word," Marilyn said. "The black children in my class used it, but it would have been terrible for somebody else to."

Sally didn't even enunciate African American the way she usually does. "This doesn't work anymore!" Sally's face reddened, her voice a harsh whisper. "So cut the Gracie Allen routine."

"I loved Gracie. So did Sid. What a woman." Marilyn rummaged her purse for a tissue or a stick of gum, anything so as not to have to look at Sally. Sally looks so much like Sid they could be in a genetics textbook: those pouty lips and hard blue eyes, prominent cheekbones and dark curly hair. Sid always told people his mother was a Cherokee and his father a Jew, that if he was a dog, like a cockapoo, he'd be a Cherojew, which Marilyn said sounded like TheraFlu, which they both like even when they don't have colds, so he went with Jewokee instead. Marilyn's ancestors were all Irish, so she and Sid called their children the Jewokirish. Sid said that the only thing that could save the world would be when everybody was so mixed up with this blood and that that nobody could pronounce the resulting tribe name. It would have to be a symbol—like the name of the artist formerly known as Prince, which was something she had just learned and had to explain to Sid. She doubts that Sally and Rusty even know who Prince is, or Nelly, for that matter. Nelly is the reason all the kids are wearing Band-Aids on their faces, which is great for those just learning to shave.

"Remember that whole routine Dad and I made up about ancestry?" Marilyn asked. She was able to look up now, Sally's hands squeezing her own, Rusty's hands on her shoulders. If she had had an ounce of energy left in her body, she would have run into Lord & Taylor's and gotten lost in the mirrored cosmetics section.

"The fact that you brought all this up is a cry for help whether you admit it or not," Sally said. "And we are here, Mother. We are here for you."

She wanted to ask why Mother—what happened to Mom and Mama and Mommy?—but she couldn't say a word.

There are some nights when Sid is dozing there that she feels frightened. She puts her hand on his chest to feel his heart. She puts her cheek close to his mouth to feel the breath. She did the same to Sally and Tom when they were children, especially with Tom, who came first. She was up and down all night long in those first weeks, making sure that he was breathing, still amazed that this perfect little creature belonged to them. Sometimes Sid would wake and do it for her, even though his work as a grocery distributor in those days caused him to get up at five a.m. The times he went to check, he would return to their tiny bedroom and lunge toward her with a perfect Dr. Frankenstein imitation: "He's alive!" followed by maniacal laughter. In those days she joined him for a drink just as the sun was setting. It was their favorite time of day, and they both always resisted the need to flip on a light and return to life. The ritual continued for years and does to this day. When the children were older they would make jokes about their parents, who were always "in the dark," and yet those pauses, the punctuation marks of a marriage, could tell their whole history spoken and unspoken.

The literature says that an intervention is the most loving and powerful thing a loved one can do. That some members might be apprehensive. Tom was apprehensive at first, but he always has been; Tom is the noncombative child. He's an orthopedist living in Denver. Skiing is great for his health and his business. And his love life. He met the new wife when she fractured her ankle. Her marriage was already fractured, his broken, much to the disappointment of Marilyn and Sid, who found the first wife to be the most loving and open-minded of the whole bunch. The new wife, Sid says, is too young to have any opinions you give a damn about. In private they call her Snow Bunny.

Tom was apprehensive until the night he called after the hour she had told everyone was acceptable. "Don't call after nine unless it's an emergency," she had told them. "We like to watch our shows without interruption." But that night, while Sid dozed and the made-for-TV movie she had looked forward to ended up (as her students would say) sucking, she went to run a deep hot bath, and that's where she was, incapable of getting to the phone fast enough.

"Let the machine get it, honey," she called as she dashed with just a towel wrapped around her dripping body, but she wasn't fast enough. She could hear the slur in Sid's speech. He could not say slalom to save his soul, and instead of letting the moment pass, he kept trying and trying—What the shit is wrong with my tongue, Tom? Did I have a goddamn stroke? Sllllmmmm—sla, sla.

Marilyn ran and picked up the extension. "Honey, Daddy has taken some decongestants, bless his heart, full of a terrible cold. Go on back to sleep now, Sid, I've got it."

"I haven't got a goddamned cold. Your mother's a kook!" He laughed and waved to where she stood in the kitchen, a puddle of suds and water at her feet. "She's a good-looking naked kook. I see her bony ass right now."

"Hang up, Tommy," she said. "I'll call you right back from the other phone. Daddy is right in the middle of his program."

"Yeah, right," Tom said.

By the time she got Sid settled down, dried herself off, and put on her robe, Tom's line was busy, and she knew before even dialing Sally that hers would be busy, too. It was a full hour later, Sid fast asleep in the bed they had owned for thirty-five years, when she finally got through, and then it was to a more serious Tom than she had heard in years. Not since he left the first wife and signed off on the lives of her grandchildren in a way that prevented Marilyn from seeing them more than once a year if she was lucky. She could get mad at him for *that*. So could Sid.

"We're not talking about my life right now," he said. "I've given Dad the benefit of the doubt for years, but Sally and Rusty are right."

"Rusty! You're the one who said he was full of it," she screamed. "And now you're on his side?"

"I'm on your side, Mom, your side."

She let her end fall silent and concentrated on Sid's breath. He's alive, only to be interrupted by a squeaky girly voice on Tom's end—Snow Bunny.

Sid likes to drive, and Marilyn has always felt secure with him there behind the wheel. Every family vacation, every weekend gathering. He was always voted the best driver of the bunch, even when a whole group had gathered down at the beach for a summer cookout where both men and women drank too much. Sid mostly drank beer in those days; he kept an old Pepsi-Cola cooler he once won throwing baseballs at tin cans at the county fair, iced down with Falstaff and Schlitz. They still have that cooler. It's out in the garage on the top shelf, long ago replaced with little red and white Playmates. Tom gave Sid his first Playmate, which has remained a family joke until this day. And Marilyn drank then. She liked the taste of beer but not the bloat. She loved to water ski, and they took turns behind a friend's powerboat. The men made jokes when the women dove in to cool off. They claimed that warm spots emerged wherever the women had been and that if they couldn't hold their beer any better than that, they should switch to girl drinks. And so they did. A little wine or a mai tai, vodka martinis. Sid had a book that told him how to make everything, and Marilyn enjoyed buying little colored toothpicks and umbrellas to dress things up when it was their turn to host. She loved rubbing her body with baby oil and iodine and letting the warmth of the sun and salty air soak in while the radio played and the other women talked. They all smoked cigarettes then. They all had little leather cases with fancy lighters tucked inside.

Whenever Marilyn sees the Pepsi cooler she is reminded of those days. Just married. No worries about skin cancer or lung cancer. No one had varicose veins. No one talked about cholesterol. None of their friends were addicted to anything other than the sun and the desire to get up on one ski—to slalom. The summer she was pregnant with Tom (compliments of a few too many mai tais, Sid told the group), she sat on the dock and sipped her ginger ale. The motion of the boat made her queasy, as did anything that had to do with poultry. It ain't the size of the ship but the motion of the ocean, Sid was fond of saying in those days, and she laughed every time. Every time he said it, she complimented his liner and the power of his steam. They batted words like throttle and wake back and forth like a birdie until finally, at the end of the afternoon, she'd go over and whisper, "Ready to dock?"

Her love for Sid then was overwhelming. His hair was thick, and he tanned a deep smooth olive without any coaxing. He was everything she had ever wanted, and she told him this those summer days as they sat through the twilight time. She didn't tell him how sometimes she craved the vodka tonics she had missed. Even though many of her friends continued drinking and smoking through their pregnancies, she would allow herself only one glass of wine with dinner. When she bragged about this during Sally's first pregnancy, instead of being congratulated on her modest intake, Sally was horrified. "My God, Mother," she said. "Tom is lucky there's not something wrong with him!"

Tom set the date for the intervention. As hard as it was for Rusty to relinquish his power even for a minute, it made perfect sense, given that Tom had to take time off from his practice and fly all the way from Denver. The Snow Bunny was coming, too, even though she really didn't know Sid at all. Sometimes over the past five years, Marilyn had called up the first wife just to hear her voice or, even better, the voice of one or more of her grandchildren on the answering machine. Now there was a man's name included in the list of who wasn't home. She and Sid would hold the receiver between them, both with watering eyes, when they heard the voices they barely recognized. They didn't know about *69 until a few months ago when Margot, the oldest child, named for Sid's mother, called back. "Who is this?" she asked. She was growing up in Minnesota and now was further alienated by an accent Marilyn only knew from Betty White's character on *The Golden Girls*.

"Your grandmother, honey. Grandma Marilyn in South Carolina."

There was a long silence, and then the child began to speak rapidly, filling them in on all that was going on in her life. "Mom says you used to teach junior high," Margot said, and she and Sid both grinned, somehow having always trusted that their daughter-in-law would not have turned on them as Tom had led them to believe.

Then Susan got on the phone, and as soon as she did, Marilyn burst into tears. "Oh, Susie, forgive me," she said. "You know how much we love you and the kids."

"I know," she said. "And if Tom doesn't bring the kids to you, I will. I promise." Marilyn and Sid still believe her. They fantasize during the twilight hour that she will drive up one day and there they'll all be. Then, lo and behold, here will come Tom. "He'll see what a goddamned fool he's been," Sid says. "They'll hug and kiss and send Snow Bunny packing."

"And we'll all live happily ever after," Marilyn says.

"You can take that to the bank, baby," he says, and she hugs him close, whispers that he has to eat dinner before they can go anywhere.

"You know I'm a very good driver," she says, and he just shakes his head back and forth; he can list every ticket and fender-bender she has had in her life.

The intervention day is next week. Tom and Bunny plan to stay with Sally and Rusty an hour away so that Sid won't get suspicious. Already it is unbearable to her—this secret. There has only been one time in their whole marriage when she had a secret, and it was a disaster.

"What's wrong with you?" Sid keeps asking. "So quiet." His eyes have that somber look she catches once in a while; it's a look of hurt, a look of disillusionment. It is the look that nearly killed them thirty-odd years ago.

There have been many phone calls late at night. Rusty knows how to set up conference calls, and there they all are, Tom and Sally and Rusty, talking nonstop. If he resists, we do this. If he gets angry, we do that. All the while, Sid dozes. Sometimes the car is parked crooked in the drive, a way that he never would have parked even two years ago, and she goes out in her housecoat and bedroom slippers to straighten it up so the neighbors won't think anything is wrong. She has repositioned the mailbox many times, touched up paint on the car and the garage that Sid didn't even notice. Sometimes he is too tired to move or undress, and she spreads a blanket over him in the chair. Recently she found a stash of empty bottles in the bottom of his golf bag. Empty bottles in the Pepsi cooler, the trunk of his car.

"I suspect he lies to you about how much he has," Rusty says. "We are taught not to ask an alcoholic how much he drinks, but to phrase it in a way that accepts a lot of intake, such as 'How many fifths do you go through in a weekend?'"

"Sid doesn't lie to me."

"This is as much for you," Rusty says, and she can hear the impatience in his voice. "You are what we call an enabler."

She doesn't respond. She reaches and takes Sid's warm limp hand in her own.

"If you really love him," he pauses, gathering volume and force in his words, "you have to go through with this."

"It was really your idea, Mom," Sally says. "We all suspected as much, but you're the one who really blew the whistle." Marilyn remains quiet, a picture of herself like some kind of Nazi woman blowing a shrill whistle, dogs barking, flesh tearing. She can't answer; her head is swimming. "Admit it. He almost killed you when he went off the road. It's your side that would have smashed into the pole. You were lucky."

"I was driving," she says now, whispering so as not to wake him. "I almost killed him!"

"Nobody believed you, Marilyn," Rusty says, and she is reminded of the one and only student she has hated in her career, a smart-assed boy who spoke to her as if he were the adult and she were the child. Even though she knew better, knew that he was a little jerk, it had still bothered her.

"You're lucky Mr. Randolph was the officer on duty, Mom," Tom says. "He's not going to look the other way next time. He told me as much."

"And what about how you told me you have to hide his keys sometimes?" Sally asks. "What about that?"

"Where are the children?" Marilyn asks. "Are they hearing all of this?"

"No," Rusty says. "We won't tell this sort of thing until they're older and can learn from it."

"We didn't," she whispers and then ignores their questions. Didn't what? Didn't what?

"The literature says that there should be a professional involved," she says and, for a brief anxious moment, relishes their silence.

"Rusty is a professional," Sally says. "This is what he does for a living."

Sid lives for a living, she wants to say, but she lets it all go. They are coming, come hell or high water. She can't stop what she has put into motion, a rush of betrayal and shame pushing her back to a dark place she has not seen in years. Sid stirs and brings her hand up to his cheek.

Sid never told the children anything. He never brought up anything once it had passed, unlike Marilyn, who sometimes gets stuck in a groove, spinning and spinning, deeper and deeper. Whenever anything in life—the approach of spring, the smell of gin, pine sap thawing and coming back to life—prompts her memory, she cringes and feels the urge to crawl into a dark hole. She doesn't recognize that woman. That woman was sick. A sick, foolish woman, a woman who had no idea that the best of life was in her hand. It was late spring, and they went with a group to the lake. They hired babysitters round the clock so the men could fish and the women could sun and shop and nobody had to be concerned for all the needs of the youngsters. The days began with coffee and bloody marys and ended with sloppy kisses on the sleeping brows of their babies. Sid was worried then. He was bucking for promotions right and left, taking extra shifts. He wanted to run the whole delivery service in their part of the state and knew that he could do it if he ever got the chance to prove himself. Then he would have normal hours, good benefits.

Marilyn had never even noticed Paula Edwards's husband before that week. She spoke to him, yes; she thought it was Paula's good fortune to have married someone who had been so successful so young. ("Easy when it's a family business and handed to you," Sid said, the only negative thing she ever heard him say about the man.) But there he was, not terribly attractive but very attentive. Paula was pregnant with twins and forced to a lot of bed rest. Even now, the words of the situation, playing through Marilyn's mind, shock her.

"You needed attention," Sid said when it all exploded in her face. "I'm sorry I wasn't there."

"Who are you—Jesus Christ?" she screamed. "Don't you hate me? Paula hates me!"

"I'm not Paula. And I'm not Jesus." He went to the cabinet and mixed a big bourbon and water. He had never had a drink that early in the day. "I'm a man who is very upset."

"At me!"

"At both of us."

She wanted him to hate her right then. She wanted him to make her suffer, make her pay. She had wanted him even at the time it was Paula's husband meeting her in the weeks following in dark, out-of-the-way parking lots—rest areas out on the interstate, rundown motels no one with any self-esteem would venture into. And yet there she had been. She bought the new underwear the way women so often do, as if that thin bit of silk could prolong the masquerade. Then later, she had burned all the new garments in a huge puddle of gasoline, a flame so high the fire department came, only to find her stretched out on the grass of her front yard, sobbing. Her children, ages four and two, were there beside her, wide-eyed and frightened. "Mommy? Are you sick?" She felt those tiny hands pulling and pulling. "Mommy? Are you sad?" Paula's husband wanted sex. She could have been anyone those times he twisted his hands in her thick long hair, grown the way Sid liked it, and pulled her head down. He wanted her to scream out and tear at him. He liked it that way. Paula wasn't that kind of girl, but he knew that she was.

"But you're not," Sid told her in the many years to follow, the times when self-loathing overtook her body and reduced her to an anguished heap on the floor. "You're not that kind."

People knew. They had to know, but out of respect for Sid, they never said a word. Paula had twin girls, and they moved to California, and to this day, they send a Christmas card with a brag letter much like the one that Sally and Rusty have begun sending. Something like: We are brilliant, and we are rich. Our lives are perfect, don't you wish yours was as good? If Sid gets the mail, he tears it up and never says a word. He did the same with the letter that Paula wrote to him when she figured out what was going on. Marilyn never saw what the letter said. She only heard Sid sobbing from the other side of a closed door, the children vigilant as they waited for him to come out. When his days of silence ended and she tried to talk, he simply put a finger up to her lips, his eyes dark and shadowed in a way that frightened her. He mixed himself a drink and offered her one as they sat and listened with relief to the giggles of the children playing outside. Sid had bought a sandbox and put it over the burned spot right there in the front yard. He said that in the fall when it was cooler, he'd cover it with sod. He gave up on advancing to the top, and settled in instead with a budget and all the investments he could make to ensure college educations and decent retirement.

Her feelings each and every year when spring came had nothing to do with any lingering feelings she might have had about the affair—she had none. Rather, her feelings were about the disgust she felt for herself, and the more disgusted she felt, the more she needed some form of self-medication. For her, alcohol was the symptom of the greater problem, and she shudders with recall of all the nights Sid had to scoop her up from the floor and carry her to bed. The times she left pots burning on the stove, the time Tom as a five-year-old sopped towels where she lay sick on the bathroom floor. "Mommy is sick," he told Sid, who stripped and bathed her, cool sheets around her body, cool cloth to her head. It was the vision of her children standing there and staring at her, their eyes as somber and vacuous as Sid's had been that day he got Paula's letter, that woke her up.

"I'm through," she said. "I need help."

Sid backed her just as he always had. Rusty would have called him her enabler. He nursed her and loved her. He forgave her and forgave her. I'm a bad chemistry experiment, she told Sid. Without him she would not have survived.

On the day of intervention, the kids come in meaning business, but then can't help but lapse into discussion about their own families and how great they all are. Snow Bunny wants a baby, which makes Sid laugh, even though Marilyn can tell he suspects something is amiss. Rusty has been promoted. He is thinking about going back to school to get his degree in psychology. They gather in the living room, Sid in his chair, a coffee cup on the table beside him. She knows there is bourbon in his cup but would never say a word. She doesn't have to. Sally sweeps by, grabs the cup, and then is in the kitchen sniffing its content. Rusty gives the nod of a man in charge. Sid is staring at her, all the questions easily read: Why are they here? Did you know they were coming? Why did you keep this from me? And she has to look away. She never should have let this happen. She should have found a way to bring Sid around to his own decision, the way he had led her.

Now she wants to scream at the children that she did this to Sid. She wants to pull out the picture box and say: This is me back when I was fucking my friend's husband while you were asleep in your beds. And this is me when I drank myself sick so that I could forget what a horrible woman and wife and mother I was. Here is where I passed out on the floor with a pan of hot grease on the stove, and here is where I became so hysterical in the front yard that I almost burned the house down. I ruined the lawn your father worked so hard to grow. I ruined your father. I did this, and he never told you about how horrible I was. He protected me. He saved me.

"Well, Sid," Rusty begins, "we have come together to be with you because we're concerned about you."

"We love you, Daddy, and we're worried."

"Mom is worried," Tom says, and as Sid turns to her, Marilyn has to look down. "Your drinking has become a problem, and we've come to get help for you."

I'm the drunk, she wants to say. I was here first.

"You're worried, honey?" Sid asks. "Why haven't you told me?"

She looks up now, first at Sid and then at Sally and Tom. If you live long enough, your children learn to love you from afar, their lives are front and center and elsewhere. Your life is only what they can conjure from bits and pieces. They don't know how it all fits together. They don't know all the sacrifices that have been made.

"We're here as what is called an intervention," Rusty says.

"Marilyn?" He is gripping the arms of his chair. "You knew this?"

"No," she says. "No, I didn't. I have nothing to do with this."

"Marilyn." Rusty rises from his chair, Sally right beside him. It's like the room has split in two and she is given a clear choice—the choice she wishes she had made years ago, and then maybe none of this would have ever happened.

"We can take care of this on our own," she says. "We've taken care of far worse."

"Such as?" Tom asks. She has always wanted to ask him what he remembers from those horrible days. Does he remember finding her there on the floor? Does he remember her wishing to be dead?

"Water under the bridge," Sid says. "Water under the bridge." Sid stands, shoulders thrown back. He is still the tallest man in the room. He is the most powerful man. "You kids are great," he says. "You're great, and you're right." He goes into the kitchen and ceremoniously pours what's left of a fifth of bourbon down the sink. He breaks out another fifth still wrapped with a Christmas ribbon and pours it down the sink. "Your mother tends to overreact and exaggerate from time to time, but I do love her." He doesn't look at her, just keeps pouring. "She doesn't drink, so I won't drink."

"She has never had a problem," Sally says, and for a brief second Marilyn feels Tom's eyes on her.

"I used to," Marilyn says.

"Yeah, she'd sip a little wine on holidays. Made her feel sick, didn't it, honey?" Sid is opening and closing cabinets. He puts on the teakettle. "Mother likes tea in the late afternoon like the British. As a matter of fact," he continues, still not looking at her, "sometimes we pretend we are British."

She nods and watches him pour out some cheap Scotch he always offers to cheap friends. He keeps the good stuff way up high behind her mother's silver service. "And we've been writing our own little holiday letter, Mother and I, and we're going to tell every single thing that has gone on this past year like Sally and

Rusty do. Like I'm going to tell that Mother has a spastic colon and often feels 'sqwitty,' as the British might say, and that I had an abscessed tooth that kept draining into my throat, leaving me no choice but to hock and spit throughout the day. But all that aside, kids, the real reason I can't formally go somewhere to dry out for you right now is, one, I have already booked a hotel over in Myrtle Beach for our anniversary, and, two, there is nothing about me to dry."

By the end of the night everyone is talking about "one more chance." Sid has easily turned the conversation to Rusty and where he plans to apply to school and to Snow Bunny and her hopes of having a "little Tommy" a year from now. They say things like that they are proud of Sid for his effort but not to be hard on himself if he can't do it on his own. He needs to realize he might have a problem. He needs to be able to say: I have a problem.

"So. Wonder what stirred all that up?" he asks as they watch the children finally drive away. She has yet to make eye contact with him. "I have to say I'm glad to see them leave." He turns now and waits for her to say something.

"I say adios, motherfuckers." She cocks her hands this way and that like the rappers do, which makes him laugh. She notices his hand shaking and reaches to hold it in her own. She waits, and then she offers to fix him a small drink to calm his nerves.

"I don't have to have it, you know," he says.

"Oh, I know that," she says. "I also know you saved the good stuff."

She mixes a weak one and goes into the living room, where he has turned off all but the small electric candle on the piano.

"Here's to the last drink," he says as she sits down beside him. He breathes a deep sigh that fills the room. He doesn't ask again if she had anything to do with what happened. He never questions her a second time; he never has. And in the middle of the night when she reaches her hand over the cool sheets, she will find him there, and when spring comes and the sticky heat disgusts her with pangs of all the failures in her life, he will be there, and when it is time to get in the car and drive to Myrtle Beach or to see the kids, perhaps even to drive all the way to Minnesota to see their grandchildren, she will get in and close the door to the passenger side without a word. She will turn and look at the house that the two of them worked so hard to maintain, and she will note as she always does the perfect green grass of the front yard and how Sid fixed it so that there is not a trace of the mess she made. It is their house. It is their life. She will fasten her seat belt and not say a word.

ANTONYA NELSON

Rear View

When I was young our winter-wear wouldn't have permitted anyone to look sexy. The look then was like the inflated figures in a Macy's parade, puffy and down-stuffed, colorful rubber boots, with pompons on the hats our mothers knitted, matching mittens hanging on yarn from our coat sleeves. Fashion then didn't have in mind sprinting along the highway on a bitter frozen day in muscle-sheathing elastic fabrics, costumed from head to foot like a superhero. The jogger on the highway shoulder outside Telluride had every straining tendon and ligament, every flex and thrust, defined in his shining black outfit. Running hard, his mouth made a white grimace under his yellow bug-like goggles. Velocity Man, on his way to save the day.

And on a Sunday, no less. I had braked when I saw him, hobbling my old Saab apologetically toward the center line to be sure he understood I knew he possessed the moral high road, hiding my smoldering cigarette beneath the dash as if he cared. I was wondering if I was pregnant, banking on a rumor I'd heard that nothing you did the first ten days of pregnancy affected the fetus in the least. A grace period, some stepping-down time from your bad habits. God's air lock. And then, amazingly, there was my brother, also on the highway shoulder, but not wearing Lycra. Not likely. He was climbing into the passenger side of his car. I pulled up behind it, assuming he'd stopped to pee or that the car had broken down again. We were two miles from town on the only road into it.

"Beer?" Sonny asked, unsurprised when I opened the driver's door. There was a box of cans on the back seat.

"No, thanks. What's going on?"

"I'm taking a break."

"From what?"

"Getting this heap home." His heater blew; the day, mid-April and barely into spring, had begun with rain down in Grand Junction, but up here, naturally, it alternated between snow and hail, soft ice or harsh. On the windshield the snowflakes melted upon contact. This was the treacherous seasonal moment when it seemed that winter might never end, that summer was a sappy dream left over from a storybook. "What are *you* up to?" he asked.

"Back from the bin." I blushed, but my brother wouldn't ask where I'd spent the night, or who with. On Saturdays I drove the hundred twenty-five miles to Grand Junction to visit my husband, then slept at another man's house. He and I went out drinking at the Junction bars, which were different from the Telluride bars. Happier, I thought. Younger, this time of year, while the junior college was still in session, and certainly no dumber. Up in Telluride the ski runs had shut down, and the party animals had gone home. Their hosts were vaguely sour, used, and disillusioned. The slopes had turned treacherous, glazed with ice like glass. Off-season.

"How's Larry doing? Close that door. It's a witch's tit."

I tossed the cigarette butt over the car and onto the bike path, then settled into the driver's seat of the Nova. Sonny had bought it just recently to restore and its interior smelled like hound dog and its prey. "You should drink whiskey, if you're so cold."

"Don't go there," he said, shaking his head, finishing the beer. His gloves were wool, without fingers because he'd snipped them off.

"He's fine," I told him, concerning Larry. "He says he meets really interesting people in the hospital. He says he's still achieving nirvana at least once a day, when they let him have the solarium to himself. He asked me to bring him his bridge books next week so he can teach one of the other patients how to play, try to wrestle up a foursome..." I sighed. "I don't think he's planning on coming home anytime soon. He likes it there."

"What's not to like? Nirvana every day?"

"That's what he claims."

"Although I could never get bridge straight."

"Me, neither."

Sonny popped another top and drained half the can. Because it was diet beer, he could drink twice as much. He'd asked me to pick up more for him, down in Junction where it was cheaper, and I'd forgotten. I was forgetful. He said, "You wanna do me a favor?"

"What's that?"

"Drive me back to my truck." He threw a thumb over his shoulder.

I craned around and saw Big Red, sitting behind a few hundred yards, also on the roadside. Its roomy cab and rounded edges made it seem homey, smiling grill and side mirrors like little ears, snow on its roof like a flattop haircut, a jolly destination on a gloomy day. "I like Big Red," I said, "but this car seems kind of cursed."

"She's been manhandled." He patted the cracked dash. Overhead, dusty material sagged. Blond dog hair clung to everything, a few downy feathers, dank undercurrent of dead fish. A hunter had owned it before he had a heart attack out in the woods alone. At auction, Sonny had been the only bidder. Such was the advantage of being so out of step with the rest of Telluride, where the Range Rovers ruled. Today, because the Nova had needed a valve job, my brother had been driving the two vehicles home by himself, leapfrogging the five miles from his friend's illegal garage down the canyon.

"Drive ahead, run on back," he explained, running his fingers like legs. "Drive ahead, run on back."

"In those boots? Why didn't you wait and let me help you this afternoon? Or tomorrow?" It went without saying that his wife wouldn't help; she wasn't finished avenging herself on him for some past bad behavior.

"I needed the car now." Sonny was simple that way; he wanted something, he went and got it, even if it meant running some portion of the distance home in freezing sleet, wearing his logger's boots and ball cap and cut-up gloves. What portion? I wondered. The whole five miles? Ten, since he had to shuttle back and forth? This was one of those story problems math teachers are always trying to persuade you will come up in your real life. "I reckon we could figure a better method," he said, "now there's two of us."

"But now there's three cars."

"Damned if they don't still have us outnumbered."

The state trooper rushed by, heading out of town with his lights on and his siren off.

"Go, Smokey, go," urged my brother, tossing his empty on the floorboard.

The bartender back in Grand Junction hadn't been the one from the night before. I was just glad the place opened on Sunday; I hadn't realized it was also a diner.

"I'm here to pick up my credit card."

He was the daytime tender, too young, soft from TV and Pop-Tarts and higher education, somebody who could handle no more difficult patron than the elders, the early risers who opened the place at ten ordering hard fried eggs and red beer. A few of them leaned over the bar, still as wax figures, occupying every other stool, eyes an easy blur behind fudgy lenses. Cigarette smoke, at this hour, smelled somehow fresh rather than noxious, like a bristling campfire at dawn, complete with the odor of bacon wafting about.

"I don't find a card," the youth reported, sniffing. He had a hell of a cold, a bead of clear mucus moving in and out of his nostril as he breathed. The inner lids of his eyes looked drawn on with red ink.

"Well." It was so exhausting, the missing credit card, the long chain reaction. And the place was warm, smelling of fried pork. I decided to delay the labor, the retracing of my steps. "How about a bloody mary?" The bartender took a second to decide whether to ask for ID; it still happened to me maybe half the time. But not for much longer.

He made the drink with Clamato. "Nautical," I said, settling at an empty stool between two men. "Naughty," I added. "Maybe the card is under the counter, with the bad checks and the lost-and-found? There might have been an altercation?"

The drunk on my right said, "That's a good breakfast drink. It's got food value. Beer has food value as well," he indicated his own glass. "This Guinness, here." We watched the creamy portion roil into the deep brown, mesmerizing as a geologic event. "But food, you know, does not have beer value." He, alone among the group, didn't even pretend to eat.

"No," I agreed. "That *is* the problem."

"Wherever your credit card is, it isn't here," the bartender said, using two fingers to plug his sneeze. I'd left the card to run a tab, then there'd been pool balls flying on account of some college girls and their boyfriends, a town-gown kind of dispute. We'd exited through the back door, the one with the panic handle that claimed to be only for emergencies, into the alley and down the block, laughing, floating. My friend was Jonathan; he said he'd seen enough bar fights to know when to leave. I was trying to fall in love with him. Escapades like this were helpful. The effort required diligence, an active imagination, an ability to overlook. I didn't recall love being so much work. *Falling in* suggested ease, the advantage of gravity. He was fifteen years younger than my husband; close to my age, in other words. Though I saw no evidence of the fracas, I knew this was the place because my car still sat in its parking lot out front, morose rusted Saab. It was remarkable what could happen one night and be utterly forgotten in the light of the morning after. This enduring establishment, named Earl's, like the human body, withstood a drunken brawling assault and resurrected itself, day after day after day. The pool balls sat racked and ready, the cues returned to their case. The trembling hands at the bar, reaching for their drinks.

My brother Sonny had once told me he'd rather die than quit drinking. I felt certain I was sitting among like minds.

"You know, you can cancel the card," the bartender said wearily. I could tell he thought he was better than any of the people he served. He probably said "You're welcome" before he was thanked.

"I have to figure out which card it is." I had a lot of credit cards, each with a low limit, because I was somebody credit-card companies thought ought to be spread thin. I paged through them in my wallet while the man beside me, old enough to be my father, gave me discouraging scenarios concerning spending sprees.

"That fella could be all the way to Mexico by now."

"By God," the Guinness drinker on my other side affirmed.

"He could be putting himself up at a swanky four-star motel, getting himself whatever he beck and calls, all on your nickel. I once had somebody charge himself airline tickets on my Visa—and you know that card never even left my billfold, I had it on my person the whole time, in my ass pocket—and here it comes charging me, anyway, some somnabitch flying from Vegas to Boston."

This line of conversation tapped into the computer nerd in the bartender, who proceeded to disabuse his old clientele of their fears concerning fraud. One phone call, he kept saying pedantically, wiping his runny nose. Easy as pie. I made the call after spreading the contents of my wallet on the bar and narrowing the options. There'd been no "activity" overnight on the missing

card, not even here at Earl's, according to the person who named
herself my representative. Did I want to wait and see if I located
it? She, like the barkeep, felt herself superior to carelessness and
its consequences.

"Nah, I should cancel that card, anyway." I should. I had debts
now that Larry was in the hospital. I didn't want to bother him
with them. Part of his trouble lay with over-assuming everybody's
problems. In his false largesse and skewed lucidity, he believed he
was capable of solving anything. He could fix the world, he
believed, if he applied the simple lessons of Zen Buddhism to
every part of his day. *"Flow,"* he'd insisted to me, two meaningful
syllables, bestowed like a blessing. He'd not slept in nearly a week
when I brought him to Junction. He'd ridden in the back seat like
a pet or child, lying with his feet up against the window, explaining the inventions he had in mind to patent, the choreography
that would transform his restaurant kitchen into a model of effi-
ciency. At his intake he was asked if he felt like killing anyone,
himself or others. No, no, no, he'd said impatiently, waving at the
air. Corporeal concerns had left him; the life of the *mind*, he
maintained. He needed time to think. That was four months ago.
Our insurance, his insurance, would cover another two before
raising much of a fuss.

"Buy you one of those?" asked the Guinness man. My glass was
empty but for the pulpy remains, a limp celery stalk, a few lime
seeds and their green rind. "I'm not going to make any moves,
sweetheart, I recognize you have some problems. I'm just offering
to buy you a drink."

"Sure."

He nodded at my shirt front. "You been at the hospital?" I
looked down to see the guest sticker still stuck to my shirt.

"Yes," I said. And, like him at this bar, I would be there again.
Meanwhile, I would spend the morning in the warm smoky haze
of avuncular concern, sipping my liquid breakfast before heading
home alone.

The day before, Jonathan had met me at the drugstore across
from the hospital, as usual. I kept waiting for my heart to leap, as
it was supposed to, at the sight of the beloved. He sat looking
exhausted—unshaven, hair savaged by his worrying hands—

wearing mint-green scrubs, playing solitaire on his laptop computer at a plastic table. The plastic chair below looked ready to give up, legs splayed beneath his massive bulk. Perhaps it was his size that allowed him to be a nurse, the knowledge that no wiseass would taunt his profession. He had the wild good looks of genetic luck, and he was indifferent about them, like money he had inherited rather than earned. No doubt he would lose his handsomeness to disregard and intemperance. His muscle, someday soon, would melt to fat.

He smiled when he saw me, a slow spreading that made wrinkles at his eyes. It was a sad smile; he worked with damaged people because he was damaged himself. He was a gentle giant, and there wasn't one of his patients he couldn't carry or restrain in his arms. His job was at the hospital psych ward, but not on Larry's floor. Jonathan's patients were confined to chairs or small padded rooms or the deeply debilitating doze of sedation. My husband, stabilized on a few helpful pharmaceuticals, lived upstairs. His stay was voluntary—necessary, it seemed, but voluntary nonetheless. Jonathan's patients had not volunteered. They'd been abandoned, or rescued, depending, but they weren't at Mercy by their own choosing.

Jonathan folded up his computer and tucked it into his armpit. "How's it going?"

"Good." I nodded, nervous, but not in love, I didn't think. I wanted to be in love. I wanted to locate love, as I had known it, and invest it somewhere, in Jonathan, if I could. He was kind, modest, complicated, a good kisser. Why didn't I love him? My love for my husband had burst into discrete pieces when he himself came undone. I could name them—concern, fear, fondness, pity—all separate like parts of a broken object it was my job to reassemble, an object whose lynchpin I seemed to have misplaced. If I'd known he was going to have a psychotic break, I would have gotten pregnant last fall and by now be halfway to a new kind of love, the love of a baby—me for it, it for me, the two of us for its father, and his for us, a perfect, impermeable system, a closed circuit. Pregnant, the barhopping and the overnights in Jonathan's bed would have been utterly unthinkable. Pregnant, I'd have installed a little cop, helping me toe the line.

"So it was a good visit?" Jonathan asked as we walked against the wind to retrieve my car. He'd made it his chivalric duty not to meet my husband, not to learn anything of him. *My husband.* When we got married, twelve years ago, I could not speak those two words with a straight face. One year ago, when it was clear that my husband was unhappy but before he went completely AWOL, I had given him permission to sleep with another woman, a waitress at his restaurant. He'd gotten as far as her bedroom, as far as a long kiss, before he changed his mind. I had been so proud of us then, me the open-minded, him the devoted, each of us choosing an unexpected course. I naïvely believed that that represented the extent of our married hardship.

"Pretty good," I lied to Jonathan.

He pulled on his sweater and hat as we went, shifting the computer around like a paperback in his large hands. "'Cause there was a suicide on his floor early this morning," he said, once inside my Saab. He sighed, unsettled. His big body absorbed bad news, trapped it inside so that it couldn't afflict anyone else.

"Larry didn't say anything."

"An Italian woman, a transfer from the ER. They treated her hypothermia over there, and then sent her our way. Nobody understood what was up with her because she wasn't talking, not in Italian, not in English, nothing. She was just about to get moved downstairs when they found her. And how she got two belts, I'll never know. One would have been hard enough. I was hoping nobody on the second floor knew about it yet."

"Belts?"

"Buddy Belts. We use them to manipulate paralytics."

"She hanged herself? That seems so..."

"Painful?" Jonathan supplied, messing his messy hair. "Desperate? Senseless? Retarded?"

"Difficult. I wouldn't even know how to tie a noose."

"Remember, she had belt notches to work with."

"I see." Italian, I thought.

"And a showerhead. If she'd weighed any more than she did, it wouldn't have held." We rode in silence to our usual first stop. "They called me to come take her down."

"I'm sorry." The car coughed when I switched off its engine, always three coughs before it quit. "Have you touched a lot of dead bodies?"

"I guess. Depending on what you think of as a lot." He breathed audibly, as large people did. "I think more than I could count on one hand, but less than on both."

"That's more people than I've had sex with," I said.

" 'People'?"

"Men. A boy or two."

"Let's drink tequila tonight," he said, shoving the computer under the seat and climbing out. He would forget it there, I thought. It would ride home with me tomorrow. "Tequila," he repeated, "even though the margaritas here taste like Gatorade."

We always started at the Alpine, where the Western coeds went. From there we would migrate toward Jonathan's duplex, stopping along the way to warm up, to sink further into the drunkenness that would allow me to make love with him later. At Earl's, fifth and final stop, where we'd been waiting for our turn at pool, he swept me smoothly out the door when he noticed the gun inside the jacket of one of the local guys playing against the college boys. The two balls that flew off the table when he took his shot hadn't been intentionally hurled, but they provoked a fight nonetheless.

"I've dealt with enough blood and guts this week," Jonathan claimed as we hustled down the alley. I felt half-carried, him large, me light with alcohol. The last woman he'd held had been dead. It was only two blocks to his duplex; our course had built into it a fail-safe drunk-driving logic. At his house we started kissing the minute we had closed the door, drama and tragedy adding, tonight, to my attraction to him: the gun tucked in the guy's jacket played a part; the Italian woman hanging from two belts dangled somewhere between us, my husband's ghostly disappearing self. *Love*, I urged myself, biting Jonathan's plump lip. He moved backward down the hall, me on his feet-tops like a child, past the second bedroom where his daughter stayed on the nights he had custody. Stuffed animals. A poster of a singing group, five scrubbed boys of varying skin tones, the United Nations of ballad crooners. They sang the kind of songs I had liked as a girl.

When Jonathan lay asleep and I gazed through his skylight into the clouds, I didn't realize I was dreaming. It seemed real: I was where I was, who I was, and who I was with. But my teeth were falling out, the roots beneath them softening and letting loose one by one. Strange, dangerous men, those from Earl's, had broken into Jonathan's house and were wreaking havoc in the kitchen, drawers crashing to the floor, the clatter of silverware, the garbage disposal ready to eat digits and limbs, if need be—a loud fantasy in a home so silent that you could hear a clock tick. A pack of clever wolves waited outside, in case we thought we could escape. And how could anyone love me now, I kept thinking, me without my teeth?

And before all that, Saturday morning at Mercy General. I was still queasy from having hit an animal with my car, still trying to eliminate the image as I crossed the parking lot, when I saw my husband at the rec room window. I had looked up accidentally, shaking off that highway event, and there was Larry, his face and hands pressed up against the glass. His tortured expression reached into my chest. I wanted to call his name out, shout a warning, make him step back immediately. I ran into the building, passing the fish-mouthed front-desk receptionist and storming up the stairs, hurrying down the hall until I found him. He wore his black cotton pants, chest and feet naked, and stood at the floor-to-ceiling window overlooking the parking lot. I was glad to know the window was reinforced. You could see the fine wires, if you stared closely into the glass, an intricate, nearly invisible web. I stood catching my breath; he hadn't heard me, perhaps hadn't even seen me down below. Larry had his hands spread reverentially on the smooth, cool surface, smearily, his cheek and chest pressed to it, too, as if absorbing the on-again, off-again sunlight, as if listening for information carried in the wires in the glass, perhaps wishing not to break through but to squeeze into its transparency, to enter the *flow*. I could see his ribs, the loose skin where once he'd been robust. His eyes were pinched shut and that was the part that most scared me. What was he praying? And why was it so anguishing? He was fifty-two years old but seemed older, the flesh on his face slack, his whiskers and chest hair white. I didn't know how to imagine what he was doing, or why he'd left our home and his business, or why this place, of all the ones, was where he wished to be.

The receptionist from downstairs caught up with me, brandishing the sign-in form on her clipboard. Her annoyance was silenced by the spectacle of my husband. "We have to have a record," she finally whispered.

For months I had entered this place murmuring my own prayer: let him be better. Last December I'd found him on the living room carpet among a pile of dirt and roots and broken pots, our houseplants pulled from their shelves and destroyed. "I can't take the responsibility," he'd said simply. "The responsibility is plaguing me." Just the need to water them once a week tormented him; he lay in the mess as if to join it, another life for someone else to nourish and encourage. I'd thought his busking at his own restaurant was a joke, him sitting out front with a hat on the sidewalk, strumming his guitar; then a week later he'd fired the entire kitchen staff and given away the contents of the walk-in, thousands of dollars worth of meat and cheese and chocolate and cream. No telling what might happen next; the head waitress had wisely locked up the wine cellar. His unhinging was erratic, some of it lighthearted. But this full-body press on the window didn't look good. It was as if he wished to sieve himself through the wired glass, disperse like powder into the landscape.

The receptionist was only too glad to retreat to her post.

"Larry," I said. "Larry, what are you doing, baby?"

He pulled himself away slowly, peeling his cheek off like a sticker. He'd left an odd imprint, fingerprints, the squashed side of his face. "My feet are freezing," he said, looking down as if he had just realized they were his, wiggling his toes. His nails needed grooming, along with every other piece of personal hygiene. That had been the first to go, caring about his appearance. And it had played such a large part before, since I was younger than he, and he wanted to feel presentable. Only the young could afford to be slovenly and still attract a mate. Even Jonathan, at thirty-five, would soon have to put out some effort.

I led Larry slowly to a couple of vinyl-covered easy chairs in the corner, grouped there near a lamp to inspire conversation, to suggest normalcy. Nurses and patients passed through the large rec room but paid no attention to us. Nobody really seemed to occupy the same universe here. There was something liberating about being among people so completely unself-conscious. Or maybe it was narcissism that made them seem nonjudgmental—they were too busy worrying about themselves to worry about others. But

there was also something terrifying. My plan, as it had been every
recent Saturday, was to have sex with Larry. Pregnancy was my
only salvation, I believed, and even if I wasn't ovulating, I wanted
to have an explanation for when Jonathan succeeded where Larry
had failed. These were the lies I lived by: not loving Jonathan,
betraying my husband. Put together, they equaled a truth, which
was that I needed a child. I was thirty-six and could no longer tol-
erate the jittery limbo of my life. Once I had a child, I would
know what to do. Every move I made would have a glowing
imperative attached like a corona, a flare of ambient light to lead
me.

I'd been having sex with Jonathan for ten weeks now, the three
most recent of them unprotected.

Larry sat breathing hard, frightened. He searched my face as if
I'd just pulled him from the sea, as if he were still in the throes of
drowning, desperate, and not quite sure that I had his best interest at heart. Did I?

"Did you take a drug holiday, hon? You know they don't like
you to do that around here. Should I run fetch something?"

"Say, Martin," he called out anxiously to a passing pajama-clad
man. Here was a familiar, safe harbor. The guy smiled, tilting his
head like a friendly dog. A piece of his fine brown hair flopped
down like that dog's ear. "You haven't met my wife. Come meet
my wife." Martin held his hand out as he approached: shake.
There was a gap in his pajama bottoms, through which his shad-
owy genitals could be glimpsed as he moved. I'd met him a few
weeks before; it was electric shock that had messed with Larry's
memory. Or maybe, in his enlightened state of mind, Larry
divined my plan for an accidental pregnancy and was rebelling,
deflecting my attention. I did not doubt his heightened con-
sciousness; it just wasn't very useful, sequestered as it was in his
mind, feeding like a worm on his physical substance, surrounded
for months now by these reinforced walls.

Martin was an English professor at Ft. Lewis College, in Duran-
go. He'd timed his stay to coincide with a sabbatical. Alarming
how thoughtful and reasonable the people on Larry's floor were,
practical in their way. Martin could, and did, recite Shakespeare.
He was preparing himself for a summer repertory production of
Hamlet. " 'Give every man thine ear,' " he'd advised me at our first

meeting, " 'but few thy voice. Take each man's censure, but reserve thy judgment.' "

"Noted," I'd said.

"Polonius," he'd said, undaunted as everyone else here by sarcasm.

He settled himself daintily on the arm of Larry's chair, his pants gap now completely open, like a grin, guileless. They began discussing the possibility of pulling together a bridge foursome. There were the two of them, and one of the orderlies, and this new admission, a young deaf woman from Italy where bridge apparently was not just for the geriatric crowd. The only problem was her not being able to hear or speak, yet they were optimistic that they could work around that. Larry held up four fingers, then made a shoveling gesture: this would be four spades. Martin put a fist on his chest, pointed to his ring finger: hearts, diamonds. But what would be clubs? And no-trump?

"I just wonder how advanced she is," Martin fretted. "You can't overestimate the importance of everyone's being somewhere near the same in terms of expertise. And maybe it's *whist* that they play in Italy? Not necessarily bridge?"

"You have to wonder if Jimbo will be able to fully concentrate, with his other duties," Larry said.

The television across the room was muted: another window into another world, this one of commercials aimed at children, Jell-O, Barbie, Play-Doh, an onslaught of action and primary colors. I could still make out the prints Larry had left on the glass of the picture window. You could probably see them from below, outside. I'd come from the windy road into the static recirculation of this room, where extraordinary minutiae made up my husband's conversation with his new friend. He hadn't seemed so banally out-of-touch, so dotty, a few minutes ago; then, he had seemed at the zenith of misery. Which did I prefer? Now Larry took my hand, stroking it benignly, the way he might a flat stone or the head of a slumbering cat. In the midst of their bridge party plans I couldn't possibly mention lovemaking—so indecorous, for starters, but also because for the remainder of my time with Larry, Martin stayed perched on the chair arm. His asexual personality overruled his open PJ fly. Every week there were different but similar circumstances to help me realize the altered and mystifying atmosphere of my marriage. I was being taught every Saturday the lesson of losing him without losing him. When the buzzer sounded that meant lunch would be served in five minutes, I rose to leave. Relieved, reprieved, ready to go find Jonathan across the street.

"Join us?" Martin asked politely. So mannerly, these nuts.

"No, thanks. You want to come with me?" I asked Larry; I knew he would say no; I asked to offset my guilt, to get away scot-free. "Maybe to a real restaurant? For a real meal?" With real people, I wanted to add. Out there in the real world.

"These are real people," he told me, well-aware of how my thoughts worked. And his sudden insight—bittersweet déjà vu—made me burst into tears. A flash of heat, mucus, helplessness. Seeing me, Martin abruptly wandered off, blinking.

Larry took my hand again, stroking. All at once a horrified expression clouded his face, and he clutched my fingers. "I forgot that you played bridge!" he said. "Honey, is that why you're crying? Oh, honey, you of *course* ought to be our fourth! How could I be so dumb, to have for—"

"It's not bridge," I said, sniffling. "Good God. *Bridge.*"

"A *Saturday* game, what was I thinking?"

"It's not bridge." My outburst was over.

"Are you sure?" He cocked his head playfully, looked under his lids, nudged his forehead toward me, as if I were being coy.

"I am positive. Absolutely."

Now he held my face and used his thumbs to wipe away tears. This role he summoned from storage, comforting me. He still performed it well. He kissed my cheeks, one, then the other, his lips so dry I could hear them chafe my face. This was as close as our bodies were going to come today.

"I love you," he said serenely. In his irises I saw vast space, the blue-green of the ocean, of the sky, of the deep and crippling uncertainty that had landed him here. And I said what every coward says when challenged by that sally: "I love you, too."

Before I left Telluride, I stopped by Sonny's house to see if he needed anything in Grand Junction. Fruit or tools or some other supply. The sky was already beginning to cloud up; my breath came in steamy puffs. He was awake early, as always, today building a dog pen out of scrap metal, old box springs and parts of a swing set, a structure he had not bothered to have sanctioned by the fussy city bureaucrats. His wife's pair of matching dogs sat watching from Big Red's truck bed, where he'd trapped them. They wore sweaters, fat Pekinese with their smashed faces and sputtering outrage. The word Sonny applied was *Warthog:* noun, verb, adjective. "That's right, Warthogs," he said when they leapt to bark and froth at me, "let's just see if you can warthog your warthog asses out of *that.*" To me he said, confidentially, "They're starting to piss me off."

Inside the house a shade slat twitched: his wife, posted at the window.

"You want me to come with?" he asked, pushing back his safety goggles, welding gun pointed at the ground. Sonny wouldn't enter the hospital proper because sick people bothered him, but he enjoyed a trip to Grand Junction regardless. We could drive in Big Red instead of my car, listen to country music, eat burgers and drink beer at Tex's, shop at The AutoZone, and come home tonight instead of tomorrow—a totally other visit, a different agenda entirely—but I knew Jane Lynn wanted him at their house. Her hand was on the blinds not fifteen feet away. They had only recently gotten back together, and one of her chief complaints against Sonny was the time he spent looking after me. And it hadn't helped that for a few months he had rekindled a flame with his old high school sweetheart, her and her four children. I liked the girlfriend better than his wife; I'd said so twenty-some years ago, when Sonny had dropped one for the other, and it was Jane Lynn I'd said it to.

The girlfriend was sweet, the kind of large happy woman whose bra strap was persistently sliding down her arm, who out of genuine affection called everyone "sugar" and hugged you goodbye wet-eyed. She had very sweet children that her complete loser of a husband had abandoned. He was in jail for manufacturing and peddling methamphetamines. I thought Sonny had made a romantic step forward, coming to her—and her children's—rescue. The first I'd known about his affair was when he'd showed up at my house wearing a nasty wound on his forearm, a dirty hankie held in place with duct tape. This was where he'd sliced off his tattoo, *Jane Lynn,* the wife he thought he was done with. Her name had been excised, and the sore was ugly. The arm festered, a sickening green fluid that escaped from beneath a rough brown patch of scab. Every shirt he owned had a rusty left sleeve.

"Didn't anyone ever teach you about infection? Or how to get out blood?" I asked him, pouring hydrogen peroxide over the mess, quelling nausea.

"I can field-dress a deer," he said stubbornly. "I can get out a tattoo."

I'd been jealous of his flushed, renewed love. It was as if he'd reclaimed his youth, gone merrily down that other path. He'd be a great father! I knew from experience as his surrogate child; for years I'd lobbied in vain for nieces and nephews. And the girlfriend had two of each, Daisy, Adam, Melanie, Mikey, their names like a lingering jingle in my head, ready-made little blond tikes young enough to adjust, squint their big blue eyes, and view my brother as their father, me the fun aunty...Then, not long ago, he'd asked Jane Lynn if he could return to their marriage.

"I got tired of the squalor over there," he said of the girlfriend's home. His arm wasn't even healed when he came back. Jane Lynn had made some conditions for his return. Probably he was supposed to stop spending so much time with me. I knew for a fact that drinking was forbidden, although that's the request he made of me Saturday morning: buy him a few cases of Bud Light. He went to the truck's dash for his wallet, taking a moment to menace the Pekinese with a hissing tongue of flame from his torch. They skittered on their nails across the slick surface of the bed.

"I found this under the seat a while back," Sonny said. He handed me a spent yellow shotgun shell. It held a rolled piece of paper with my name on it and a date more than ten years past: 8-8-88. Since I was born on 6-6-66, I found dates noteworthy. I'd engraved 7-7-77 all over town when that day came; same with the 8's and 9's. I left my phone number on napkins tucked under the glass-tops of tables, my initials carved in the soft walls of saunas, in the boards of fences, the bark of trees. A part of a poem, a line from a song, a lovelorn query, moony messages sent into the universe in search of an answer, a responding soul, that alleged prince. At a bar in Junction called Earl's, I'd penned my initials in an equation with Jonathan's on the wall of the women's room stall: J.J. + S.S. = LOVE. This winter I had marked 02-02-02, and for the first time felt a discouraging downward tilt, imagining somehow a gravestone, that other public place where dates were registered. These notes had once been a record of my own fantastic hopefulness. Beneath Big Red's front seat I'd tucked this one, the reverse side of which read *All the little emptiness of love...* Those eloquent ellipses I'd drawn in, a trail of sentimental crumbs that wished to dispute the claim.

"That's yours, right?" Sonny asked.

"Yep." So far as I knew, he was the only one who'd ever found any of my messages.

"You want me to put that back under the seat?" Big Red was a fixture, could be used like a safety deposit box. My brother held out his hand, and I returned the scroll in its ribbed tube.

On the road to Grand Junction I got teary, feeling sorry for myself. The landscape turned an Impressionistic mess before my eyes, a set of blurry yellow warning lights, construction cones, slow curves, bare trees furred into ash-colored fluff. My father had taught me to drive on this road, unhappy passenger pulling air between his teeth and clutching the chicken handle, stomping at what would have been the brake. When he and my mother moved away, he told Sonny to look after me. That explained Sonny's consternation when I started dating Larry—a man older than himself—since the match wouldn't have pleased my father. But surely they were relieved that I was finally doing the things grown-ups did. And Larry eventually endeared himself to my family. He had taken good care of me until lately. Then in stepped Jonathan the nurse; the first time we met he was tending me after I'd fainted. Hospital odor: that nauseating alchemy of blood and antiseptic, the cool fluorescence of the halls, like walking into a refrigerator where half-dead people were stored, living only by the grace of machinery and medical personnel. Why should that place, the epicenter of need, the headquarters of help, send me limp to my knees? Jonathan sat cross-legged beside me on the floor, unalarmed, instructing me to breathe slowly and lower my head. When I told him my name was Sissy, he disagreed, "No, no, don't worry. People faint all the time."

"No, I don't mean I'm a sissy, I mean that's my name." My brother was Sonny, my parents' son, and I was his sister, Sissy.

"Sissy," said Jonathan.

And now, driving to Grand Junction, I thought of how I'd lied to Jonathan. I *was* a sissy. I would tell him so, since it was, in fact, Jonathan I was going to see. It was Jonathan to whom I'd turned myself over.

Down the familiar highway I rolled, through the little towns and the bigger ones, away from the brooding winter clouds of Telluride and into the mild high desert outside Grand Junction. Down from the ski village to the fruit orchards, the stands selling juice and jerky. On the last long stretch of flatlands, just before the big sign that announced the city limits, a notorious speed trap where you had to drop from sixty to thirty-five in an instant, I saw the marmot. This was where I'd been cited, three different costly times these past months; now I knew better. Today, instead of a motorcycle cop holding a speed gun like a hair dryer, the marmot sat in the sign's shadow, poised, quizzical, nervy. Whistling pig, big as a beaver. "Don't move, buddy," I murmured, tapping the brake. "Don't you dare—" I had failed to note his partner, who suddenly dashed from the other side of the road, his brown fur the rich thick pelt of a Russian hat. I swerved but felt him bump under the back tire, soft yet fatal. I screamed, braking, putting my fingers in my mouth, and looking to the rearview mirror, where I saw the animal thrashing madly on the pavement. "Oh my God, you damn dummy!" Injured, in violent agony, squealing. A fine spray of blood from its gasping mouth. His friend had disappeared; there was no human traffic except me. I'd hit animals, yet never before left a survivor. My obligation was to put it out of its misery, anybody knew that. "Sorry, sorry, sorry," I murmured, looking once more in the rearview, longing to see another vehicle come finish what I'd begun, my brother in Big Red, for instance, its bright rounded hood and headlights and grill familiar as a face bearing down. Some agent of mercy to do the right thing, aim his wheel at the creature's chest swiftly and without hesitation—sparing what suffered, killing with kindness.

But I couldn't do it. No matter how painful that backward glance—and I kept looking behind, long after the animal was out of sight—I couldn't stop myself from driving away.

Reading in His Wake

"At last," my husband said, when I had locked up for the night and come to bed.

"You knew I would," I said.

"But I didn't know when." Propped up in the recently rented hospital bed, he peered more closely at my chosen book. A novel by Patrick O'Brian. "Wait, no, no," he said. "You must begin at the beginning."

"But I like the sound of this one," I said, drawing out the swish of *The Mauritius Command.*

"Ah, but you want to be there when Aubrey and Maturin meet."

"I can always go back," I said, only slightly petulant, aware that at another time we'd never see again I would have been reading favorites, Trevor, Atwood, or Munro. Or tapping into the wall of biographies across from our beds, Rowley's Christina Stead, or Ellman's Joyce. Continuing through the poetry at the top of the stairs: Rivard, Roethke, Ruefle, Solomon, Szymborska.

His eyes gleamed. "But Aubrey and Maturin meet at such an unlikely place—especially to begin the series. They meet at a concert. Italians on little gilt chairs are playing Locatelli." He stopped, out of breath. "Never mind."

"So what's the first one?" If I was going to do this, give him this gift, so to speak, I must do it right. He named *Master and Commander,* and, ignoring the irony, I did as commanded and retrieved *Master and Commander* from his study next door. Carefully I settled in beside him, our old queen set flush to his new bed, and embarked. In running commentary over years of hurried breakfasts and long dinners, he'd extolled to me Patrick O'Brian's sheer genius; how in the first novel he delivers to the reader in dramatic scenes of tense negotiation a detailed account of everything that Jack Aubrey must buy to outfit a ship circa 1859.

Four pages and an "introduction" later, I said, "I see what you mean. A most prickly meeting. Maturin delightfully pissy because a rapt Aubrey, from his seat in the scraggly audience, is audibly 'conducting' the quartet a half beat ahead."

"Don't forget their terse exchange of addresses as if for a duel," he said, laughing and coughing. I looked toward the oxygen machine, then at him. He shook his head.

Relieved, I slid the damp shoulder of his nightshirt into place. "Conflict on page one," I said, making us both happy.

Fifty pages later, when I murmured, "Mmmmmm," he said, "What? Tell me." He turned on the pillow with an effort and put aside his own O'Brian, *The Truelove*. So I read for him: *"... the sun popped up from behind St. Philip's fort—it did, in fact, pop up, flattened sideways like a lemon in the morning haze and drawing its bottom free of the land with a distinct jerk."*

"... distinct jerk," he repeated.

I said again *"... drawing its bottom free of the land with a distinct jerk."* A shared blanket of satisfaction settled over us, and we went back to our books, companionably together, and companionably apart.

When I stopped reading to bring him a fresh glass of water to chase his myriad pills, he wanted to know where I was now. I slipped back into bed and tented the book on my flannel chest as I described how Mowett, an earnest member of the square-rigged ship's crew, is explaining sails to a queasy Maturin, and here my husband smiled wryly in queasy recognition of feeling queasy. I took his hand, and went on to describe how Maturin affects interest, although he is exceedingly dismayed to be getting this lesson at the appalling height of forty feet above the roiling seas. "Meanwhile, the reader is getting the lesson, too—and drama at the same time. Here," and I read, *"The rail passed slowly under Stephen's downward gaze—to be followed by the sea... his grip on the ratlines tightened with cataleptic strength."*

"It makes me want to start all over again," my husband said. Then, not to be seen as sentimental, he held up his book to show he'd just finished the most recent O'Brian. It slipped to the rug, and we left it there.

"You could read Dave Barry now," I said, acknowledging the only good thing about our new sleeping arrangement. My husband used to read Barry's essays in bed, laughing so hard the bed would shake, shake me loose from whatever I was reading.

Annoyed, I'd mark my page and say, "Okay, read it to me." The ensuing excerpt was a tone change and mood swing one too many times, because I finally banished Dave Barry from the bed after his column titled "There's Nothing like Feeling Flush," which had my husband out of bed and pacing with laughter. In it, Dave Barry refers to an article published in a Scottish medical journal, "The Collapse of Toilets in Glasgow." Barry says, "The article describes the collapsing-toilet incidents in clinical scientific terminology, which contrasts nicely with a close-up, full-face photograph, suitable for framing, of a hairy and hefty victim's naked wounded butt, mooning out of the page at you, causing you to think, for reasons you cannot explain, of Pat Buchanan." We said it again and again. It answered everything: "for reasons you cannot explain."

"Do you want a Barry book?" I asked. He didn't answer. He was either sleeping or wishing I would shut up.

When we were about to leave for radiation, he was still bereft of a new O'Brian. I found him standing in his study, leaning on a walking stick from his collection, now no longer an affectation.

"The W's are too high," he said, stabbing the air with his stick. "It's Wodehouse I'm after."

"Why Wodehouse?" I said. Jeeves, the perfect valet and gentleman's gentleman, would be totally disapproving of how my husband's shirts went un-ironed and how his trousers drooped on his thinning hips. "I'm almost finished with Trevor's *After Rain*, it has that startlingly dark story about—"

"I think I'll read Wodehouse," he said, his jaw set. Out of breath, he slumped into his desk chair and pointed again. "But I can't reach him." On the shelves behind where my husband was pointing ranged the two hundred-plus books he'd edited at a Boston publishing house, and the four he'd written, the last novel, *A Secret History of Time to Come*, included by the New York Museum of Natural History in a time capsule that would outlast us all. "We have too many books," he said.

"That's what you always say," I said. Hitching up my skirt before the wall of English and European Fiction, I mounted the wobbly wooden ladder we swore at on principle every time we retrieved an out-of-reach book. WaughWintersonWodehouse. I called down three titles before he nodded at the fourth. *The Code of the Woosters.* "Why Wodehouse?" I asked again on my descent.

"Ah, you haven't read Wodehouse yet. Arch, mannered humor. You'll see." Then, as if anticipating my early mutiny against O'Brian in deference to Wodehouse, his eyes narrowed, and he instructed, "Keep with the O'Brians for now."

We left for the hospital, armed with our respective books. On the way, I mentioned that Raymond Chandler, also English, and Wodehouse had both attended the posh prep school Dulwich College. "Dul-ich, but spelled Dulwich," my husband said, surprised by Chandler.

Our bookish, competent doctor always wanted to know what we were reading. My husband waved the Wodehouse at him. "It has a blurb by Ogden Nash," he said, and read, "*In my salad days, I thought that P. G. Wodehouse was the funniest writer in the world. Now I have reached the after-dinner coffee stage, and I know that he is.*"

"Woadhouse," the doctor said, making a note on his prescription pad.

"W-o-o-d. I hope he's still funny," my husband said, peering at the doctor over his glasses. "I'm way past the after-dinner coffee. I've reached the medicine stage."

A week later, we were again side by side, my husband's bed rising smoothly and electronically to a barely comfortable position I tried to match with pillows, despairing of the difference in height. I'd finished *Master and Commander* and put it in a safe place because the doctor had meticulously written his home phone number inside its cover. *Post Captain* was next. My husband's long fingers, thin and bony, were oddly free of books because he was listening to the tape of O'Brian's latest Aubrey/Maturin, *The Wine-Dark Sea.* His eyes were alertly closed beneath the Walkman's earphones curving over his new, silky growth of hair.

When he stopped listening to take his pills, I asked him to recall what he'd liked best about *Post Captain.* I closed my eyes against a hysterical welling up of water. And when he'd told me, I thought yes, yes, after years of reading and rereading, arguing, damning, and praising, I knew now almost exactly what he would say. Although I didn't tell him this—but tested more. I badgered him about the repetition of one battle scene after another, asked him to name his favorite title in the series, asked him if Maturin ever dies. I moved on to Ford's *The Good Soldier*. Didn't the narrator's equivocation grate on his nerves? Yes and no. Who was Dante's best translator? Yes, yes. And what did he think of the poem in *Pale Fire*?

"Stop it," he said, his voice stronger than it had been in days. "Enough."

The next evening, when he had finished both sides of the first tape, he told me to look in his desk for a second Walkman. Why didn't matter. "Now, listen to this tape," he said.

"You're still seducing me with literature," I accused him.

He took the tape from his Walkman and inserted it into mine.

"No. No. I can't," I said. "I'll get the plots mixed up." Already I was awash in the unfamiliar world of sloops and frigates, admiring of royals, baffled by masts and yards, and dipping in and out of *A Sea of Words: A Lexicon and Companion for Patrick O'Brian's Seafaring Tales*, chastely beside me on the bed. In love again.

"Here," he said. "Listen."

I donned the earphones, and because he was watching, I closed my eyes. Across the tiny gulf between our beds, his hand found my hand as a calming voice began, *"A purple ocean, vast under the sky and devoid of all visible life apart from two minute ships racing across its immensity."*

Until my husband's hand slipped from mine, until his breath failed, until I called 911, until the ambulance arrived to provide our last voyage together, on that last evening I sailed precariously in two different seas, astride two listing vessels, keeping a third in view against a dark horizon, reading in his wake.

Justice—A Beginning

One day, waiting for a bus, standing on a street corner in Lower Manhattan, somewhere near Canal, having completed jury duty, having in fact judged another human being and found him guilty, she thought of justice, that heavy word. As a member of the general worldwide mothers' union, she had watched the man's mother. She leaned on the witness bar, her face like a dying flower in its late-season, lank leafage of yellow hair, turning one way then the other in the breeze and blast of justice. Like a sunflower maybe in mid-autumn, having given up on the sun, Faith thought, letting wind and weather move her heavy head.

Still the man had held a real gun to the head of the old grocer and taken his half-day's profit of about twenty-seven dollars. Immediately Faith thought as she often did of the great gun held at the world's head and the cheaper guns pointing every which way at all the little nations that had barely gotten their heads up. She probably said Oh shit or even Fuck. Many people, some friends, really hated the way she moved from daily fact to planetary metaphor. Others thought she was absolutely right.

She leaned against someone's car, looked up and around, and saw the high six-story wall of a building whose old companion had been torn down, leaving a pale green New York imprint of old staircases, landings, some mysterious verticals and horizontals. She sighed not cosmically this time, but with an appreciation for the delicate but extraordinary designs of time and decadence. A man, passing, stopped, watched her looking and sighing. Well, he said, what do you think, lady? It's like the rest of us. It's going to deteriorate any minute, right?

At home she was surprised by Anthony visiting. It was the middle of the workweek. Here's Judy, he said. Remember her? Of course, she said. Then she told him that she was exhausted and thought she might deteriorate any minute, probably because of justice and her own wintry visage.

But Ma, he said, your visage isn't wintrier than it was last week. Right, said Judy. It's more late October or early November, don't you think, Anthony? He smiled to encourage her. She was shy but sometimes made good sentences. Anthony rolled his eyes round and round. When they rested, he said, Honest, folks, that wasn't a comment, it was only yoga.

Okay, okay, Faith said, there's some good stuff in the fridge. She wanted to go to her room and sit on the nice chair she'd recently bought for herself so as to be comfortable when writing things down. She needed to think more about the jury system, mainly her companion jurors. Also the way that capitalism was getting to be a pain in the world's neck. She thought she might try to make a poem out of that opposition.

After about an hour Anthony knocked on the door. Ma, when you're finished being private, come out and have some tea with us. We have some really bad news for you. This wasn't true, but if he'd said, Let's have tea and pie, and we have some wonderful news for you, she'd never leave her room.

Okay, she said, coming to the door. I'm ready, I guess. For God's sake, tell me.

The Bad Thing

We found the kittens in a pile, too young to even stagger, the mother too hungry herself to feed them, or caught by the dogs. We had a big old plastic purse with a blanket inside, and we put them all in there and hauled them around in the wagon. I liked them, they were a little town of their own, part of our gang to defend against the Polish kids that lived right next to the tracks, or the Irish kids in the houses down by the river. Gang warfare, but our gang was only us. We boys kept our pockets full of rocks, small ones to chuck at the dogs. Now and then the City would clean the stray dogs out of the rail yard, put out poisoned meat. We'd see carcasses dropped in the ditch round back of the tracks, like the dogs crawled there on purpose when they knew something was wrong. Some City worker emptied bags of lime over them, shaking the bags with his gloved hands, rolling a wheelbarrow along. Sleep dust for the dogs. We'd see him, and he'd shoo us away, angry, like we'd caught him at murder. But it was just a benediction, like Father Salvadore gave in the shape of the cross after services. Grass grew up over the dogs, high and green, till they were only bones, and the rangy pups who'd survived were big enough to slink after us, compete with the cats for mice and rats, hunt the cats. Those dogs' faces were so scarred they looked painted in thin white lines.

I was a murderer myself. The first time, my dad made me, showed me how. He put that passel of kittens we brought home into a burlap sack like they pour wood pulp into at the sawmill. He made me hold it open and put in the rocks. The rocks were heavy, and I put them under the kittens, like a hard bed. The kittens were so young they barely had their eyes open. The rocks were too hard, so I put in some of the soft rags we kept around for washing cars or cleaning motors, wiping oily grime off carburetors. Even then, we had a car that worked and a car that didn't, for fooling with. My dad told me it was fine to cushion the rocks, and I could let these kittens go a few blocks away, but they'd die of starvation or something would kill them, and they would suffer. If I brought them back here, he said, or any other passel of animals so young he couldn't chase them off, we'd have to do all this again, and he'd personally escort me to the riverbank and watch me throw in the bag. Rule one, he said, you don't make a baby and then leave it, unless you're dead yourself. Plenty around here might have been taught this simple rule. That was about all he ever said about my mother. Or any of the other fathers and mothers missing in the neighborhood. One father we knew had died a soldier, and that seemed honorable. Other people should take care of what he was forced to leave, no matter how hard that might be. Here I'd intervened in something, my dad said, and I should be a man and finish it. He struggled to keep us fed and clothed. No one was going to bottle-feed these kittens and find them homes over on Fairmont Hill, where the rich people kept their cats indoors and fed them out of cans. He was right. Where we lived on the alley, so close to the rail yard, people thought cats were diseased vermin, and they shot them and chased them and kicked them. This was the cleanest and strongest those kittens were ever going to be.

So I took them to the riverbank, to the tunnel under the rail bridge. I put the bag on the ground, and I could see the kittens shifting around in the burlap and hear them mewling. They sounded loud in the tunnel, where the air was different, enclosed in a high space, like at church. We kids always went there, but I'd never been there alone. It was deep and shady under the rail bridge in the summer, with the river beside, and you could watch the trains overhead sometimes and see them cross the river. Trains came barreling across from the rail yard over us. Just at the midpoint, a stone support of the same thick rock stood up in the deepest water of the river. It was built to look like the tunnel bridges on either side, but it was only half as big, and bore the most stress. It stood out of the water like a man with a massive weight on his shoulders. As a train reached it, I had to fight not to hold my breath, then the train streaked across to the other side and filled the entire span before it lost itself around the bend of the hill. At dusk you could see town lights come on up and down the riverbank, but the other bank was darkness and trees. There was a brushy mound of island in the middle of the river, not far from the central support of the bridge. Might have been slag at one time because it was treeless, but the river had risen and fallen over it enough times to deposit a rich layer of sediment. The island was green every summer with grass and flowering weeds and brush that died back in winter. Deer swam out to it from the other side of the river. You could see them plain if they were standing on top of the mound, one or two or three of them. They'd look up when a train passed, then fall to grazing again, safe from whatever hunted them in the woods.

It was quiet that day. There were no trains. Even the kittens had got quiet. They must have fallen asleep on those soft rags, all curled up into one another. There wasn't a sound when I put them in the water.

After that I wouldn't let anyone take kittens from the rail yard until they were well onto their feet, and then we'd let them loose by the river where there were toads and minnows and mice and lizards. They could take their own chances. Death was not the bad thing. Leaving something behind when you gave up or walked away was the bad thing.

Fast Sunday

Sarah was nine-about-to-be-ten. The world was taking its sweet time. And she was in the world. It was Easter, but it was also Fast Sunday, because Easter had fallen on the first Sunday of the month this year, so all the meetings were in a row, Sunday school, then fast and testimony meeting, which was always longer than regular sacrament meeting, because people could get up and talk as long as they wanted, *as long as the spirit moved them.* Some year Easter would fall on her birthday, her mother had told her, it had when she was five, but this year her birthday would be two weeks after Easter. Because it was Fast Sunday, Sarah and her brothers could not eat any of the candy in their Easter baskets until after dark. On Fast Sundays, they had to fast from nightfall on Saturday to nightfall on Sunday. This was one of the commandments. Not one of the Ten Commandments, but one of the other ones. One of the many she knew by heart, like the Word of Wisdom: *Thou shalt run and not be weary, and walk and not faint.*

But when she didn't eat for a whole day, she felt faint. And her head hurt. The only thing that would pass her lips all day was the sacrament—a little piece of torn-up Wonder bread, followed by a tiny fluted paper cup of water, like the ones they had at the dentist's office—passed hand to hand down the pews by the deacons on metal trays after the priests had blessed them: *That they may have His spirit to be with them.* The priests seemed old to her, though they were only sixteen, and the deacons were twelve. They joked outside on the steps after church, but when they were passing the sacrament, they were serious. Girls couldn't be deacons or priests or elders or anything but mothers and primary or Sunday school or MIA or Relief Society teachers. When boys turned twelve, they received the priesthood. Then the boys and the girls would be in separate Sunday school classes, and the boys would go to early morning priesthood meetings.

Sarah imagined receiving the priesthood must be something like receiving the gift of the Holy Ghost, but the priesthood was conferred in secret. Only the men could see. The day after she was baptized, nearly two years ago, she had been blessed in front of the whole congregation, along with the other children who had turned eight in the past month and a few converts, who always seemed strange and too large next to the children. What would it have been like not to have been born into the church? she wondered. She felt the converts were lucky the missionaries had found them in time. Both her mother and her father had been missionaries, her father in Scotland and her mother in Mexico. It was the only time either of them had ever traveled outside the United States. The onyx bookends in the living room had come from Mexico; the sheepskin rug in her parents' bedroom had come from Scotland. Her father sometimes sang songs in a funny Scottish accent. And her mother taught her and her brothers Spanish. *Me llamo Sarah. Yo soy una hija de Dios.*

"Remember who you are: you are a child of God," her parents said repeatedly, when she left for school in the morning, when she went to a friend's house to play, when she asked why she couldn't do something she wanted to do.

"Thank you for that lovely prelude, Sister Erickson. And now, Brother Meredith, President of the Quorum of Seventies, will lead us in the opening prayer, following which we will sing hymn #194, 'There Is a Green Hill Faraway.'"

Bishop Anderson was presiding at fast and testimony meeting. Sarah always thought he looked slightly uncomfortable when he was wearing a suit and tie. His wrists hung down below his shirt cuffs. During the week, he worked as an electrician, and he always wore blue coveralls with his name, Don Anderson, in red curlicue script on his left pocket. He was a very tall man with a blond crewcut. Usually, bishops were doctors or dentists or businessmen, but everyone said that Bishop Anderson was truly a man of the spirit.

"Heavenly Father," prayed Brother Meredith, "we are grateful to be gathered here in Thy name today in this beautiful house of worship which Thou hast provided for us. We ask that Thou wilt bless us and guide us in the path of righteousness. Bless those who will speak to us today that their mouths will be filled with Thy holy presence. In the name of the Father, and of the Son, and of the Holy Ghost, Amen."

"Amen," echoed Sarah with the rest of the congregation.

Two years ago, when her father and the other elders and high priests had stood in a circle around her and put their hands on her head to confirm her and give her the gift of the Holy Ghost, Sarah had expected that she would feel the Holy Ghost enter her body, that it would be like drinking a cold glass of milk too fast or like holding her breath too long underwater. She expected that she would feel something or see something, the way she assumed, the first time she crossed the state border from Utah into Nevada, that the states would be different colors the way they were on a map. When nothing had changed colors, when the road and the salt flats and the sagebrush looked exactly the same on one side of the state line as the other, Sarah couldn't help exclaiming, "Nevada's the same color as Utah."

"Oh, it's a little different," her father had said, "you'll see."

But it wasn't, just more sand and more road and maybe hotter. On one trip across Nevada, though, they saw a giant cloud billow up in the distance. The air was full of brilliant particles, like dust, only it wasn't dust.

"It's pretty," said her brother Drew, uncharacteristically. Usually, he was too busy poking Sarah in the ribs or tickling Danny to notice what was outside the car. "It's like Tinkerbell or angels."

"It's the Test Site," said her father. "Like Hiroshima, only in the desert, where there are no people. It's so we won't have war ever again."

This was also the day that Drew would be confirmed. As always, for Easter, her mother had stayed up all night finishing the matching outfits she made for herself and Sarah and her brothers. Dresses for her mother and Sarah, shirts for the three boys, all made out of the same material. This year the cloth was an orange-and-brown plaid, which really didn't seem like Easter colors, more like fall. Sarah knew that it must have been one of the only fabrics inexpensive enough and with enough material left on the bolt for two dresses and four shirts. Only her father, in his blue suit and maroon tie with squiggles on it, didn't match. She had thought that maybe her mother wouldn't make the Easter clothes this year, since she'd been sick so long. But when Sarah and Drew and Danny and Tyler woke up early to look for their Easter baskets, even though they knew they wouldn't be able to eat anything from them, they found the row of clothes laid out on the back of the couch from left to right, from biggest (Sarah) to smallest (Tyler), just the way they always were, so Sarah knew she couldn't say anything about not liking the color of the fabric. Or the pattern—it was too babyish; her mother had used the same pattern last year, just made it a little bigger. Sarah felt she was too old for puffed sleeves and rickrack.

Now, sitting on the pew between her mother and Danny, with Tyler on the other side of her mother, she watched Drew. He was up on the dais in the choir seats with the four other children who were about to be confirmed. Her father was also on the dais, behind a table on one side, not the sacrament table, but like it. He was the ward clerk now; he had to write everything down that was said in the meeting. Sarah knew he didn't like it, even though he had been ordained.

"Why was I called to this position?" he asked their mother frequently. "Why can't I be the Gospel Doctrine teacher?"

"This, too, shall pass," her mother always said.

She wondered if Drew would feel something when they gave him the gift of the Holy Ghost. He was a little afraid of it, she could tell. Now he would have to be good, because he had reached the age of accountability. When you were eight, you knew the difference between right and wrong. That is why you were baptized then, and not when you were a baby. She remembered how the bishop asked her, right before she was baptized, if she knew that she would be making a solemn covenant between herself and the Lord. She knew, she assured him, she knew with all her heart. But she had always been good; Drew had not. He talked back, and had his mouth washed out with soap. She had had her mouth washed out with soap once, and that was enough. Now she would bite her cheek so she wouldn't say a bad thing, but Drew would say it. He was proud of saying bad words and said he liked the taste of Ivory soap. Sometimes when their parents weren't there, he would bite off a tiny piece, fill his mouth with water, and spit small bubbles at her.

* * *

Sacrament was over. The priests folded the white lace tablecloth over the trays, and moved down to sit with the rest of the congregation. Bishop Anderson got up to say a few words. There were two babies to be blessed, before the five gifts of the Holy Ghost, so it would be a long time before the testimonies even started. This is not what Bishop Anderson said, but Sarah could see it was going to be a long Fast Sunday, not a short Fast Sunday. He said not to forget the Relief Society bazaar and potluck supper next Saturday night. He said that he hoped our special prayers would be with Sister Nelson, who had broken her hip after a fall.

Sister Nelson usually led the choir. She had dark black hair with one thick white stripe in it, starting at her forehead and going all the way down the back of her head. Sarah's mother said it was a widow's peak, but it looked like a skunk to Sarah, only the stripe wasn't right in the center the way a skunk's would be. Sister Nelson had been kind to Sarah, though; she gave her a book after she was baptized. And it wasn't even a religious book, like the other ones she got, her own leather-bound copy of the *Book of Mormon* and the *Doctrine and Covenants* and *The Pearl of Great Price,* a triple combination, or a three-in-one, it was called, like the tin of oil her mother used for the sewing machine. Sister Nelson had given her *Five Children and It.* Sarah had tried some of the spells. The one that was most successful was the one where, before you went to sleep, you concentrated really hard, and banged your head on the pillow the number of times for the hour you wanted to wake up—six for six o'clock, seven for seven o'clock. It always worked. She wanted to be like the children in English storybooks, having adventures all day in the hedgerows—she imagined the hedgerows as being a little like the tunnel she and her cousins made through the honeysuckle bushes in Grandma Hart's garden—and drinking ginger beer. She didn't know what ginger beer was, but it probably wasn't allowed, the way Coca-Cola wasn't allowed. Latter-day Saints could have root beer, though. Sometimes, after all six of them piled in the station wagon and before they would go to the drive-in movie, they would go to the Arctic Circle and have root beer floats.

Oh, she was hungry now. She shouldn't have thought about food. It was bad to think about food on Fast Sunday, not bad because it wasn't allowed, but bad because it would be too hard to get through the whole day without eating if she thought about food. On regular Sundays, they would have a big meal between Sunday school and sacrament meeting. Her mother would start a pot roast or a stewed chicken cooking before Sunday school, then they would smell it first thing when they got in the door after church. Tyler didn't have to fast, because he was only two. But when it was Fast Sunday, even he couldn't have the dry Cheerios her mother would usually bring to church to keep him quiet. Her mother had given Tyler her handkerchief to fuss with instead. He was playing peek-a-boo with Sister Holmgren in the pew behind them. Sister Holmgren had seven children, but they were all grown-up now and had children of their own.

The babies had been brought up to the front of the chapel and blessed—they hardly ever cried while they were spoken over and bounced in the men's arms, but often cried when they were given back to their mothers, Sarah noticed—and now it was almost Drew's turn to receive the gift of the Holy Ghost. Today, because it was Easter besides Fast Sunday, there were flowers in the chapel, white trumpet-shaped blossoms on tall green stems. They smelled the way Sarah imagined the Celestial Kingdom must smell. They looked the same as the flowers in one of the picture books she had seen at Grandma Hart's house, a big book with gold on the edges of the pages. The flowers were in a blue vase on a checkerboard floor between Mary—her grandmother said it was Mary-the-mother-of-Jesus—and an angel, with wings, though everyone knew angels didn't have wings.

Sarah wished there were flowers in the chapel all the time, not just Easter and Christmas and missionary farewells and funerals. In the church she went to once with her friend Emma, called St. Sebastian's, there were flowers everywhere and paintings and colored glass in the windows and candles in tall, gold candlesticks and pink velvet cushions on the seats and a smell of something burning, but sweet, and, most surprising of all, a huge wooden cross with Jesus nailed on it at the front of the church. Sarah couldn't stop looking at it. It was scary, but beautiful, too. Jesus didn't look unhappy; he looked peaceful. When she asked her mother about it later, her mother said Latter-day Saints weren't allowed to have crosses in their churches or to wear crosses, because it reminded them of the bad part of Jesus' life, and that they wanted to think of the good part, when Jesus rises out of the tomb and says, *I am the resurrection and the light.*

Latter-day Saints weren't supposed to go inside other people's churches, either, but her mother had let her go, just that once. She wished she could go there again; there were so many more things to look at there than in their own chapel, which had plain white walls, brown benches with no cushions on them, and frosted-glass windows you couldn't see through, like the ones in bathrooms, so you couldn't even see whether it had started to rain. Outside she knew the apricot trees were in blossom. *I looked out the window and what did I see: popcorn popping on the apricot tree.* Val Verda, the neighborhood where they lived, used to be all orchards, no houses, her father had told her.

The only thing she could do when she got bored at her church meetings was to play with the hymnbook. She knew practically all the hymns by heart. She would make up new words to some of them. *Cherries hurt you* instead of *Cherish virtue. God be with you till we eat again* instead of *God be with you till we meet again.* She especially liked it if they sang that one on Fast Sunday, but today unfortunately they wouldn't. Today the closing hymn would be #136, "I Know That My Redeemer Lives." The numbers of the hymns they would sing were posted on a little wooden board above her father's head. He was bent over, writing, writing, writing. He had to write down the names of everyone who was in church that day and everything that happened. Sarah wondered what happened to the black notebooks after they were full. Did they keep them in a vault somewhere? In a temple, maybe? Were they to give to God when the millennium came? But didn't He know everything already? Why did it have to be written down?

"Heavenly Father," Brother Wickham's voice boomed out. His prayers were always louder than anyone else's, and he was praying over his own daughter, Karen, so he was especially loud. Sister Spackman said that man's voice would reach all the way to heaven. Karen stood up after the blessing and adjusted the sash on her pink, embroidered, store-bought dress. Brother Wickham was a doctor, and Sister Wickham didn't have to make her own or Karen's clothes. Then it was Drew and their father's turn to come down and join the circle of men. Her father prayed "that the spirit of the Holy Ghost might guide Drew and direct him in all his endeavors throughout his life, that the still, small voice would stay his hand from evil. In the name of the Father and of the Son and of the Holy Ghost, Amen."

"Amen," the men in the circle repeated and took their hands off Drew's head. Sarah remembered that when the hands had been lifted off her head, she felt as if she might float up, the way if you pressed the backs of your hands against a door frame for long enough, when you stepped away your hands would rise up, magically, by themselves, sometimes even above your head. Drew looked a little stunned as he climbed back up on the dais.

Two more confirmations followed, then finally the testimonies began. Some people bore their testimonies every single Fast Sunday. Sarah almost knew by heart what Sister Spackman, in her pale gray, much-washed shirtwaist dress, would say when she got up: "I'm grateful for the church and my family and for the strength to live each day and to be a witness for the truth of the gospel." Sister Spackman was a widow, and her youngest son had a disease. He would always stay a child. He couldn't hold the priesthood, even though he was already old enough to be a deacon.

Sarah hoped her parents wouldn't bear their testimonies this time. They had gotten up often in the months since her mother had had her operation. The Fast Sunday after her mother had come home from the hospital, even Sarah had risen to say that she knew the church was true and that Joseph Smith was a prophet and that she was grateful her prayers had been answered and that her mother was back home. She was still frightened, though, that her mother would not be all right. Sarah found it harder to pray now, harder to have faith the way she was supposed to. She was afraid God wasn't listening to her anymore, that maybe He was looking at her, and that He didn't like what He saw.

Sarah's mother was still weak; her father did all the grocery shopping, and Sarah did most of the cooking and ironing. That was why it was so surprising that her mother had made their Easter clothes this year. Her mother looked very tired; the skin around her mouth seemed yellowish next to the red lipstick. Sarah glanced over at the bodice of her mother's dress. You couldn't tell with her clothes on. She had let Sarah hold the pad that she slipped into her bra every morning. It was surprisingly heavy. She had also shown Sarah the two long red scars, and let her touch them so she wouldn't be frightened. One started at her left armpit, curved across her chest and down almost all the way to her navel; the other started at her navel and went straight down her whole belly. The scars were flat and wide and hard and criss-crossed with marks, like bumpy railroad tracks.

Her mother would have sewn herself up more neatly than the doctors did, thought Sarah. Her mother was such a good seam-stress that she even made wedding dresses and Temple clothes. She had taught Sarah how to sew, too, and embroider. Sarah made a cross-stitched sampler that read "I will bring the light of the gospel into my home." Her mother had taught her how to make lots of different kinds of stitches: tacking stitch, basting stitch, running stitch, overhand stitch, blind stitch, hem stitch, seed stitch, pearl stitch, invisible stitch.

Sarah's mother was even thinner now than she used to be. She couldn't have any more children, she had told Sarah. She had wanted to have twelve, like her friend, Sister Barber, who was Mrs. Utah one year. Sarah couldn't imagine more children—three brothers were enough—though it would have been nice to have had a sister. A sister could have helped with the cooking and dish-washing, so Sarah wouldn't have to do it all by herself. She could have had secrets with a sister; they could have slept in the same bed together, the way Drew and Danny did. And when they grew up, they could go on double dates together and marry brothers, the way Annie and Abby Holmgren had. They even had their first babies at the same time.

The church was suddenly quiet. Sarah looked up. Sister Spack-man had finished her testimony and sat down. A man she had seen only a few times at church was walking up the aisle. Most people just stood up to speak from where they were sitting, but some people came up to the podium on the dais. The man was tall, and had wavy brown hair and blue eyes. He looked a little bit like her oldest cousin, Shep, who was on a mission in Brazil, but he was older than Shep. This man was old enough to be a father, but as far as Sarah knew, he didn't have a wife and children. No one had ever come to church with him, and he always had left quickly after sacrament meeting, not standing around shaking hands after the service, the way the other men did. Since he had never spoken before in church, Sarah was curious. Maybe he would say something about his wife and children. Maybe they had all died in a fire. People talked about things like that in fast and testimony meeting. Sarah didn't always understand what people meant when they spoke, but usually her mother would explain things later, like when Brother Watkins moved out of his house for six months, leaving Sister Watkins and their five children behind. When he came back, he repented in front of the whole congregation.

"Brothers and sisters," the man began, his hands gripping the edges of the podium, "most of you don't know me. I have only lived in this ward for a few months. My name is John Perry. I was born in Moscow, Idaho. My great-great-grandfather Perry crossed the plains with a handcart and my great-grandfather Williams converted in England during the early days of the church."

This was like Sarah's family and most of the people she knew. She wondered if he was going to tell his whole genealogy. She knew, though no one would say much about it, that her great-grandfather on her mother's side had been a polygamist. When relatives did talk about it, they called it "living the principle." Her great-grandfather had only three wives, though. Not nearly as many as Brigham Young. But because of polygamy, Sarah did seem to have a lot of relatives, the usual aunts and uncles and cousins, but also great-aunts once removed, second cousins twice removed, and honorary uncles.

"I was raised in the church, went to Ricks College for a year, then served my mission in the Netherlands. After I returned from my mission, I went to BYU and completed my degree in business administration. Then I married my high school sweetheart in the Temple, for Time and all Eternity. We went to live in Boise, and we prospered in the Lord and were blessed with three fine children."

So far, this still sounded like the story of almost every other grown-up. But then he said something Sarah didn't expect.

"I fell in love with another woman. My wife cast me out. That is why I came back here, to Bountiful, to the heart of the church. Because here, I thought, I would find kindred souls, as it is written in Helaman, Chapter 5, Verse 14: *And they did remember his words; and therefore they went forth, keeping the commandments of God, to teach the word of God among all the people of Nephi, beginning at the city of Bountiful.* I've been watching you, in the short time I've lived in this ward, and I decided that today would be the day to tell you what I was brought to this earth to accomplish."

Bountiful, Sarah thought. She had never connected her Bountiful with the Bountiful from olden days in the *Book of Mormon.* Sarah felt her mother stir beside her. She saw her father lift his pen from the record book and look more closely at the man on the podium. Drew was putting rabbit ears behind Karen Wickham's head, so maybe he hadn't changed too much yet.

"Brothers and sisters," Brother Perry continued, "*Straight is the way and narrow the gate that leads to the Kingdom of Heaven.* I believe that the church has taken a wrong turn on the path. I believe in the continuing power of revelation, and God has revealed to me that we should return to the old covenant, that men should take unto themselves more wives, that we should prepare to enter the Celestial Kingdom as God has planned by giving as many souls as possible their mortal bodies. I have seen all those spirits waiting in the preexistence, waiting to receive their terrestrial bodies, and God has told me that we must make more bodies, soon, before the millennium. It's time, brothers and sisters, to redouble and triple our efforts. We are the Chosen People, and we cannot allow only the Gentiles to populate this terrestrial plane. Every man and every woman of childbearing age must join together to make new temples to house the spirits waiting in the preexistence."

My body is a temple, Sarah thought. That was in a song she had learned when she was very little. *My body is a temple.* How could a body be a building? What about her mother—did the operation mean her mother's body couldn't be a temple anymore? What if her father decided to marry someone else? Her mother was clasping her hand tightly now, and Sarah, in turn, had taken Danny's hand on her left.

The man paused for a moment. Members of the congregation started to murmur and look at each other. Sarah noticed that Bishop Anderson was whispering to Brother Jenson, the first counselor, sitting on his right. "Sarah," her mother said, "maybe you shouldn't listen. Tell Danny not to listen, too. He might be bearing false witness." But Sarah had to listen, just the way she had to read everything in the World Book and all the biographies of composers in the library. Maybe he would say something that would help her make sense of what had happened to her mother, even though her mother was so very good.

"Brothers and sisters, I ask you to remember with me the tidings of 3 Nephi 11:1: *And now it came to pass that there were a great multitude gathered together of the people of Nephi, round about the temple which was in the land Bountiful; and they were marveling and wondering one with another, and were showing one to another the great and marvelous changes which had taken place.* We have the opportunity now, in Bountiful, to fulfill our great spiritual destiny, to come and be numbered with the house of Israel. I have chosen you to join with me and restore the principle we are meant to follow. All those of you who truly hunger and thirst after righteousness, come follow me now. Come follow me into the hills of Zion, and we will start a new era of brotherly and sisterly love. Come follow me or be cast down into the pit of wickedness."

The man stepped down from the dais and walked across the front of the chapel. He opened the door by the sacrament table, letting in the surprising blue light of the day, like the stone being rolled away from the tomb. He cupped his hands in front of him, like a picture Sarah had seen of Jesus speaking to the disciples. "Come follow me," he said one last time, and stepped outside.

No one moved.

Finally, Bishop Anderson got up. He said, "And now, brothers and sisters, difficult as it is, we must act. As we know from 1 Nephi 22:19, *all who fight against Zion shall be cut off,* and from Moroni 6:7, *the names of the unrighteous are blotted out.* We must never speak of John Perry again. Because he has apostatized, he will be cut off temporally and spiritually from the presence of God. And it is our duty as followers of the gospel and members of the true church to excommunicate him. After the close of testimony meeting, I ask all the elders, seventies, and high priests to meet with me in a special priesthood meeting. But now it is even more important than ever for us to continue to bear our testimonies."

Bishop Anderson bore his, then one by one, almost all the members of the congregation stood up to bear theirs. When

Sarah's mother rose, she said, "I know I was put on this earth for a special purpose, and, even though my strength has been tested by illness, I love the gospel more than ever. I know this church is true and that Joseph Smith was a prophet of God and that we are guided today by a prophet, seer, and revelator."

Even Drew and Danny got up to speak. Drew sounded very grown-up when he said how grateful he was to have been baptized into the true church and to have received the gift of the Holy Ghost. He even recited part of a hymn, *"The witness of the Holy Ghost, / As borne by those who know, / Has lifted me again to thee, / O Father of my soul."* Danny simply said he was thankful for his family and glad that it was Easter.

But Sarah felt something hard inside herself, as if she had accidentally swallowed the pit of an apricot. Why couldn't she stand up like everyone else to bear her testimony? It was Easter, the holiest day of the year. Where were the words that used to come so easily?

It was dark by the time everyone finished speaking and sang the final hymn; one of the lines, *"He lives my hungry soul to feed,"* leapt out at Sarah. On a normal Fast Sunday, she and Drew might have repeated that line over and over instead of singing the rest of the hymn, or they might have giggled at *"He lives, my ever-living Head,"* but now she sang straight through, without changing any words, and it looked like Drew was singing his heart out on the dais.

After the final amen after the final prayer, Sarah rushed outside. She knew that the women would stand in the foyer and talk while the men gathered in the gospel doctrine room for the special priesthood meeting. Her mother would probably ask Sister Holmgren for a ride home, since the men might meet for hours more. Sarah wanted to see if John Perry was still around. She walked to the edge of the parking lot. Along with the scent of apricot blossoms, she could smell a faint tang of smoke from the oil refineries next to the Great Salt Lake. Down in the valley, she could see the chain of lights from Slim Olson's, the huge gas station where her father was a bookkeeper. Even in the dark, she could see the sheen of the white screen of the drive-in movie, which hadn't yet opened for the season. But no sign of John

Perry. So she walked back toward the chapel. By the side of a red pickup truck, she saw him. No one else was near. She wanted to say something to him, but she didn't know what. She wanted to ask him if he knew whether her mother would ever get well again. As she walked closer, she could see he was crying. She pulled her new Easter handkerchief out of her patent-leather purse. Without a word, she gave it to him. He looked down at her. "You believe me, don't you," he said in a soft voice. "You'll know I'm right when you get older. I can see that; I can see you're a thoughtful child."

"Good luck," Sarah said, but that didn't seem quite enough, so she added, "God bless," then turned away. She knew her mother would be looking for her by now, or wondering if she'd taken a ride with Sister Spackman, who lived nearby. When she saw her mother in the foyer with Sister Holmgren, Sarah ran towards her, but stopped before hugging her. She was afraid her mother, so thin already, would dissolve at her touch. She knew she would never be able to tell her parents about seeing John Perry outside the chapel.

Sarah and her mother and brothers rode home in Sister Holmgren's big car. Drew got in the middle of the back seat right away, without even fighting Sarah for a window seat. Sarah opened the window a crack so she could smell the blossoming trees. She was hungry, so hungry, and she felt that she occupied a very small corner in the world, a corner into which no hands could reach to comfort her.

A Flower for Ginette

Giverny, 1907

Quickly Émile took out the green wooden rowboat to lift fall-en leaves off the pond. When Monsieur would come out of the pink stucco house at six in the morning, it had to be just right. With no breeze yet, the water lay like a liquid mirror, and Monsieur would want to paint the rosy clouds reflected among the water lilies. Émile trimmed a few errant lily pads overgrowing the shapes Monsieur ranted about keeping just so. He knew what Monsieur wanted.

At the pond's edge, he leaned to the side of the boat to cut off agapanthus, irises, azaleas, and rhododendrons that were spent, careful not to leave a blunt end visible. He could not reach the lily of the valley spilling over in bunches and sending its slightly acid scent out through its inverted cups. He'd have to snip them on foot. The other workers did the fertilizing, watering, and green-house work with bulbs and seedlings, but Émile did the pruning, for that was an art. Twenty years had taught him how much Mon-sieur wanted left—a profusion of plants just short of the point of excess. He had to create anew, every day, that single point the mas-ter wanted between the presence and absence of a gardener's hand.

One enormous deep violet blue bearded iris thrust itself before a fan of sword-shaped leaves. He'd been watching it grow. No doubt Monsieur had noticed it, too, but as far as Émile could tell, he hadn't begun a painting of it. Today was the day. The bloom was at its bursting peak, puffed out like a dowager queen in regal velvet wearing a dewdrop jewel. There was not sky enough to con-tain it. He might be able to get it home and be back before Mon-sieur came out to paint. Ginette would think it spectacular. She always received the flowers he brought her with that round O her lips made at surprises, and then the hint of a sigh. Blossoms would not last. No matter how moist the flesh under the velvet skin, the petals were already dead the moment their stems were cut.

What would Ginette do for flowers after he was gone? The

thought troubled him more since the pricks of pain had begun in his chest.

He looked over his shoulder at the windows in the house and snipped off the iris for his wife, feeling only a fraction of the guilt he'd felt the first time. God would forgive him in the name of love, even if Monsieur wouldn't.

The porch door banged, and rapid footsteps crunched the coarse sand pathway.

"Émile," Monsieur bellowed.

He felt a tiny pain, or was it his imagination? He hid the iris behind his feet under the boat's crossbench.

"Clemenceau is coming. On Sunday. And Jean and Blanche. To see the tulips and cherry trees in bloom. Everything must be at its best. Transplant if you need to." Still in his dressing gown, Monsieur waved his arm toward the pathway. "Nasturtiums are invading us. Keep the *sense* of it overgrown, though not actually. Leave space for two to walk abreast. Will you have time to repaint the rest of the woodwork?"

Émile had finished the green porch railing and morning bench—Prussian green, Monsieur would call it—and, the day before, he'd repainted the underside of the Japanese bridge from the rowboat so that green would reflect in the water. His neck still ached. What remained were the clematis trellis along the wall and the large railed storage boxes for unfinished canvases situated in unobtrusive spots in the garden.

"Of course," Émile said.

Monsieur stopped moving suddenly and looked curiously at the spot on the bank where the giant iris had grown. A scowl darkened his face, and his big fingers curled into a fist. Émile shifted in the boat to hide the iris better. A bee buzzing near his feet threatened to give him away. Monsieur snapped his head to peer at him for a long moment. How could he not know? Ever since they kneeled together to plant that first pansy bed and Émile had snipped off a violet and yellow pansy face and hid it up his full sleeve—but this iris was no mere pansy. It was the grandest bloom in an Eden of blooms. Had he gone too far?

"*Alors, bien,*" Monsieur said, gave an abrupt nod, and strode back to the house.

Even with the quick trot home midmorning to take the iris to

Ginette, by noon Émile had finished the tulip beds and tied the clippings in burlap to lay out to dry behind the wall for burning. He was pleased, now, to put away his clippers and take out his brushes and paint can.

Monsieur's morning work apparently went well, too. Émile heard no lion's roar across the pond. Monsieur was prone to fits of despair that often led to rash acts. Madame Alice always said the right thing to her husband, and so effortlessly, but Émile had to think out the words to say ahead of time in case she wasn't there.

Once, painting from his floating studio on the Epte, Monsieur had bellowed a loud "ooff." Hearing the clatter and splash, Émile had called to Madame Alice and rowed quickly out to the Epte, thinking that Monsieur had fallen in. His easel and canvas were floating. "I'm through, Émile," he said and threw in his palette, tubes, and brushes. He stepped from the large flatboat into Émile's rowboat. "I'm not a painter. Row me home."

Émile tried to save the canvas. "Let it go, Émile!" Coming into the pond in the rowboat, he saw Alice and repeated, "I'm not a painter, Alice."

"Today, maybe not. But tomorrow, yes," she said. "In the meantime, this afternoon you've got to plan the colors for the new flower bed with Émile."

By the next morning Monsieur had a new idea and was calling for more paints. To be so little at peace—Émile felt sorrow for him. What he painted was as a happy man would see it, but he wondered whether Monsieur was happy the way he was happy, hurrying the perfect iris home to Ginette.

Only last month, Monsieur had begun to slash for burning thirty of the water lily canvases. "Once I'm dead no one will destroy any of my paintings, no matter how bad they are," he'd said.

Madame Alice stood on the porch and watched, gripping the railing with hands as white as her hair. "Help him, Émile. He can't be dissuaded. He'll paint more, and better ones."

With aching heart, Émile had helped to lay the fire.

"Isn't there one of these you wouldn't mind if I took for Ginette?"

"No," he bellowed. "Burn them all." With his razor Monsieur hacked another canvas out of its frame and threw it to the ground.

The bonfire rose into the night sky, and Monsieur watched it behind the glowing tip of his cigarette until the work of a year was only embers. Émile took care to pour water on the mound before he went home.

"You mean to say you've broken your back for him all these years, and he wouldn't even give you one painting he didn't want?" Ginette had said. "You, who dug that pond with your bare hands and created something that made him rich and famous? He'd rather burn them than give you a scrap!"

Émile shrugged and fell into bed exhausted, smelling the smoke on his skin and mustache.

Early the next morning he found that they had overlooked one elongated triangle of sliced canvas. It was covered with ashes and dirt, but still intact. He swept it up and stuffed it under his shirt, apologizing to God for his disobedience, and only then looked around to see if someone was watching. No one was up yet. He'd hardly seen the thing, and as he felt it stiff and scratchy against his skin while he bent to prune the roses, he was agitated with curiosity.

When the sun finally dipped behind the plum trees, he tramped home through the field of wild red poppies, his heart hammering in his chest. He didn't take out the slash of canvas until he had bolted the door behind him. Gently he washed off the ashes and dirt. Brush strokes of lavender, blues, and greens swirled in what might be an oval if the piece were larger. Just colors, he thought, sinking into a chair, until he turned it upside down. Thick paint rose in ridges for part of a lily. Next to it, smooth for a willow leaf. It *was* something.

Breathless, he showed it to Ginette.

"What is it?" she asked.

"A hanging willow leaf and half a lily. A flower that will last."

"He gave that to you?"

"No. If he knows I have it, he'll be raving mad."

"And you'll be fired for sure, and then what will become of us?"

"It's for you, Ginette. For our bedroom. Don't tell a soul."

That Sunday, he worked all afternoon to fit the joints for a little triangular wooden frame. He sanded it smooth as satin and painted it with Monsieur's green paint he had taken in a pickle jar. Nothing else seemed so right. And every night since, before he turned out the light, he looked at the sliver of painting above Ginette's dressing table with satisfaction. Ginette would always have a flower.

Now, after the midday supper, Émile lifted a veil of blue, pink, and white clematis away from the trellis so he could paint it.

"Painting again?" Felix, the newest gardener, asked with a tone of derision.

"Clemenceau is coming. If you feed the geraniums on the porch, they might open out by Sunday."

"Why paint the back? It's up against the wall. Monsieur can't see it."

"No, but I can. And you can."

Felix shrugged and went on by. He's too young to understand my satisfactions, Émile thought.

With the corner of his brush Émile lifted off a bristle that had stuck to the wood. He liked painting things almost as much as gardening, and so would not give it up to the younger men. He liked that creamy feeling of dipping the brush. He often said a little prayer, "à la grâce de Dieu," before that treacherous moment of swinging the loaded brush from can to trellis, over the clematis so not a single drop would mar a leaf or petal. Then there came the pleasure of the smooth spread of shining color until he felt a slight drag on the brush telling him he needed more paint. He loved all these feelings just as much as Monsieur did. He was certain of that.

"Ooff! It's maddening," Monsieur cried from somewhere near the pond. "It's a damned obsession."

The poor man's railing again, Émile thought, pained by his disquietude. He finished the trellises and started on a storage box in a swirl of perfumes—the spicy clovelike scent of pink dianthus and the sweetness of roses like a balm.

"I'm no better than a pig. I know nothing!" he heard.

Monsieur's *sabots* scraped the pebbled path. Émile smelled his cigarette and saw out of the corner of his eye Monsieur's fist hanging like a small ham. "Don't you ever find it hard to do what you have in mind?" Monsieur asked and lifted his slouch hat to wipe his forehead with his handkerchief.

"No. I just keep things in mind that are possible."

"Where's the joy in that?"

"Look around you. This garden. It's full of joy. Always we keep the possible in mind. Now you want the impossible. You'll want to paint the scent of flowers next."

"Right now I just want to paint the reeds underwater, the water's surface, and the sky reflected, all of that at once. What's impossible about that?"

"Only God—"

"*I* want to do it."

"You will, God willing. You are."

Monsieur was looking at a white clematis blossom as though he'd never seen one before. "My God, how exquisite." He shook his head. "What a confounded profession. No matter what beautiful thing I see, it's too hard. It's beyond an old man's powers."

Émile dipped his brush and watched the bristles puncture the smooth green surface of the paint in the can.

"Hand me that brush," Monsieur demanded. "Let me paint something I can."

"No!"

The word struck like a deep bell in the quiet garden. He had never contradicted him before. Monsieur stood for a long time with his big hand out for the brush. The air thickened with the will of his temperamental genius. Émile took only shallow breaths.

He had come to work for Monsieur when the Japanese cherry trees were only spindles. Together they'd kneeled to plant the first blue forget-me-nots to harmonize with mauve tulips and pink peonies. He'd been here before there was a Japanese bridge, before the roses climbed the arching trellises of the Grande Allée. All those years. Never a disagreement.

Émile drew the brush across the wood. "This is mine to do," he said. "You do yours." He felt a ping in his chest. Even if he had to fight him, ridiculous at their age, he would not give over the brush. He tightened his grip, in case the man would grab.

A thrush sang a short flutelike song, and after a long pause, did it again, as though he couldn't help it. They waited without moving for the third song, and at last it came. Monsieur turned and walked back to his canvas. By then the light had changed. Émile heard him shove the painting into a garden box. He didn't move until he heard him pull out another.

Something about the way he'd said "beyond an old man's powers" touched him more than Monsieur's ravings ever had. They were both old men, but Émile was older, and likely to die first. And then what about Ginette's little scrap of painting? She might try to sell it—need might force her—and Monsieur might learn of it.

But there was something else. Monsieur had a right to choose what remained of him, just like he did—the smooth green coating on this box, for example—and if Monsieur thought a single lily was beyond his powers, then it should not remain. He could not violate the man that way.

He finished the box and cleaned his brush carefully, thinking again—what would she do for flowers after he was gone? If he took the lily from her?

He hurried out the gate, across the field through wilting poppies, promising *grâce à Dieu*, praying that God would not let him stumble and break a leg and die in the dirt track, would not let his heart stop beating before he could get home to build a little fire of kindling in the grate and place on it the slice of both their masterworks. He knew what Monsieur wanted.

ABOUT ALICE HOFFMAN

A Profile by Maryanne O'Hara

Alice Hoffman is a prolific writer with a bent toward the magical and luminous, and it's easy to imagine her at some fantastical loom, spinning tales of daily life turned to myth. In the real world, though, she works quietly and consistently out of an old Victorian house near Boston that she shares with her husband, two sons, and three dogs.

One early *New York Times* review said her work had "the quality of folk tale—of amazing events calmly recounted." Countless reviews since then speak of her skill in fusing the mysterious with the practical, the dark with the optimistic. In her novel *The River King,* she describes a great flood that consumes an entire town: "Whole chimneys floated down Main Street, with some of them still issuing forth smoke." It's the kind of matter-of-fact, Hoffman-esque line that makes a reader do a double-take. Could such a thing really happen? Does it matter?

Hoffman doesn't think so. She is endlessly surprised when people make a fuss over the uncanny aspects of her fiction, and points to pregnancy as a prime example of the fact that life itself is magical. "Magic in fiction is a long tradition," she says. "One of the reasons we like fables and fairy tales is that they're emotionally true, and page-turners at the same time."

Her strong reader base might say that statement summarizes her own work. She is the bestselling author of fifteen novels, one book of short fiction, and five books for children; she also wrote, with her husband, Tom Martin, an average of two screenplays a year for twenty-five years, so it's surprising to hear that this hardworking author grew up with no real ambitions, thinking she might perhaps cut hair for a living. "I'd have cut a lot of hair," she says wryly. "I always have to be doing something—have four things going at once."

Born in 1952 in New York, she grew up in a working-class Long Island town, positioned, as she says, to be a lifelong observer. Her parents divorced when she was eight, at a time when parents did

Debi Milligan

not divorce, and her mother worked at a time when mothers did not work. Though both her parents had attended college, they were the only people in her neighborhood who had, and Hoffman never really considered college as an option for herself. Certainly she did not expect to make words a career. Though she was always writing, she says, "I was a secret writer." So what got her writing for the rest of the world?

Her first job, at age seventeen, was a push in the right direction. She worked, ironically, at the Doubleday factory—publisher of her most recent novel, *The Probable Future*. "I stayed till lunch and then quit," she says. One morning was enough to show her that eight hours a day in a world where you had to ask permission to go to the bathroom wasn't for her. There is still some wonder in her voice when she says, "I think it was the first time I ever really *thought*." At the same time, most of the friends she'd grown up with were drowning in serious heroin addictions. "A lot of people were lost." She didn't want to be one of them.

She enrolled in night school at Adelphi University. She's not sure that she would have stayed in college if she'd had to abide by "a lot of rules and regulations. But it was the sixties. One year it was Kent State, and we never finished the semester." She took writing classes and had the good fortune to study with excellent teachers who encouraged her. She left with a degree in English and anthropology, and applied to the Stanford University Creative Writing Center. Not only was she accepted, she was offered, out of the blue, a Mirrielees fellowship. At Stanford, she met Albert Guerard, who became her mentor. Guerard and his wife, the writer Maclin Bocock Guerard, helped her publish her first story in the literary magazine *Fiction*. Legendary editor Ted Solotaroff then beckoned—did she have a novel? She quickly began to write one. *Property Of* was published in 1977 when she was twenty-five years old.

Hoffman has enjoyed early and continued success. Her work has been published in more than twenty translations and one hundred foreign editions. Her novels have repeatedly received mention as notable books of the year by *The New York Times, The Los Angeles Times, Library Journal,* and other periodicals. *Practical Magic* was made into a film starring Nicole Kidman. *Here on Earth* was chosen by Oprah's Book Club. *At Risk,* a novel about a family coping with a child with AIDS, is on the reading lists of numerous secondary schools and universities.

Yet she says, "I really struggle every time. I have terrible self-doubt. I've had periods where I've had writer's block and then I haven't, and I feel like I've had periods where I've had to learn to write all over again. It took me a long time to be able to tell anyone I was a writer."

And the glamour doesn't attract her. "How do you become a writer if you're interested in all that? Because if you want to be a writer, you want to be alone in a room."

She spends a lot of time alone in a room. But she calls her life normal, and like all normal lives, hers has not been without hardship. For years, she struggled with phobias. It is impossible to read *Illumination Night* and not feel that you know what it is to suffocate in the bell jar of agoraphobia. Hoffman intersperses third-person narrative with relentless second-person panic, as in this passage of agoraphobic Vonny attempting to board a plane:

> Her legs will not move. Her skin is cold. She is not quite sure why but she knows that if she walks into the plane she will die.
>
> *Your heart is beating much faster than a human heart.*

A believer in writing as an act of healing, Hoffman helps her characters find ways to heal, too. By the end of the book, Vonny begins to come out the other side:

> When your safe place begins to feel dangerous it can mean your pattern of phobias is breaking down. This can be a sign of recovery...one morning you go out and drive back and forth in the driveway. By the time you have made your third run down the driveway you have stopped asking yourself why you have to start all over again. You are simply a woman practicing the art of real life.

Real life is hard life in Hoffman's books, which tend to feature outsiders—strong women, single women, struggling women, children facing danger. Even though she has enjoyed a long marriage and raised two children, she continues to mull on themes that have long preoccupied her. This is natural, she believes. "Very often what you're writing about is what you've experienced as a child."

In *Illumination Night,* she wrote: "It is terrifying how people can misjudge each other." Years later, *Turtle Moon*'s Lucy reflects: "It hits her, all in a rush, that she may have not been the only one who was unhappy in their marriage—a possibility she has never once considered before." And most recently, *The Blue Diary* depicts a contented married couple suddenly exposed to the fact that the husband committed a brutal rape fifteen years before. All beg the question: can a person ever completely know another?

"I think it's much easier to know your dog," Hoffman says, quite seriously. In *Turtle Moon,* an embittered young boy bonds with a dog. When Hoffman writes, "No one has ever known him the way this dog does," you believe her.

It's a line that recognizes that life is uncertain, a fact which was made poignantly clear to Hoffman in 1998 when she learned, after a prolonged period of illnesses and deaths in her family, that she herself had breast cancer. In a 2000 *New York Times* article entitled "Sustained by Fiction While Facing Life's Facts," she writes of her reaction to the news: "I was certain my doctor was phoning to tell me the biopsy had come back negative. I was absolutely sure of it, but then she said, 'Alice, I'm sorry.' I could hear the concern and sadness in her voice, and I understood that some things are true no matter how and when you're told."

More than ever, she found that writing sustained her during her months of treatment. "When I became too ill to sit up for long, I moved a futon into my office and went from desk to bed, back and forth until the line between dreaming and writing was nothing more than a thin, translucent thread."

She has been healthy since those twilight months of treatment ended. In recent years, she has written for younger readers. She sees a lot of mother-daughter duos at readings, and decided she wanted to write to both generations, because "what you read when you're twelve stays with you in such a deep way."

She also wanted to include her younger son in her writing life, so they wrote a book together. "He's been able to experience the whole process, and how incredibly long it takes," she says. *Moondog*, by Alice Hoffman and Wolfe Martin, will be published by Scholastic on Halloween 2004.

Besides writing? "What else is there to do? I walk with a friend every morning. I go to the beach, the Cape. Mostly I work, and I always feel like there's not enough time. I always feel like I'm so lucky to be a writer."

That feeling of luck translates into a desire to give back. Years ago, she donated her advance from *At Risk* to AIDS research and funding for People with AIDS. After September 11, she wrote *Green Angel*, a kind of apocalyptic fairy tale for young adults. Proceeds benefit the New York Women's Foundation. Proceeds from *Local Girls*, a collection of interrelated stories, benefit breast cancer.

"I've been lucky," she says. "And I feel like fiction needs to matter in the real world."

The real world, like life in Hoffman's fictions, is uncertain and wondrous and generally resistant to our attempts to control it. But Hoffman herself increasingly embraces all of her worlds. Recently an elderly driver hit the gas instead of the brake and crashed into Hoffman's backyard. "And I thought, Well, this is a message," she says. "Here's someone telling you something. You might as well live."

COHEN AWARDS Each year, we honor the best short story and poem published in *Ploughshares* with the Cohen Awards, which are wholly sponsored by our longtime patrons Denise and Mel Cohen. Finalists are nominated by staff editors, and the winners—each of whom receives a cash prize of $600—are selected by our advisory editors. The 2003 Cohen Awards for work published in *Ploughshares* in 2002, Volume 28, go to Joan Silber and Scott Withiam. (Both of their works are accessible on our website at www.pshares.org.)

JOAN SILBER *for her story "The High Road" in Fall 2002, edited by Margot Livesey.*

Joan Silber grew up in Millburn, New Jersey, where her father was a dentist and her mother was a schoolteacher. At Sarah Lawrence College, Silber studied writing with Jane Cooper and Grace Paley. After she graduated, she moved to Manhattan and spent most of her twenties waitressing and working various odd jobs. Eventually she went back to school and got her M.A. at New York University, then taught at NYU.

Her first novel, *Household Words,* won the PEN/Hemingway Award in 1981, and was followed by *In the City* in 1987. She received grants from the Guggenheim Foundation, the National Endowment for the Arts, and the New York Foundation for the Arts. She moved from novels to short stories and put together a collection that was published as *In My Other Life* in 2000. Stories from the book appeared in *The New Yorker, Ploughshares,* and other magazines. She published a third novel, *Lucky Us,* in 2001, and a new book of stories, *Ideas of Heaven,* which includes "The High Road," will be released in the spring of 2004 by W.W. Norton. The story has also been selected for *Prize Stories 2003: The O. Henry Awards* and *The Pushcart Prize XXVIII.* She lives in New York City and teaches writing at Sarah Lawrence College, as well

as in Warren Wilson College's M.F.A. program. She is now working on a new novel: "It started with the idea of travel, but has
moved into the question of how different cultures think people
should carry their emotions. Some of the book is set in Asia,
where I have been traveling as much as I can in recent years."

About "The High Road," Silber says: "Before I wrote the story, I
wrote another one loosely based on an incident someone had told
me, in which a woman is humiliated by her dance coach. And then
I wanted to give Duncan, the coach, his own story. He was even
worse, more darkly scornful, in the first story. I knew that he would
end up a fool for love in some way and that this devotion without
reward would do him good. Gaspara Stampa, an actual Venetian
poet, is the teller of the next story in this cycle. I'd heard of her because Rilke mentions her in the *Duino Elegies,* and when I went to
find her poems, they really did seem like blues lyrics to me."

SCOTT WITHIAM *for his poem "Walk Right In" in Spring 2002,
edited by Cornelius Eady.*

Scott Withiam grew up in Interlaken, a rural village in the Finger Lakes region of upstate New York, and graduated from SUNY
Geneseo in 1975 with a B.S. in education. He wanted to study the
visual arts, to be a sculptor, but says he had neither the portfolio
nor the confidence to pursue that path, and so fell back on education as a livelihood. He moved to the Boston vicinity in 1976,
where he worked as a public school teacher, Section 8 property
manager, and newspaper reporter. He became interested in poetry
while attending Lesley College in the early eighties. "I was supposed to be pursuing a graduate degree in arts in education," he
says, "but decided to give up education to pursue art again. I fell in
love with poetry as a cheap means of making art, no studio
required. No supplies, just the discipline." He earned his M.F.A.
from Vermont College in 1997, and has since taught writing and
literature at Vermont College's Adult Degree Program, the Massachusetts Maritime Academy, and Western New England College.
His poems have appeared in *The Beloit Poetry Journal, 5 A.M.,
Green Mountains Review, Field, Harvard Review, Marlboro Review,
The Massachusetts Review, The Notre Dame Review, Puerto del Sol,
Sonora Review, Sycamore Review, Third Coast, Ploughshares, The
Sun,* and elsewhere. His first book, *Arson & Prophets,* will be out
this fall from Ashland Poetry Press. Since 1986, he has lived in

Wareham, Massachusetts, with his partner, Pam, and their three children.

About "Walk Right In," he says: "Often my first impulse is to make some daily encounter or remembered snippet into a story. And I often do set it down on paper like a story, but then I don't want it to be a story, I want it to be a poem, dammit. I don't know how many times I've been told that a poem I'm working on would be better off as a story, and I've always fought that. The impulse for 'Walk Right In' came years ago. Fresh out of college, I worked in a shelter workshop for mentally disabled adults. I overheard a claim by a tattooed man of a couple who worked there, a claim that the two of them were able to enter each other's dreams while they slept. For a long time this image kept coming back to me. What eventually entered into the drafts of this poem was the setting. I spent a few too many hours of my youth with my father in bars. I was never comfortable in bars. Too often I saw or heard the sadness or discontent beneath all the banter and celebration. Enter the couple who enter each other's dreams, who make us ask, 'Why would anyone want to do such a thing?' And the barmaid who has the answer that everyone probably knows but is not interested in hearing."

MORE AWARDS Our congratulations to the following writers, whose work has been selected for these anthologies:

BEST STORIES ZZ Packer's "Every Tongue Shall Confess" and Sharon Pomerantz's "Ghost Knife," both from the Fall 2002 issue edited by Margot Livesey, will be included in *The Best American Short Stories 2003*. The anthology is due out this October from Houghton Mifflin, with Walter Mosley as the guest editor and Katrina Kenison as the series editor.

BEST POETRY Joshua Clover's "Aeon Flux: June," from the Winter 2001–02 issue edited by Jorie Graham, will appear in *The Best American Poetry 2003* this September from Scribner, with Yusef Komunyakaa as the guest editor and David Lehman as the series editor.

PUSHCART Valerie Laken's story "Before Long," from the Winter 2002–03 issue edited by C. D. Wright, and Joan Silber's story

"The High Road," from the Fall 2002 issue edited by Margot Livesey, have been selected for *The Pushcart Prize XXVIII: Best of the Small Presses,* which will be published by Bill Henderson's Pushcart Press this fall.

o. henry Joan Silber's "The High Road" has also been chosen for *Prize Stories 2003: The O. Henry Awards* by editor Laura Furman. The anthology will be published in September by Anchor Books.

departure We're sad to announce that Susan Conley has moved to Maine and will no longer be serving as our Associate Poetry Editor. She had worked for *Ploughshares* in various capacities since 1996. We thank her for her dedicated service, and we wish her the best.

How to Breathe Underwater, *stories by Julie Orringer:* The three stories that open this debut collection are pure gems, rollicking along with scintillating prose and surety. Just when you think they will stop—and lesser writers would stop—they keep going with inexorable momentum. Almost all of the stories involve youths imperiled—by accidents, illness, fate, and, most interestingly, by siblings and other children, who bring new meaning to "cruel and unusual" punishments. (Knopf)

Thieves' Latin, *poems by Peter Jay Shippy:* This prize-winning first collection provides proof that, as Peter Jay Shippy writes, "writ happens"—and that sometimes it is wonderful "writ." With a gift for breathtakingly original language, he leads us through the vast orchard of his imagination, where we can pluck and taste its astonishing fruit. *Thieves' Latin,* with its madnesses, its great and tragic hilarity, its wild imaginings, and its equally great and tender heart, will be treasured for a long time to come. (Iowa)

Built in a Day, *a novel by Steven Rinehart:* The hero of this ambitious and smart debut novel, following on the heels of the story collection *Kick in the Head,* is a deceptively dangerous thirty-something dropout who is not above sleeping with his dead wife's dead son's teenaged girlfriend. Ultimately, this relentlessly entertaining story demonstrates how the difficulties of being so desperate for affection can render all intimacies boundary-less. (Doubleday)

George Garrett recommends *Do I Owe You Something,* a memoir by Michael Mewshaw: "Novelist and nonfiction writer Mewshaw here offers a focused memoir concerning writers he has known well over many years. At the still point where memory and gossip become history, he gives us candid and surprising portraits of giants and pygmies of the literary scene, including, among others, William Styron, James Dickey, Peter Taylor, James Jones, Anthony Burgess, Paul Bowles, Graham Greene, and Gore Vidal. Good stories and great fun." (LSU)

DeWitt Henry recommends *A Tragic Honesty,* a biography by Blake Bailey: "Richard Yates comes fully alive as an artist and as a man in this meticulously researched, judicious, and critically perceptive biography. Blake Bailey has done for Yates what Carlos Baker did for Hemingway, allowing Yates himself to speak from letters, archives, reported conversations, and from autobiographical passages from the fiction, while organizing the narrative into a gripping story of literary career, proud values, and accomplishment." (Picador)

Jane Hirshfield recommends *Ripe,* poems by Roy Jacobstein: "Roy Jacobstein's *Ripe,* winner of the Felix Pollak Prize, is a book of balance, precision, vision, courage, and wit. Each poem feels solidly present in what it knows, each poem is fragrant with lived life— just as its title implies, here is a poet come into his ripeness." (Wisconsin)

Philip Levine recommends *Feeding the Fire,* poems by Jeffrey Harrison: "It's thrilling to read an entire book of poems written with such pleasure and gusto. Harrison writes with remarkable confidence about a range of ordinary things—salt, rowing a boat, discarded books, a stinking pond—and he gets more out of his subjects than seems possible. How does he do this without ever being pretentious? He's an artist." (Sarabande)

C. D. Wright recommends *Alphabet,* poems by Inger Christensen: "A book to break up the psychic mumbo jumbo within, and to help you fight the actual threats from without. A true singer of the syllables." (New Directions)

EDITORS' CORNER

*New Books by
Our Advisory Editors*

Sherman Alexie, *Ten Little Indians,* stories: In this powerful, exuberant new collection, Alexie presents stories about Native Americans who find themselves at personal and cultural crossroads that test their notions of who they are and who they love. (Grove)

Marilyn Hacker, *Desesperanto,* poems: In her brilliant tenth collection, with typical wit, brio, and intelligence, Hacker refines the themes of loss, exile, and return that have consistently informed her work. (Norton)

Donald Hall, *Willow Temple,* stories: There are twelve stories here—five from *The Ideal Bakery* and six collected for the first time, as well as one new tale—and the volume attests to Hall's

mastery as a storyteller, the prose lyrical and elegiac as he movingly unfolds each character's frailties. (Houghton Mifflin)

Fanny Howe, *Gone,* poems: With verve and clarity, Howe illuminates the interstices between the known and unknown worlds with motifs of advance and recovery, doubt and conviction, in her extraordinary new book. (California)

Maxine Kumin, *Bringing Together,* poems: These poems from nine earlier collections crackle with intensity, offering Kumin's refreshing and singular perspective on everyday experiences, examining the pain of loss, the idealism of youth, and the endurance of the natural world. (Norton)

Jay Neugeboren, *Open Heart,* memoir: In this inspiring book, Neugeboren thoughtfully recounts his emergency bypass surgery and ruminates on the state of doctor-patient relationships through discussions with four friends from high school, all prominent physicians. (Houghton Mifflin)

C. D. Wright, *One Big Self,* text and photographs: Wright and photographer Deborah Luster collaborate to produce intimate, haunting, and oddly gorgeous portraits of prisoners in Louisiana, giving voice to their isolation, heartache, and individualism. (Twin Palms)

CONTRIBUTORS' NOTES

Fall 2003

ELIZABETH BERG is the author of eleven novels, a collection of short stories, and two nonfiction books. She lives in Chicago.

PETER HO DAVIES is the author of the story collections *The Ugliest House in the World* and *Equal Love*. His work has appeared in *The Atlantic, Harper's,* and *The Paris Review,* among others, and has been selected for *The Best American Short Stories* and *Prize Stories: The O. Henry Awards.* He was recently named one of *Granta's* Best of Young British Novelists. He currently directs the M.F.A. program at the University of Michigan.

KIM EDWARDS is the author of the story collection *The Secrets of a Fire King,* an alternate for the PEN/Hemingway Award. Her stories have been performed at Symphony Space and have won many honors, including the Nelson Algren Award, the National Magazine Award for excellence in fiction, and inclusion in *The Best American Short Stories* and *The Pushcart Prize* anthologies. She is the recipient of a 2002 Whiting Writer's Award.

KARL HARSHBARGER lives with his wife in Germany, where he teaches English as a foreign language. His stories have appeared or are forthcoming in many magazines, including *The Atlantic Monthly, The Iowa Review, The Antioch Review,* and *The Prairie Schooner.*

ELIZABETH L. HODGES has published poetry in *The North American Review, New Virginia Review,* and *Connecticut Poetry Review.* She has traveled extensively to Russia. She works as an attorney in New Hampshire, where she lives with her husband and son.

PERRI KLASS is a practicing pediatrician in Boston, and the Medical Director of Reach Out and Read, a national literacy program for children. Her books include *Other Women's Children,* a novel, *Baby Doctor: A Pediatrician's Training,* a collection of essays, and, most recently, *Love and Modern Medicine,* a collection of short stories. (Lines from *One Fish, Two Fish, Red Fish, Blue Fish* by Dr. Seuss used by permission of Random House Children's Books.)

GREGORY MAGUIRE is the author of four novels, including the recent *Mirror Mirror.* His first novel, *Wicked,* is the basis for a new musical expected to open on Broadway this fall. Another book, *Confessions of an Ugly Stepsister,* was adapted into an ABC movie. He has written editorials, essays, and signal reviews for *The New York Times Book Review, Boston Review,* and *The Christian Science Monitor.*

ALEXANDRA MARSHALL's latest novel is *The Court of Common Pleas,* which recently appeared in paperback. She has published four other novels, *Something Borrowed, Gus in Bronze, Tender Offer,* and *The Brass Bed,* as well as *Still Waters,* a book about a New England pond. She has been a film critic for *The American Prospect* and has written for many other journals, including *The Boston Globe* and *The New York Times.*

TOM MARTIN lives near Boston, where he is currently working on a novel.

ALICE MATTISON's story "In Case We're Separated," which first appeared in *Ploughshares,* was reprinted in *The Best American Short Stories 2002.* Her novel *The Wedding of the Two-Headed Woman* will appear next year. She is the author of three previous novels, including *The Book Borrower* and *Hilda and Pearl,* three books of short stories, and a collection of poems. She lives in New Haven and teaches in Bennington College's M.F.A. program.

JILL MCCORKLE is the author of five novels and three collections of stories, most recently *Creatures of Habit.* She teaches in Bennington College's M.F.A. program and lives near Boston with her husband and two children.

ABELARDO MORELL was born in Cuba in 1948. His work has been exhibited and collected by The Museum of Modern Art, the Whitney Museum of American Art, and The Metropolitan Museum of Art in New York; the Art Institute of Chicago; and over forty other museums and institutions worldwide. He has been the recipient of several awards, including a Guggenheim fellowship. He is a professor at the Massachusetts College of Art and lives in Brookline, Massachusetts.

ANTONYA NELSON is the author of seven books of fiction, including *Female Trouble* (Scribner, 2002). She teaches in Warren Wilson College's M.F.A. program, as well as at the University of Houston, where she shares, with her husband, Robert Boswell, the Cullen Chair in Creative Writing. She lives in Houston and Telluride.

PAMELA PAINTER is the author of two story collections, *Getting to Know the Weather* and *The Long and Short of It.* She is also the co-author of *What If? Writing Exercises for Fiction Writers.* Her stories have appeared in *The Atlantic Monthly, Harper's, The Kenyon Review,* and *Story.* She has received grants from the NEA and the Massachusetts Artists Foundation, and has won two Pushcart Prizes. A founding editor of *StoryQuarterly,* she lives in Boston and teaches at Emerson College.

GRACE PALEY is the author of *The Little Disturbances of Man, Enormous Changes at the Last Minute, Later the Same Day, The Collected Stories, New and Collected Poems,* and a gathering of essays, *Just As I Thought.* Her many honors include an NEA Senior Fellowship, a Guggenheim fellowship in fiction, the Edith Wharton Award, the National Institute of Arts and Letters Award for short story writing, a Lannan Award, and a citation as the First Official New York State Writer.

JAYNE ANNE PHILLIPS is the author of three novels, *MotherKind, Shelter,* and *Machine Dreams,* and two books of stories, *Black Tickets* and *Fast Lanes.* She is the recipient of Guggenheim, NEA, and Bunting fellowships, and was awarded the Sue Kaufman Prize and an Academy Award in Literature from the American Academy of Arts and Letters. She is presently Writer in Residence at Brandeis University.

SUE STANDING's poems have appeared in many journals, including *Agni, APR, The American Scholar, The Atlantic Monthly, The Nation,* and *Southwest Review.* Her most recent poetry collection is *False Horizon* (Four Way Books, 2003). The recipient of grants from the NEA and the Bunting Institute, she teaches creative writing and African literature at Wheaton College, where she directs the creative writing program.

SUSAN VREELAND's novels include *Girl in Hyacinth Blue,* a finalist for the Book Sense Book of the Year Award for 1999, and *The Passion of Artemisia,* both *New York Times* bestsellers. *The Forest Lover,* another art-related novel, is due out in January 2004, and a story collection, *Life Studies,* which includes "A Flower for Ginette," will be published in January 2005, both from Viking.

～

GUEST EDITOR POLICY *Ploughshares* is published three times a year: mixed issues of poetry and fiction in the Spring and Winter and a fiction issue in the Fall, with each guest-edited by a different writer of prominence, usually one whose early work was published in the journal. Guest editors are invited to solicit up to half of their issues, with the other half selected from unsolicited manuscripts screened for them by staff editors. This guest editor policy is designed to introduce readers to different literary circles and tastes, and to offer a fuller representation of the range and diversity of contemporary letters than would be possible with a single editorship. Yet, at the same time, we expect every issue to reflect our overall standards of literary excellence. We liken *Ploughshares* to a theater company: each issue might have a different guest editor and different writers—just as a play will have a different director, playwright, and cast—but subscribers can count on a governing aesthetic, a consistency in literary values and quality, that is uniquely our own.

～

SUBMISSION POLICIES We welcome unsolicited manuscripts from August 1 to March 31 (postmark dates). All submissions sent from April to July are returned unread. In the past, guest editors often announced specific themes for issues, but we have revised our editorial policies and no longer restrict submissions to thematic topics. Submit your work at any time during our reading period; if a manuscript is not timely for one issue, it will be considered for another. We do not recommend trying to target specific guest editors. Our backlog is unpredictable, and staff editors ultimately have the responsibility of determining for which editor a work is most appropriate. Mail one prose piece or one to three poems. No e-mail submissions. Poems should be individually typed either single- or double-spaced on one side of the page. Prose should be typed double-spaced on one side and be no longer than thirty pages. Although we look primarily for short stories, we occasionally publish personal essays/memoirs. Novel excerpts are acceptable if self-contained. Unsolicited book reviews and criticism are not considered. Please do not send multiple submissions of the same genre, and do not send another manuscript until you hear about the first.

No more than a total of two submissions per reading period. Additional submissions will be returned unread. Mail your manuscript in a page-size manila envelope, your full name and address written on the outside. In general, address submissions to the "Fiction Editor," "Poetry Editor," or "Nonfiction Editor," not to the guest or staff editors by name, unless you have a legitimate association with them or have been previously published in the magazine. Unsolicited work sent directly to a guest editor's home or office will be ignored and discarded; guest editors are formally instructed not to read such work. All manuscripts and correspondence regarding submissions should be accompanied by a self-addressed, stamped envelope (s.a.s.e.) for a response; no replies will be given by e-mail or postcard. Expect three to five months for a decision. We now receive well over a thousand manuscripts a month. Do not query us until five months have passed, and if you do, please write to us, including an s.a.s.e. and indicating the postmark date of submission, instead of calling or e-mailing. Simultaneous submissions are amenable as long as they are indicated as such and we are notified immediately upon acceptance elsewhere. We cannot accommodate revisions, changes of return address, or forgotten s.a.s.e.'s after the fact. We do not reprint previously published work. Translations are welcome if permission has been granted. We cannot be responsible for delay, loss, or damage. Payment is upon publication: $25/printed page, $50 minimum and $250 maximum per author, with two copies of the issue and a one-year subscription.

~

THE NAME *Ploughshares* 1. The sharp edge of a plough that cuts a furrow in the earth. 2a. A variation of the name of the pub, the Plough and Stars, in Cambridge, Massachusetts, where the journal *Ploughshares* was founded in 1971. 2b. The pub's name was inspired by the Sean O'Casey play about the Easter Rising of the Irish "citizen army." The army's flag contained a plough, representing the things of the earth, hence practicality; and stars, the ideals by which the plough is steered. 3. A shared, collaborative, community effort. 4. A literary journal that has been energized by a desire for harmony, peace, and reform. Once, that spirit motivated civil rights marches, war protests, and student activism. Today, it still inspirits a desire for beating swords into ploughshares, but through the power and the beauty of the written word.

NATIONAL ENDOWMENT FOR THE ARTS

massculturalcouncil.org

IN MEMORIAM
LEONARD MICHAELS
1933–2003

A Girl with Monkey
Time Out of Mind
To Feel These Things
Sylvia
Shuffle
The Men's Club
I Would Have Saved Them If I Could
Going Places

Join our selective and close-knit community of writers
at a first-rate university in the cultural mecca
of Austin, Texas. Students are fully funded
by annual fellowships of $17,500.

James A. Michener Center for Writers

MFA in Writing

THE UNIVERSITY OF TEXAS AT AUSTIN

RESIDENT & RECENT VISITING FACULTY

Fiction
Michael Adams
Laura Furman
Zulfikar Ghose
Elizabeth Harris
R.R. Hinojosa-Smith
Peter LaSalle
J.M. Coetzee
James Kelman
Joy Williams
Denis Johnson
David Bradley
Anthony Giardina

Poetry
Judith Kroll
Khaled Mattawa
David Wevill
Thomas Whitbread
August Kleinzahler
Heather McHugh
Naomi Shihab Nye
Marie Howe

Screenwriting
Robert Foshko
Stephen Harrigan
Charles Ramirez-Berg
William Hauptman
Anne Rapp
Tim McCanlies

Playwriting
Suzan Zeder
Lee Blessing
Naomi Iizuka
Sherry Kramer

www.utexas.edu/academic/mcw
512-471-1601

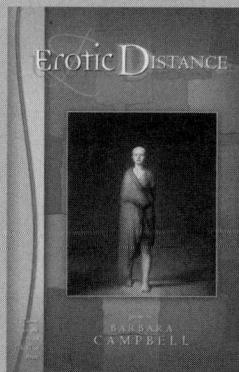

BENNINGTON WRITING SEMINARS

MFA in Writing and Literature
Two-Year Low-Residency Program

A. BLAKE GARDNER

FICTION
NONFICTION
POETRY

Partial Scholarships Available
For more information contact:
Writing Seminars
Box PL
Bennington College
Bennington, VT 05201
802-440-4452, Fax 802-440-4453
www.bennington.edu

CORE FACULTY

FICTION

Douglas Bauer	Sheila Kohler
Martha Cooley	Alice Mattison
Elizabeth Cox	Jill McCorkle
Lynn Freed	Askold Melnyczuk
Amy Hempel	

NONFICTION

Sven Birkerts	George Packer
Susan Cheever	Bob Shacochis
Phillip Lopate	

POETRY

April Bernard	E. Ethelbert Miller
Amy Gerstler	Ed Ochester
Jane Hirshfield	Liam Rector
David Lehman	Jason Shinder

WRITERS-IN-RESIDENCE

Robert Bly	Lyndall Gordon
Donald Hall	Rick Moody

PAST FACULTY IN RESIDENCE

Agha Shahid Ali	Carole Maso
Lucie Brock-Broido	Christopher Merrill
Robert Creeley	Sue Miller
Susan Dodd	Honor Moore
Mark Doty	Marjorie Perloff
Karen Finley	Robert Pinsky
William Finnegan	Robert Polito
George Garrett	Katha Pollitt
Vivian Gornick	Alastair Reid
Judith Grossman	Mary Robison
Barry Hannah	Roger Shattuck
Edward Hoagland	Ilan Stavans
Richard Howard	Mac Wellman
Marie Howe	Tom Wicker
Jane Kenyon	

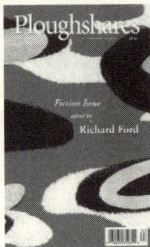